"IT IS CLEAR THAT SINGER IS A WRITER OF FAR GREATER THAN ORDINARY POWERS."

—*New York Times Book Review*

"Tale about Yasha Mazur, who makes his living in the circuses and theaters of 19th-century Poland. He can skate on the high wire, eat fire...and, above all, charm any woman."

—*Time*

"SINGER SHARES WITH SAUL BELLOW, BERNARD MALAMUD AND PHILIP ROTH THE ABILITY TO TAKE THE DRAMA OF THE SOUL CAUGHT BETWEEN GOOD AND EVIL AND WRITE OF IT IN CONCRETE, HUMAN, EVEN HUMOROUS TERMS."

—*Library Journal*

Also by
Isaac Bashevis Singer

The Magician Of Lublin

ISAAC BASHEVIS SINGER

FAWCETT CREST • NEW YORK

The Magician Of Lublin

ONE

That morning Yasha Mazur, or the Magician of Lublin as he was known everywhere but in his home town, awoke early. He always spent a day or two in bed after returning from a trip; his weariness required the indulgence of continual sleep. His wife, Esther, would bring him cookies, milk, a dish of groats. He would eat and doze off again. The parrot shrieked; Yoktan, the monkey, chattered; the canaries whistled and trilled, but Yasha, disregarding them, merely reminded Esther to water the horses. He need not have bothered with such instructions; she always remembered to draw water from the well for Kara and Shiva, their brace of gray mares, or, as Yasha had nicknamed them, Dust and Ashes.

Yasha, although a magician, was considered rich; he owned a house and, with it, barns, silos, stables, a hay loft, a courtyard having two apple trees, even a garden where Esther grew her own vegetables. He lacked only children. Esther could not conceive. In every other way she was a good wife; she knew how to knit, sew a wedding gown, bake gingerbread and tarts, tear out the pip of a chicken, apply a cupping-glass or leeches, even bleed a patient. In her younger days she had tried all sorts of remedies for barrenness, but now it was too late—she was nearly forty.

Like every other magician, Yasha was held in small esteem by the community. He wore no beard and went to synagogue only on Rosh Hashonah and Yom Kippur; that is, if he happened to be in Lublin at the time. Esther, on the other hand, wore the customary kerchief and kept a Kosher kitchen; she observed the Sabbath and all the laws. Yasha spent his Sabbath talking and smoking cigarettes among musicians. To the earnest moralists who attempted to get him to mend his ways, he would always answer: "When were you in heaven, and what did God look like?"

It was risky to debate with him since he was no fool, knew how to read Russian and Polish, and was even well-informed on Jewish matters. A reckless man! To win a bet, he had once spent a whole night in the cemetery. He could walk a tightrope, skate on a wire, climb walls, open any lock. Abraham Leibush, the locksmith, had wagered five rubles he could make a lock that Yasha could not open. He had worked over it for months, and Yasha had picked it with a shoemaker's awl. In Lublin they said that if Yasha had chosen crime, no one's house would be safe.

His two days of lounging in bed were over, and that morning Yasha rose with the sun. He was a short man, broad-shouldered and lean-hipped; he had unruly flaxen hair and watery blue eyes, thin lips, a narrow chin and a short Slavic nose. His right eye was somewhat larger than his left, and because of this he always seemed to be blinking with insolent mockery. He was now forty but looked ten years younger. His toes were almost as long and tensile as his fingers, and with a pen in them he could sign his name with a flourish. He could also shell peas with them. He could flex his body in any direction—it was said that he had malleable bones and fluid joints. He rarely performed in Lublin but the few who had seen his act acclaimed his talents. He could walk on his hands, eat fire, swallow swords, turn somersaults like a monkey. No one could duplicate his skill. He would be imprisoned in a room at night with the lock clamped on the outside of the door, and the next morning he would be seen nonchalantly strolling through the market place, while on the outside of the door the lock remained unopened. He could manage this even with his hands and feet chained. Some maintained that he practiced black magic and owned a cap which made him invisible, capable of squeezing through cracks in the wall; others said that he was merely a master of illusion.

Now he got out of bed without pouring water

over his hands as he should have done, nor did he say his morning prayers. He put on green trousers, red house slippers, and a black velvet vest decorated with silver sequins. While dressing, he capered and clowned like a schoolboy, whistled at the canaries, addressed Yoktan, the monkey; spoke to Haman, the dog, and to Meztotze, the cat. This was only part of the menagerie he kept. In the courtyard were a peacock and peahen, a pair of turkeys, a flock of rabbits, even a snake which had to be fed a live mouse every other day.

It was a warm morning, just before Pentecost. Green shoots had already appeared in Esther's garden. Yasha opened the stable door and entered. He inhaled deeply the odor of horse-droppings and petted the mares. Then he currycombed them and fed the other animals. Sometimes he returned from a trip to find one of his pets gone, but this time there had been no deaths.

He was in good spirits and he strolled about his property aimlessly. The grass in the courtyard was green, and a host of flowers grew there: yellow, white, speckled buds, and tufted blossoms that dispersed with every breeze. Brush and thistle reached almost to the roof of the outhouse. Butterflies fluttered this way and that, and bees buzzed from flower to flower. Every leaf and stalk had its inhabitant: a worm, a bug, a gnat, creatures barely discernible to the naked eye. As always, Yasha marveled at them. Where did they come from? How did they exist? What did they do in the night? They died in winter but, with summer, the swarms came again. How did that happen? When he was in the tavern, Yasha played the atheist but, actually, he believed in God. God's hand was evident everywhere. Each fruit blossom, pebble, and grain of sand proclaimed Him. The leaves of the apple trees were wet with dew and sparkled like little candles in the morning light. His house was near the edge of the city and he could see great fields of wheat which were green now but in six weeks would be golden-yellow, ready for the harvest. Who created all this? Yasha would ask himself. Was it the sun? If so, then perhaps the sun was God. Yasha had read in some holy book that Abraham had worshiped the sun before accepting the existence of Jehovah.

No, he was not illiterate. His father had been a learned man, and Yasha had even studied the Talmud as a boy. After his father's death, he had been advised to continue his education, but instead had joined a traveling circus. He was half Jew, half Gentile—neither Jew nor Gentile. He had worked out his own religion. There was a Creator, but He revealed Himself to no one, gave no indications of what was permitted or forbidden. Those who spoke in His name were liars.

2

Yasha amused himself in the courtyard and Esther prepared his breakfast: a hard roll with butter and cottage cheese, scallions, radishes, a cucumber, and coffee which she had ground herself and which she brewed with milk. Esther was small and dark, had a youthful face, a straight nose, black eyes in which both joy and sorrow were reflected. There were even times when those eyes would sparkle mischievously. When she smiled her upper lip turned up playfully, revealing small teeth, and her cheeks dimpled. Since she was childless, she associated with the girls rather than with other married women. She employed two seamstresses with whom she was always joking, but it was said that when alone she wept. God had sealed her womb, as it is written in the Pentateuch, and it was rumored that she spent much of what she earned on quacks and miracle workers. Once she had cried out that she even envied those mothers whose children lay in the cemetery.

Now she served Yasha his breakfast. She sat opposite him on the bench and studied him—wryly, appraisingly, curiously. She never bothered him until he had had time to recover from his trip, but this morning she saw from his face that his period of recuperation was over. His being away so much had had its effect upon their relationship; they did not have the intimacy of long-married couples. Esther's small talk might have been exchanged with a casual acquaintance.

"Well, what's new out in the great big world?"

"It's the same old world."

"And how about your magic?"

"It's the same old magic."

"What about the girls? Have there been any changes there?"

"What girls? There aren't any."

"No, no. Of course not. I just wish I had twenty silver pieces for every girl you've had."

"What would you do with such a vast amount of money?" he asked, winking at her. Then he returned to his food, chewing as he stared off into the distance beyond her. Her suspicions never left her, but he admitted to nothing, reassuring her after each trip that he believed in only one God and one wife.

"Those who run around with women don't walk tight ropes. They find it hard enough to creep around on the ground. You know that as well as I do," he argued.

"Just how could I know it?" she asked. "When you're on the road I don't stand at the foot of your bed."

And the smile that she gave him was a mixture of affection and resentment. He could not be watched over like other husbands—he spent more time on the road than at home, met all sorts of women, wandered further than a gypsy. Yes, he was as free as the wind, but, thank God, he always returned to her and always with some gift in his hand. The eagerness with which he kissed and embraced her suggested that he had been living the life of a saint during his absence, but what could a mere woman know of the male appetite? Often Esther regretted that she had married a magician and not some tailor or cobbler who sat at home all day and was constantly in view. But her love for Yasha persisted. He was both son and husband to her. Every day that she spent with him was a holiday.

Esther continued to study him as he ate. Somehow he did things differently from the usual run of people. While he was eating, he would suddenly pause as if in deep thought, and then begin chewing again. Another of his odd habits was to dally with a piece of thread, idly tying knots in it, but so skillfully that an equal space would remain between each knot. Esther would gaze often into his eyes trying to penetrate their artifice, but his impassivity always defeated her. He concealed much, seldom spoke in earnest, always hid his vexations. Even if he were ill, he would walk around burning with fever, and Esther would be none the wiser. Frequently she questioned him about the performances which had made him famous throughout Poland, but he either dismissed her questions with a curt reply or evaded them with a joke. One moment he would be on the most intimate terms with her, and the next he would be equally remote, and she never grew tired of wondering about each move he made, each word, each gesture. Even when he was in one of his exuberant moods and babbled like a schoolboy, everything he said had meaning. Occasionally, it was only after he had left and was once more on the road, that Esther would understand what he had said.

They had been married twenty years, but he was still as playful with her as he had been on the first days after their wedding. He would tug at her kerchief, tweak her nose, call her ridiculous nicknames such as Jerambola, Pussyball, Goose Gizzard—musician's jargon, she knew. Days, he was one thing, and nights another. One moment he crowed elatedly like a rooster, squealed like a pig, whinnied like a horse, and the next was inexplicably melancholy. At home he spent most of his time in his room, occupied with his equipment: locks, chains, ropes, files, tongs, all sorts of odds and ends. Those who had witnessed his stunts spoke of the ease with which they were performed, but Esther had witnessed the days and nights spent perfecting his paraphernalia. She had seen him train a crow to speak like a man; watched him teach Yoktan, the monkey, to smoke a pipe. She dreaded his overworking or being bitten by one of the animals, or falling from the tightrope. To Esther he was all sorcery. Even at night, in bed, she would hear him clicking his tongue or snapping his toes. His eyes were those of a cat; he could see in the dark; he knew how to locate missing articles; he was even able to read her thoughts. Once she had had a quarrel with one of the seamstresses and Yasha, coming in late that night, had scarcely spoken to her before divining that she had had an argument that day. Another time she had lost her wedding ring and searched everywhere for it before she had told him of the loss. He had taken her by the hand and had led her to the water barrel where the ring lay at the bottom. She had long since come to the conclusion that she would never be able to understand all his complexities. He possessed hidden powers; he had more secrets than the blessed Rosh Hashonah pomegranate has seeds.

3

It was midday and Bella's tavern was almost deserted. Bella was dozing in a back room and the bar was tended by her small assistant, Zipporah. Fresh sawdust had been sprinkled on the floor, and roast goose, jellied calf's foot, chopped herring, egg cookies, pretzels, had been laid out on the counter. Yasha sat at a table with Schmul the Musician. Schmul was a large man with bushy black hair, black eyes, sideburns, and a thin mustache. He was dressed in the Russian manner: a satin blouse, tasseled belt, and high boots. For several years Schmul had worked for a Zhitomir nobleman, but having become involved with the wife of his patron's steward, had had to flee. Considered Lublin's most accomplished violinist, he always performed at the more exclusive weddings. This, however, was the period between Passover and Pentecost, a time of no weddings. Schmul had a mug of beer before him; he leaned against the wall, one eye screwed up, the other contemplating the beverage, as if debating whether to drink or not. On the table was a roll and on the roll a large golden-green fly, which also seemed unable to come to a decision: Should it fly off or not?

Yasha had not yet tasted his beer. He seemed entranced by the foam. One by one the bubbles in the brimming glass disintegrated until it was only three-quarters full. Yasha murmured, "Swindle, swindle, bubble, bubble." Schmul had just been bragging about one of his amorous adventures, and now at the end of one story and before the beginning of another, the men sat silently thoughtful. Yasha enjoyed listening to Schmul's stories; he could have replied in kind had he wished, but with the pleasure evoked by Schmul's story, came an inner gnawing, an ominous feeling of doubt. Let's assume he's telling the truth, Yasha thought, then who is deceiving whom? Aloud he said, "It doesn't sound like much of a triumph to me. You captured a soldier who wanted to surrender."

"Well, you've got to catch them at the right moment. In Lublin it's not as easy as you think. You see some girl. She wants you, you want her— the problem is how can the cat climb the fence? Let's say you're at a wedding; when it's over she goes home with her husband and you don't even know where she lives. And even if you do know, what good is it? There's her mother, her mother-in-law, her sisters, and her sisters-in-law. You don't have such problems, Yasha. Once you're on the other side of the city gate, the world is yours."

"All right, come along with me."

"You'd take me?"

"I'll do more than that. I'll pay your expenses."

"Yes, and what would Yentel say? When a man has children, he's not free any more. You won't believe me, but I'd miss the kids. I leave town for a few days and I'm half crazy. Can you understand that?"

"I? I understand everything."

"Despite yourself, you get involved. It's as if you took a rope and tied yourself with it."

"What would you do if your wife carried on like the one you were telling me about?"

Schmul's face suddenly became serious. "Believe me, I'd strangle her," and he lifted the mug to his lips and drained its contents.

Well, he's no different from anyone else, Yasha thought as he sipped his beer. It's what we're all after. But how do you manage it?

For quite some time now Yasha had been involved in this very dilemma. It disturbed him day and night. Of course he had always been a soul-searcher, prone to fantasy and strange conjecture, but since the advent of Emilia, his mind was never quiet. He had evolved into a regular philosopher. Now instead of swallowing his beer, he rolled the bitterness around on his tongue, gums, and palate. In the past he had sowed every variety of wild oats, had tangled and disentangled himself on numerous occasions, but in some final sense his marriage had remained sacred to him. He had never concealed that he had a wife and he had always made it clear that he would do nothing that would jeopardize this relationship. But Emilia demanded that he sacrifice everything: his home, his religion—nor were these all that were required. Somehow or other he must raise a vast amount of money. But how could he accomplish that honestly?

No, I must end the thing, he told himself, and the sooner the better.

Schmul twirled his mustache and moistened it with saliva to get the ends nicely pointed. "How's Magda?" he asked.

Yasha woke from his reverie, "How should she be? She's just the same."

"Her mother still living?"

"Yes."

"Have you taught the girl anything?"

"Some things."

"What, for instance?"

"She can spin a barrel with her feet and do somersaults."

"Is that all?"

"That's it."

"Someone showed me a newspaper from Warsaw and there was a great to-do about you in it. What a fuss! They say you're as good as Napoleon the Third's magician. What sleight of hand, eh, Yasha? You really are a master of deception."

Schmul's words jarred him; Yasha did not like to discuss his magic, and for a moment he disputed with himself, finally deciding: I won't answer at all. But aloud he said, "I don't deceive anyone."

"No, of course not. You really swallow the sword."

"Of course I do."

"Go tell that to your grandma."

"You big simpleton, how can anyone deceive the eye? You happen to hear the word 'deception' and you keep repeating it like a parrot. Do you have any idea what the word means? Look, the sword does go down the throat and not into the vest pocket."

"The blade goes into your throat?"

"First the throat, and then the stomach."

"And you stay alive?"

"I have so far."

"Oh Yasha, please don't expect me to believe that!"

"Who gives a damn what you believe?" Yasha said, suddenly becoming weary. Schmul was nothing but a loud-mouthed fool who could not think for himself. They see with their own eyes but they don't believe, Yasha thought. As for Schmul's wife, Yentel, he knew something about her that would have driven that big blockhead insane. Well, everyone has something that he keeps to himself. Each person has his secrets. If the world had ever been informed of what went on inside of him, he, Yasha, would have long ago been committed to a madhouse.

4

The dusk descended. Beyond the city there was still some light, but among the narrow streets and high buildings it was already dark. In the shops, oil lamps and candles were lit. Bearded Jews, dressed in long cloaks and wearing wide boots, moved through the streets on their way to evening prayers. A new moon arose, the moon of the month of Sivan. There were still puddles in the streets, vestiges of the spring rains, even though the sun had been blazing down on the city all day. Here and there, sewers had flooded over with rank water; the air smelled of horse and cow dung and milk fresh from the udder. Smoke came from the chimneys; housewives were busy preparing the evening meal: groats with soup, groats with stew, groats with mushrooms. Yasha said goodbye to Schmul and started for home. The world beyond Lublin was in turmoil. Every day the Polish newspapers screamed war, revolution, crisis. Jews everywhere were being driven from their villages. Many were emigrating to America. But here in Lublin one felt only the stability of a long-established community. Some of the town's synagogues had been built as long ago as the time of Chmelnicki. Rabbis were buried in the cemetery, as well as authors of commentaries, legists, and saints, each under his tombstone or chapel. Old customs prevailed here: the women conducted business and the men studied the Torah.

Pentecost was still several days off, but the cheder boys had already decorated the windows with numerous designs and cutouts; there were also birds moulded out of dough and eggshells, and leaves and branches had been brought in from the countryside in honor of the holiday, the day on which the Torah had been given on Mount Sinai.

Yasha paused at one of the prayerhouses and glanced in. The worshipers were chanting the evening services. He heard a tranquil buzz; they were saying the Eighteen Benedictions. Pious Jews who served their Creator the year round beat their breasts, crying: "We have sinned;" "We have transgressed." Some raised their hands, others their eyes—heavenward.

A gabardined old man with a high crowned hat over two skullcaps, one behind the other, tugged at his white beard and moaned softly. Shadows danced on the walls to the flickering of the one memorial candle in the menorah. For a moment, Yasha lingered at the open door inhaling the mixture of wax, tallow, and something musty—something which he remembered from childhood. Jews—an entire community of them—spoke to a God no one saw. Although plagues, famines, poverty, and pogroms were His gifts to them, they deemed Him merciful and compassionate, and proclaimed themselves His chosen people. Yasha often envied their unswerving faith.

He stood there for a moment before continuing. The streetlamps were lit but it made little difference. They scarcely illumined their own darkness. Since there were no customers in sight, it was hard to understand why the shops remained open. Kerchiefs on their shaven skulls, the shopwomen sat darning their men's socks or sewing little aprons and undershirts for their grandchildren. Yasha knew them all. Married at fourteen or fifteen, they had become grandmothers in their thirties. Old age, prematurely invited, had puckered their faces, stolen their teeth, and left them benign and affectionate.

Though Yasha, like his father and grandfather, had been born here, he remained a stranger—not simply because he had cast off his Jewishness but because he was always a stranger, here and in Warsaw, amongst Jews as well as Gentiles. They were all settled, domesticated—while he kept moving. They had children and grandchildren; there were none for him. They had their God, their saints, their leaders—he had only doubt. Death meant Paradise to them, but to him only dread. What came after life? Was there such a thing as a soul? And what happened to it after it left the body? Since early childhood he had listened to tales of dybbuks, ghosts, werewolves, and hobgoblins. He, himself, had experienced events unexplained by natural law, but what did it all mean? He became increasingly confused and withdrawn. Within him, forces raged; passions reduced him to terror.

In the darkness as he walked, Emilia's face loomed before him: narrow, olive-skinned, with black Jewish eyes, a Slavic turned-up nose, dimpled cheeks, a high forehead, the hair combed straight back, a dark fuzz shadowing the upper lip. She smiled, shy and lustful at once, and eyed him with an inquisitiveness both worldly and sisterly. He wanted to put out his hand to touch her. Was his imagination so vivid, or was this truly a vision? Her image moved backwards like a holy placard in a religious procession. He saw details of her coiffure, the lace around her neck, the earrings in her ears. He yearned to call her by name. None of his past affairs could compare with this one. Asleep and awake, he hungered for her. Now that fatigue had left him he could scarcely wait for the Pentecost to pass so that he could be with her in Warsaw again. He had not assuaged his passion through Esther, though he had tried.

Someone jostled him. It was Haskell, the water bearer, with two buckets of water on his yoke. He seemed to have sprung out of the earth. The red beard picked up glints of light from somewhere.

"Haskell, is it you?"

"Who else?"

"Isn't it late to carry water?"

"I need money for the holidays."

Yasha rummaged in his pocket, found a twenty-groschen piece. "Here, Haskell."

Haskell bristled. "What's this? I don't take alms."

"It's not alms, it's for your boy to buy himself a butter-cookie."

"All right, I'll take it—and thanks."

And Haskell's dirty fingers intertwined for a moment with Yasha's.

Yasha came to his house and looked into the window. The seamstresses were working on a trousseau for a bride. The thimbled fingers sewed swiftly. In the lamplight, a seamstress' red hair seemed aflame. Esther bustled around the stove, adding pine twigs to the tripod on which the supper was cooking. A trough of dough in the center of the room was covered with rags and a cushion; Esther was about to bake a batch of butter-cookies from it for the Pentecost. Can I leave her? Yasha thought. During all these years she's been my only support. Were it not for her devotion, I would have long since drifted like a leaf in a windstorm. . . .

He did not go immediately into his rooms, but walked down the corridor into the courtyard to look in on the mares. The courtyard was like a patch of country in the midst of a city. The grass was dewy, the apples green and raw, but already fragrant. The sky here seemed lower, more dense with stars. As Yasha walked into the courtyard, a star somewhere in space detached itself and plummeted, trailing a fiery wake. The air smelled half-sweet, half-acrid, alive with rustlings, ferment, and crickets' chirping—which, every once in a while became a loud ringing. Field mice scurried about. Moles had burrowed humps in the ground, birds' nests were in the branches of trees, in the barn, and the roof-eaves. Chickens dozed in the hayloft. Each night the fowl bickered quietly over the disputed porch-space. Yasha breathed deeply. Strange, that every star was larger than the earth, and millions of miles beyond it. If one were to dig a ditch thousands of miles deep into the earth, one would come up in America. . . . He opened the stable-door. The horses loomed mysteriously, shrouded in the darkness. The pupil-filled eyes were flecked with gold or fire. Yasha recalled what his father—blessed be his memory—had told him: that animals could see the forces of evil. Kara swished her tail and pawed the earth. A gripping animal devotion exuded from the mare to her master.

All the temples, prayerhouses and Hasidic assembly rooms were jam-packed for the Pentecost. Even Esther put on the hat she had made for her wedding, took her gold-engraved prayer book and headed for the women's synagogue. But Yasha remained at home. Since God did not answer, why address Him? He began to read a thick Polish book on the Laws of Nature that he had bought in Warsaw. Everything was explained therein: the law of gravity, how each magnet had a north and a south pole, how likes repelled and opposites attracted. It was all here: why a ship floated, how a hydraulic press operated, how a lightning rod drew the lightning, how steam moved a locomotive. This information was as vital to Yasha professionally as it was interesting. He had been walking the tightrope for years without knowing that he had stayed up only because he managed to balance the center of his gravity directly over the rope. But after he had finished this illuminating book, many questions remained unanswered. Why did the ground pull the rock to it? What, actually, was gravity? And why did a magnet attract iron but not copper? What was electricity? And from where had it all come: the sky, the earth, the sun, the moon, the stars? The book mentioned Kant's and Laplace's theory of the solar system, but somehow it did not ring true. Emilia had presented Yasha with a volume on the Christian religion written by a professor of theology, but the story of the immaculate conception and the explanation of the trinity—the Father, the Son, and the Holy Ghost—seemed to Yasha even more unbelievable than the miracles which the Hassidim attributed to their rabbis. How can she believe this? he asked himself. No, she only pretends. They all pretend. The whole world acts out a farce because everyone is ashamed to say: I do not know.

He paced back and forth. His thoughts were always stimulated when he was alone in the house, while others were at temple. How had it come about? His father had been a pious Jew, an impecunious hardware-dealer. His mother had died when Yasha was seven and the father had not remarried; the boy had had to raise himself. He would go to cheder one day, skip the next three days. An abundance of locks and keys were to be found in his father's store and Yasha had been curious about them. He would fumble and fuss with a lock until it opened without a key. When magicians came to Lublin from Warsaw and other big cities, Yasha would follow them from street to street, observing their tricks, and later he would attempt to duplicate them. If he saw someone do a card trick, he would play around with a deck of cards until he mastered it. He watched an acrobat walk the tightrope and went home promptly to try it. After falling, he would mount again. He scampered over rooftops, swam in deep water, leaped from balconies (into straw discarded from mattresses before Passover), but somehow nothing harmed him. He cheated in his prayers and desecrated the Sabbath, but continued to believe that a guardian angel watched and protected him from danger. Despite his reputation as an unbeliever, rascal, and savage, a respectable girl, Esther, had fallen in love with him. He roamed about with a circus, a bear trainer, even with a Polish wandering troupe which performed in firehouses, but Esther waited for him patiently, forgiving all his peccadilloes. It was because of her that he had his home, his estate. The knowledge that Esther awaited him had fired him with the ambition to raise his station, to aspire to the Warsaw circus, and the summer theaters, to become famous throughout Poland. He was no street performer now, who drags about with an accordion and a monkey—he was an artist. The newspapers hailed him, called him a master, a great talent; noblemen and *grand dames* came backstage to greet him. Everyone said that had he lived in Western Europe, he would be world-famous by now.

The years had passed but he could not say where. At times he felt as if he were still a boy, at other times he seemed a hundred years old. He had taught himself Polish, Russian, grammar, and arithmetic; he had read textbooks on algebra, physics, geography, chemistry, and history. His mind was crammed with facts, dates, information. He remembered everything, forgot nothing. One glance determined a person's character for him. Someone need only open his mouth and Yasha would know what was about to be said. He could read while blindfolded, was expert at mesmerism, magnetism, and hypnotism. But what was happening between Emilia—a high-born professor's widow—and himself, was something different. It was not he who had magnetized her, but the other way around. Although they were miles apart, she never left him. He felt her gaze, heard her voice, inhaled her aroma. He was tense as though walking the tightrope. As soon as he went to sleep, she would come to him—in spirit, but vibrantly alive, whispering sweet nothings, kissing, embracing, showering him with affection and, strangely enough, her daughter, Halina, would be there too.

The door opened and Esther came in, prayerbook in one hand, the train of her silken gown, with the tucks and stripes, in the other. Her feathered hat reminded Yasha of the first Saturday after the wedding, when Esther, the bride, had been led to the temple. Her eyes sparkled with joy now—the high spirits of one who has shared ceremonies with others.

"Happy holiday!"

"Happy holiday to you, Esther!"

He embraced her and she blushed like a bride. The long periods of separation had preserved in them the eagerness of newlyweds.

"What's new at the temple?"

"The men's or the women's?"

"The women's."

Esther laughed.

"Women are women. A little praying and a little gossip. You should have heard the hymn of

Acdamuth. It was glorious. Compare it to your finest opera!"

She immediately began to prepare the holiday meal. No matter what Yasha chose to be, she was determined to have a good Jewish home like the others. She placed a carafe of wine, a benediction winecup, twin jars of salt and honey, a Sabbath loaf, and a pearl-handled breadknife, on the table. Yasha said a benediction over the wine. It was one thing he dared not refuse her. They were alone, and this always reminded Esther of her infecundity. Children would have made all the difference. She smiled sadly and wiped away a tear with the edge of an embroidered apron. She served the fish, the noodles with milk, the kreplach with cheese and cinnamon, the dessert of stewed prunes, butter-cake, and coffee. Yasha was always home for the holidays; it was the only time they were together. Esther looked at her husband as she ate. Who was he? Why did she love him? She knew he led a wicked life. She did not reveal all she knew; only God knew how far he had fallen. But she could hold no grudges against him. Everyone villified him and pitied her, but she preferred him above any man, no matter how exalted—even a rabbi.

After the meal, the couple retired to their bedroom. Man and wife don't usually lie together in the daytime, but when he went outside to close the shutters, she did not protest. As soon as he put his arm around her she was aroused, like an adolescent—since a woman who has not been pregnant, remains virginal forever.

TWO

The Pentecost was over. Yasha again prepared to go on the road. During his last night home, he said things that frightened Esther.

"How would you feel if I never returned?" he asked her. "What would you do if I died on the road?"

Esther silenced him with her hand over his mouth, and begged him never to speak like that, but he persisted. "Such things do happen, you know. Only recently I climbed the tower of a city hall; I could easily have slipped right there and then." He also mentioned his will and admonished her not to mourn him for too long a period, should he pass away. Then he showed her a hiding place where he had secreted a few hundred rubles in golden ducats. When Esther protested that he was ruining the last few hours they had before their next meeting on the Days of Awe, he countered: "Well, suppose I'd fallen in love with someone else and were going to leave you. What would you say to that?"

"What? Have you fallen in love with someone else?"

"Don't be ridiculous."

"You'd better tell me the truth."

He kissed her and vowed eternal love. These scenes between them were not new. He liked to tease her with all sorts of contingencies and vex her with puzzling questions. How long would she wait for him if he were imprisoned? Or if he went to America? Or if he contracted consumption and were confined to a sanitarium? Esther always offered the same reply: She could love no one else; without him, her life would end. But he often resorted to this kind of interrogation. He now demanded, "What would happen if I became an ascetic and, to repent, had myself bricked into a cell without a door like that saint in Lithuania? Would you remain true to me? Would you give me food through a slit in the wall?"

Esther said, "It's not necessary to seal one's self in a cell to repent."

"It all depends on what sort of passion one is trying to control," he answered.

"Then I would seal myself in with you," she said.

It all ended with fresh caresses, endearments, and protestations of undying love. When Esther later fell asleep, she suffered a terrifying nightmare and on the following day fasted until noon. She quietly uttered a prayer which she'd found in a prayer-book: "God Almighty, I am Yours and my dreams are Yours. . . ." She also dropped six groschen into the alms box of Reb Mayer, The Miracle Worker. She asked Yasha to give his holy promise never again to torment her with such idle talk, since, what could a person know of the future?—Everything was ordained in Heaven.

The holidays were over. Yasha hitched up the wagon and prepared to leave on his journey. He took along the monkey, the crow, and the parrot. Esther cried so much that her eyes swelled. One side of her head ached, a weight seemed to press against her left breast. She was not a drinker, but for the first days after his departure she always sipped cherry-brandy to uplift her spirit. The seamstresses suffered from her grief; she found fault with every stitch. Strangely enough, the girls sulked as well after Yasha left—he was that "lucky."

He went on a Saturday night. Esther accompanied him all the way to the highway with his wagon. She would have gone further, but he playfully drove her back with his whip. He did not want her walking back so far alone in the dark. He kissed her for the last time and left her standing there—tearful and with arms outstretched. For years they had parted this way but the leave-taking seemed more difficult now than ever.

He clicked his tongue and the horses broke into a trot. The night was mild, a three-quarter moon hung in the sky. Yasha's eyes misted; after a while he gave the horses free rein. The moon rode with him. In the gloriously moonlit fields, the tips of the green wheat gleamed bright and silvery. He could distinguish every scarecrow, every path, every cornflower along the road. The dew descended like flour from a heavenly sieve. There was a seething in the fields, as if unseen grains poured into an unseen mill. Even the horses occasionally turned their heads. One could almost hear the roots sucking the earth, the stalks growing, the underground streams trickling. Occasionally a shadow, as of a mythical bird, crossed the fields. At times a droning became audible, neither human nor animal, but as if a monster hovered somewhere in space. Yasha breathed deeply and fingered his pistol, which he carried as protection against highwaymen. He was on the road to Piask. There, outside of town, lived Magda's mother, the widow of a blacksmith. In Piask itself, he numbered among his acquaintances notorious thieves, as well as one Zeftel, a deserted wife, with whom he was having an affair.

Soon the smithy, a sooty structure, its crooked roof torn apart like an abandoned nest, its walls askew, its window a hole, materialized. Once, Adam Zbarski, Magda's father, had forged axes and plough-shares here. The son of a nobleman ruined by the uprising in 1831, he had sent Magda to a school in Lublin and had later perished during an epidemic. For eight years Magda had been Yasha's assistant. Since she was an acrobat, she had short hair and wore a leotard during the performances, where she turned somersaults, spun a barrel on her feet and handed Yasha his juggling paraphernalia. In the Old City of Warsaw they shared the same apartment. She was registered with the municipal authorities as his maid.

The horses must have recognized the smithy for they went faster. Now they moved through buckwheat and potato fields, past a roadside shrine where the Virgin Mary held the Christ child in her arms. In the moonlight the statue appeared strangely alive. On a hill further on, the Catholic cemetery stood, surrounded by a low fence. Yasha focused his eyes. Here lay the ones who rested eternally. In cemeteries, he always sought omens of life after death. He had heard all kinds of stories of little flames which flickered between the graves—as well as of shades and phantoms. It was said of Yasha's own grandfather that he had revealed himself to his children and even to strangers weeks and months after his death. It was even said that he once rapped on his daughter's window. But Yasha could see nothing now. The birch trees, leaning together, looked petrified. Although there was no wind, their leaves rustled as if self-stirred. The tombstones gazed at each other with the silence of beings who had had their final say.

2

The Zbarskis had been expecting Yasha; neither mother nor daughter had retired for the night. Elzbieta Zbarski, the smith's widow, was a stout woman, built like a haystack. Her white hair was pinned up in back and her face was gentle despite her size. She sat playing patience. Although she could neither read nor write, having been orphaned at an early age, her knowledge of cards indicated irrevocably an aristocratic descent. Once, she must have been beautiful since even now her features were regular: her nose well cut and slightly turned up, her mouth thin and shapely, without a tooth missing, her eyes bright. But she had a broad double-chin, underhung with a goiter which extended nearly to the breast; her bosom jutted out like a balcony; her arms were uncommonly thick and weighty; her torso like a sack stuffed with flesh of which little mounds burst out here and there. She had bad feet and had to use a cane, even around the house. The deck of playing cards was soiled and wrinkled. She mumbled to herself, "Again the ace of spades! It's a bad sign. Something is going to happen, children, something is going to happen! . . ."

"What's going to happen, Mother? Don't be so superstitious!" Magda cried out.

Magda had already packed her possessions in a chest with brass hoops—a present from Yasha. She was in her late twenties but appeared younger; audiences thought her no more than eighteen. Slight, swarthy, flat-chested, barely skin-and-bones, it was hard to believe she was Elzbieta's child. Her eyes were grayish-green, her nose snub, her lips full and pouting as if ready to be kissed, or like those of a child about to cry. Her neck was long and thin, her hair ash-colored, the high cheekbones roseola-red. Her skin was pimply; at boarding school she had been nicknamed the Frog. She had been a surly, introspective schoolgirl with a furtive air, given to preposterous antics. Even then she had already proved unusually agile. She could scurry up a tree, master the latest dance, and, after lights-out, leave the dormitory by way of the window and later return the same way. Magda still spoke of the boarding-school as a hell hole. Inept at her studies, she had been taunted by her schoolmates because her father had been a smith; even her teachers had been hostile. Several times she had tried to run away, quarreled frequently with other students, and, once, after punishment, had spat in a nun's face. When her father died, Magda left the school without a diploma. Soon afterwards, Yasha hired her as his assistant.

When Magda was younger it had been said that a man in her life would drive the rash out, since it was obviously due to virginal frustration; but she had been Yasha's mistress for years and her skin was as bad as ever. Magda made no secret of the relationship with her master. Each time that Yasha spent the night at the Zbarski's, she slept with him in the wide bed in the alcove, and in the morning her mother even brought the bedded couple tea with milk. Elzbieta called Yasha "my son." In the past, Bolek, Magda's younger brother, furious at Yasha, had sworn revenge, but eventually even Bolek became accustomed to the situation. Yasha supported the family, gave Bolek money for his carousing and his gambling at cards and dominoes. Each time the drunken Bolek threatened to avenge himself upon this damned Jew who had disgraced the name of Zbarski, Elzbieta would beat her head with her fists and Magda would say, "You touch a hair of his head and both of us will die! You'll come with me to the grave. I swear it on Father's memory. . . ."

And she'd rear back and hiss and spit like a cat at a dog.

The family had sunk low. Magda tramped about with a magician. Bolek drove for the Piask thieves. They sent him with their loot to those who received stolen goods and he often slept among cut-throats. Elzbieta, on the other hand, had become a glutton. She was so huge she could barely get through the doorway. From early dawn to the last "Holy Father" before retiring, she nibbled at various delicacies: sausages with sauerkraut, cakes baked in lard, eggs fried with onions and fat drippings, or fritters filled with meat or groats. Her legs had become so heavy that she no longer went to church, even on Sundays. She would lament to her children, "We are forsaken, forsaken! Since your father, may his soul find peace in Heaven, passed away, we're nothing but dirt. . . . No one cares about us. . . ."

The neighbors said that Elzbieta had sacrificed Magda because of Bolek. Elzbieta adored him blindly, indulged his every whim, justified all his excesses, surrendered to him her last groschen.

Although she no longer went to church, she still prayed to Jesus, lit candles to the saints, and genuflected before the holy images, mouthing the prayers from memory. Elzbieta was possessed by one fear—that something would happen to their benefactor, Yasha; that he might, God forbid, lose interest in Magda. The family owed its existence to his generosity. She, Elzbieta, was like a broken shard with her arthritic limbs, pain-wracked spine, the varicose veins in her legs, and the lump in her breast grown hard as a pebble—a constant worry to her lest it spread as had her mother's, may she rest in Paradise. . . .

Bolek had gone to Piask in the morning and no one could say whether he would spend the night with that rabble, as Elzbieta had branded the band of thieves. He also had a sweetheart in town. Thus, Elzbieta was expecting either Yasha or Bolek that night, and the game of Patience served not only to predict the future, but to tell her which of the two would arrive first—and at what time. Each card signified something to her. And, whenever the deck was shuffled, the same king, queen, or jack would take on another expression. The printed portraits were alive to her, knowing and mysterious. When she heard her dog, Burek, bark, and the wagon wheels rasp, she crossed herself gratefully. Blessed be Jesus, he was here, her precious boy from Lublin, her benefactor. She knew that he had a wife in Lublin, and associated with that gang of rogues in Piask, but she would not permit herself to dwell upon this—to what avail? One had to take what one could get. She was an impoverished widow, her children were orphans, and—how could one fathom the ways of a man? It was still better than sending her daughter to toil in the factories where she'd cough out her lungs, or to a brothel. Each time that Yasha's wagon approached, Elzbieta felt the same sensation—the forces of evil had conspired to engulf her but she had vanquished them with her prayers and supplications to the Saviour. She clapped her hands and looked triumphantly at Magda, but her daughter, proud as ever, remained impassive, although her mother well knew that she was inwardly delighted. Yasha was both lover and father to the girl. Who else would bother with such a dried-up snip, thin as a twig, and with a bosom so flat?

Elzbieta began to sigh, pant, and scrape her chair backwards, in an effort to raise herself. Magda hesitated a little while longer, then dashed outside and ran to Yasha with open arms: "Darling! . . ."

He dismounted, kissed and embraced her. Her skin felt almost feverish. Burek had been fawning upon the visitor from the beginning. The parrot scolded from her cage, the monkey screeched, the crow cawed and spoke. Elzbieta waited for Yasha to finish with her daughter before she appeared on the threshold. She stood there—large and ungainly as a snowman, waiting patiently for him to come and kiss her hand like a gentleman. Every time he came, she would embrace him, kiss his forehead, and offer the same greeting: "A guest in the house—God in the house. . . ."

And then she would weep and dab at her eyes with her apron.

3

Elzbieta looked forward to Yasha's visits not only for her daughter's sake, but for her own as well. He always brought her something from Lublin: some delicatessen, liver, halvah, or store-bought pastry. But even more than the delicacies, she longed for someone with whom to converse. Bolek refused to listen despite her sacrifices and servitude. As soon as she began a story he would interrupt brutally, "That's right, Mama, keep lying, keep lying."

And at his impudence the words would choke in Elzbieta's throat. She would begin to cough and turn apoplectically red. Gasping, hiccuping, she had to allow this same foul brute of a Bolek to fetch water and pound her nape and back in order to subdue the lump in her throat.

Magda, on the other hand, scarcely spoke. One could address her for three hours, relating the most unusual events, and she would not even blink an eye. Only Yasha, the Jew, the magician, would draw Elzbieta out, encourage her to express herself, treat her as a mother-in-law should be treated, not as a hated mother-in-law, but as one beloved. He, the poor boy, had himself been orphaned at an early age and Elzbieta was like a mother to him. She secretly felt that Magda owed it to her that Yasha had remained with them these many years. She, Elzbieta, cooked his favorite dishes for him, offered him all sorts of practical advice, warned him to beware of enemies, even interpreted his dreams. She had presented him with a miniature elephant, an heirloom from her grandmother's estate, which he wore under his lapel whenever he walked the tightrope or performed any other of his dangerous stunts.

Although when he arrived he insisted he was not hungry, Elzbieta always had a meal ready for him. Everything had been prepared beforehand: the freshly laundered tablecloth, the kindling wood for the stove, the porcelain cup from which he drank, the blue-patterned platter from which he ate. Nothing was missing, not even the table napkin. Elzbieta was considered an excellent housekeeper. Her husband might have been a blacksmith but her grandfather, the Squire Czapinski, had owned an estate of four hundred peasants, and had hunted with the noble Radziwills.

Elzbieta had already eaten supper but Yasha's arrival rekindled her appetite. After the first warm exchanges, Yasha and Magda retired to the alcove and Elzbieta occupied herself preparing the meal. Her weariness vanished miraculously; her legs, which usually felt leaden at night, seemed to have had their numbness exorcised by an amulet. In no time she had the fire started in the stove, she cooked and fried with an astonishing agility. She sighed pleasurably. Was it any wonder Magda adored him? He even breathed new life into her, Elzbieta.

The events followed their usual pattern. He assured her that he was not hungry, but the food was already before him, its aroma permeating every corner of the room. She had prepared blintzes with cherries and cheese, sprinkled with sugar and cinnamon. A bottle of cherry-brandy stood on the table as well as the sweet liquor Yasha had brought from Warsaw during a previous visit. As soon as Yasha tasted the food, he immediately requested more. Magda, who had a shrunken stomach and also suffered from constipation, suddenly developed a healthy appetite. The dog, tail wagging, hovered at Yasha's knee. After the coffee and the lard-cookies, Elzbieta began to reminisce: of how devoted her late husband had been to her, how he had carried her around in his arms, how once the Czar's carriage had stopped before the smithy to replace a lost horseshoe and the Czar, himself, had gone into their house while waiting, and she, Elzbieta, had given him a drink of vodka. Her greatest adventure had been during the time of the uprising of 1863 when she had given refuge to condemned rebels and had warned the Polish troops of the approaching Cossacks. Eloquently, tearfully, she had saved a noblewoman from being lashed by Russian soldiers. Magda had been only a child then but Elzbieta turned to her for confirmation. "Don't you remember, Magda? You sat on the general's lap, he was wearing the trousers with the red stripes and you sat there and played with his medals. You don't remember? Ah, children . . . they have heads like cabbages. . . . Eat, darling boy, take another blintze. It won't hurt you.

My grandma, may she intercede for us in heaven, used to say, 'The intestine is endless.' "

One story led to another. Elzbieta had suffered all sorts of illnesses. She had had a breast cut open and sewn up again with a needle. She lowered her blouse to show the scar. Once she'd been at the point of death—the priest had given her extreme unction and they had measured her for a coffin. She lay as if dead and saw angels, ghosts, and visions. Suddenly her dead father appeared and drove away all the phantoms, shouting, "My daughter has small children. She must not die! . . ." and in that moment she had begun to sweat drops of perspiration large as sugar beans.

The clock with the wooden weights indicated midnight already, but Elzbieta was only warming up. She still had dozens of stories waiting. Yasha listened courteously, asked the proper questions, nodded at required intervals. The miracles and omens she described sounded oddly similar to those told by the Jews in Lublin. Magda began yawning and blushing.

"Last time, Mama, you told the same story entirely differently."

"What are you saying, child? How dare you? You disgrace me before my precious boy. Yes, your mother is a humble widow without money, without honor, but a liar—never!"

"You forget, Mother."

"I forget nothing. My whole life stands before my eyes like a tapestry." And she began telling a new tale of a terrible frost. The winter had begun so early that year that the Jews had been unable

to use the booths during the Feast of the Tabernacles. The winds had blown away the thatch.
The raging torrents had destroyed the sluice-
gates in the mill, pierced the dam, and inundated
half a village. Afterwards, such deep snowdrifts
had formed that people had sunk in them as if in
swamps and their bodies were not recovered until
the following spring. Starving wolves had deserted the forests to invade the villages and snatch
babies out of cribs. So severe had the frosts been
that the oaks had burst. Just then, Bolek
swaggered in, a young man of medium height,
husky, with a red pock-marked face, pale blue
eyes, yellow hair, and a snub nose with nostrils
wide as a bulldog's. He wore an embroidered
waistcoat, jodhpurs, high boots, and a hat with a
feather—the picture of a huntsman! A cigaret
drooped from the corner of his mouth. He came
whistling, and stumbled on the threshold like a
drunkard. When he spied Yasha, he laughed—
then promptly grew serious, even grim.

"Well, well—so you are here."

"Kiss each other, brothers-in-law!" Elzbieta
trilled. "You are kin, after all . . . As long as
Yasha is with Magda, he is like your brother,
Bolek—even closer, closer."

"Stop it, Mama!"

"What am I asking, after all? Only for peace.
The priest once preached that peace was like the
dew that falls from heaven and satiates the fields.
It was the time the Bishop from Czestochow
came to us. I remember as if it were today—he
wore a red skullcap."

And Elzbieta could say no more. Her tears had begun to flow again.

Yasha was anxious to start for Warsaw, but he was compelled to linger a day or two. After a while he retired for the night in the wide bed in the alcove. Elzbieta had stuffed fresh straw into the mattress and covered the pillow and comforter with fresh linen. Magda did not come to him immediately. She first washed and combed her hair. Her mother helped soap her down, and afterwards dressed her in a long nightgown with lace at the hem and bosom. Yasha lay quietly, amazed at his own behavior. "It's all because I'm so bored," he said to himself. He listened intently. Mother and daughter were bickering over something. Elzbieta liked to offer Magda advice before she went to bed. She also tried to make her daughter tie a lavender sachet on her person. Bolek snored, stretched out on the bench-bed. Funny, but he, Yasha, lived his whole life as if walking the tightrope, merely inches from disaster. One false move on his part, and Bolek would surely plunge a knife into his heart.

Yasha dozed off and dreamt that he was flying. He rose above the ground and soared, soared. He wondered why he had not tried it before—it was so easy, so easy. He dreamt this almost every night, and each time awoke with the sensation that a distorted kind of reality had been revealed to him. Often he wondered if it had been a dream or simply a train of thought. For years now he had been fascinated by the idea of putting on a pair of wings and flying. If a bird could do it, why not man? The wings would have to be large enough and made of a strong silk like the kind used in balloons. They should be sewn onto ribs and should be able to fold and unfold like an umbrella. And if the wings were not enough, a sort of web, like a bat's, could be attached between the legs to assist buoyancy. Man was heavier than a bird, but eagles and hawks were not exactly light either, and they could even lift a lamb and fly away with it. Whatever time Yasha could spare from thoughts of Emilia, he dedicated to this problem. He had drawers full of plans and diagrams, bales of clippings from newspapers and magazines. Of course, many of those who'd tried to fly had been killed, but it was a fact that they had flown, if only temporarily. Simply let the material be strong enough, the ribs elastic, the man agile, light, and sprightly, and the deed must be accomplished. What a sensation it would cause throughout the world if he, Yasha, flew over the rooftops of Warsaw or better still— Rome, Paris, or London.

He apparently dozed off again, for when Magda got into bed he woke with a start although he had been lying there with his eyes open. She brought with her the odor of camomile. She was, and always had been, shy. She came to him like a timid virgin, smiled as if apologizing. She lay down next to him—bony, icy, in a nightgown too spacious, her hair still damp from combing. He ran his hand down her emaciated ribs.

"What's the matter with you? Don't you eat?"

"Yes, I eat."

"It would be easy for you to fly. You weigh about as much as a goose."

Once they were on the road they grew quite familiar, but now after the long absence—the weeks he'd spent away from her with his wife, Esther—they had grown apart and had to reacquaint themselves. It was like a wedding night. She lay with her back to him and he had to court her silently to make her turn to him. She still felt ashamed before her mother and brother. When he made too loud a sound she placed her palm over his mouth to silence him. He embraced her and she fluttered like a pullet in his arms. She whispered to him so quietly he could barely hear her. Why had he stayed away so long? She had certainly feared he would never come again. Mother went around talking a blue streak, complaining . . . worrying about his abandoning her, Magda. Bolek was in with that pack of thieves. It was a disgrace, a disgrace. He might be thrown in jail. And he drank too much. Got drunk and went around looking for trouble. And what had Yasha been doing in Lublin all those weeks? The days had gone slowly like molasses.

It was astonishing that this shy girl could grow so passionate, as if bewitched. She showered Yasha with kisses, surrendered herself to him in all the ways he had taught her—but in silence, afraid that her brother or mother might waken.

It was like a secret rite they performed before a night spirit. Although she had been taught a flawless Polish at the school, she now babbled in a rustic gibberish which he could scarcely understand; uttered words—strange, stilted, inherited from generations of peasants.

He said, "If by chance I should leave you, remember that I'll come back. Be true to me."

"Yes, beloved, until death!"

"I'll put wings on you, make you fly."

"Yes, my Lord . . . I'm flying now."

5

It was market day in Piask. Bolek had gone to Lublin right after breakfast. Yasha started out by foot to Piask, claiming that he had to make some purchases in the stores. Elzbieta tried to deter him, desiring his presence at lunchtime, but Magda stopped her with a shake of the head. She never interfered with him. He kissed her and she said, humbly, "Don't forget the way home."

The market had opened at daybreak but late-arriving peasants were still walking down the road. One led a scrawny cow ready for the slaughter, another a hog, or a goat. Women with wooden frames under their headkerchiefs—signifying married status—carried their wares in bowls, pitchers, and baskets covered with linen cloths. They laughed and called out to Yasha. They remembered his touring the villages with his act years ago. A wagon appeared and, in it, a peasant bride and groom and a band of musicians. The team was decorated with green twigs and garlands of flowers. Musicians, sawing small fiddles, chanted a long drawn-out melody. From a wagon of peasant girls jammed together like geese rose a song vowing revenge upon men:

> *Black am I, oh black.*
> *I'll blacken myself some more*
> *I'll be the blackest thing, dear lad,*
> *That ever made you care.*

> *White am I, oh white.*
> *I'll whiten myself some more*
> *When you look at me, dear boy,*
> *You'll long, but I won't care.*

Zeftel, the deserted wife, lived on a hill behind the slaughterhouses. Her husband, Leibush Lekach, had, some time ago, escaped from the Yanov prison and his present whereabouts were unknown. Some said that he had fled to America, others thought he was somewhere deep in the wilds of Russia. For many months there had been no word from him. The thieves, who had their own brotherhood—with elders and by-laws—gave Zeftel two gulden every week as they usually did when the man of the house was in prison; but it was becoming apparent that Leibush had vanished permanently. The couple had been childless. Zeftel, who was not a local girl, came from somewhere on the other side of the Vistula. Usually, the wives of imprisoned thieves conducted themselves honorably, but Zeftel was considered suspect. She wore jewelry even on weekdays, kept her head uncovered, and cooked on the Sabbath. Any day now her allowance would be cut off.

Yasha was aware of all this, but he had involved himself with the woman, nevertheless; he came to her through back-alleys and gave her three-ruble bills. He now carried a present for her from Warsaw—a coral necklace. It was madness. He had a wife, he had Magda, he was wildly infatuated with Emilia,—what was he looking for on top of this dung-heap? He had repeatedly decided to break off, but whenever he came to Piask he was again drawn to her. He now ran towards her house with the fear and anticipation of a schoolboy about to go to bed with his first woman. He approached her house not by Lublin Street but through the back way. Although it was past Pentecost, the ground here was still slimy and soggy, but Zeftel's house was clean inside, with curtains, a lamp with a paper-fringed shade, a cushion on the bed, the floor freshly scrubbed and sprinkled with sand as if on Friday night for the benediction of the candles. Zeftel was standing in the center of the room—a young-looking, curly-haired woman with eyes black as a gypsy's, a beauty patch on her left cheek and a string of glass beads around her neck. She smiled cunningly at him, revealing her white teeth, and spoke in her other-side-of-the-Vistula dialect, "I thought you surely weren't coming!"

"I come when I say I will," Yasha replied sternly.

"An unexpected guest!"

It was all humiliating to him, the kissing, the offering of the present, the waiting while she fetched the coffee with chicory, but just as the thieves had to steal money—he had to steal love. She bolted the door to avoid interruptions, and stuffed paper into the keyhole. She was as much disposed to dawdle as he was to hurry. He kept looking meaningfully at the bed, but she drew the calico curtain, indicating that it was not yet time.

"What's going on in the world?" she asked.

"I don't know myself."

"Who would know if you don't? We're stuck here but you roam about as free as a bird."

She sat down near him, her round knee against his. She arranged her skirt so that he could see the tops of her black stockings and her red garters.

"I see you so seldom," she complained, "that I forget from one time to the next."

"Have you heard anything from your husband?"

"Gone—like a stone in the sea." And she smiled—humbly, arrogantly, deceitfully.

He had to hear her out since a woman who is loquacious is passionately so. Even as she complained, the words shot out—smooth and round, like peas from a peashooter. What did the future hold for her here in Piask? Leibush would never return. The other side of the ocean might as well be the other world. She was practically a widow already. They doled out the two gulden a week to her, but for how long would this continue? Their

treasury was bare. Half the brotherhood was behind bars. And what could she buy with this
chicken feed? Water for groats. She was in debt
to everybody. She didn't have a thing to wear. All
the women were her enemies. They gossiped
about her constantly and her ears were forever
burning. While it was still summer she could bear
it, but as soon as the rains came she would go out
of her mind. And while Zeftel spoke of doom, she
continued to trifle with the loop of her necklace.
A dimple suddenly appeared in her right cheek.

"Oh, Yashale, take me with you."

"You know I can't."

"Why not? You have a team and wagon."

"What would Magda say? What would your
neighbors say?"

"They say it anyhow. Whatever that Polack of
yours can do, I can do as well. Maybe even a little
better."

"Can you turn a somersault?"

"If I can't, I'll learn."

It was all idle chatter. She was too stout to become an acrobat. Her legs were too short, her hips
too broad, her bosom too protuberant.

She could never be anything but a servant—
and one other thing, Yasha thought. Although
he, Yasha, surely did not love her, he grew momentarily jealous. How did she behave all the
weeks he was on the road? Well, this is the last
time I'll come here, he thought. It's only because
I'm so bored and I want to forget for a little
while—he justified his conduct to himself. Like a
drunkard who drowns his sorrow in alcohol, he

thought. He could never understand how other people managed to live in one place and spend their entire lives with one woman without becoming melancholy. He, Yasha, was forever at the point of depression. He suddenly drew three silver rubles and with childish gravity placed them upon her leg beneath the dress—one near the knee, the other a trifle higher, the third upon her thigh. Zeftel watched him with a curious smile.

"This won't help."

"It certainly won't hurt any."

He addressed her crudely—at her own level. It was one of his attributes to adjust to any character. It was a useful factor when applied to the art of magnetism. Deliberately, Zeftel collected the coins and deposited them in a mortar on the dresser.

"Well, thanks anyhow."

"I'm in a hurry."

"What's the rush? I've missed you. For weeks I don't hear a word from you. How have you been, Yashale? We are good friends, too, after all."

"Yes, yes . . ."

"Why the wool-gathering? I know—it must be a new girl! Tell me, Yashale, tell me. I'm not the jealous type. I know what's going on. But to you women are like flowers to a bee. Always a new one. A sniff here, a lick there and 'whist!'—you buzz away. How I envy you! It would be worth surrendering my last pair of drawers to be a man!"

"Yes, there is a new one," Yasha said. He needed to talk to someone. With Zeftel, he felt as uninhibited as with himself. He feared neither her jealousy nor her wrath. She yielded to him as a peasant girl to a squire. Her eyes began to sparkle. She smiled the bitter smile of those who are wronged and take pleasure in this.

"Didn't I know it? Who is she?"

"A professor's widow."

"Widow, eh? Well, well."

"Well nothing."

"Are you in love with her?"

"Yes, a little."

"If a man says 'a little,' he means a whole lot. What is she—young? Pretty?"

"Not so young. She has a daughter of fourteen."

"Which one is it you love, the mother or the daughter?"

"Both."

Zeftel's throat moved, as if she had swallowed something. "You can't have both, brother."

"For the present, I'll be satisfied with the mother."

"What's a professor like—a doctor?"

"He used to teach mathematics at the university."

"What's mathematics?"

"Figuring."

She thought it over for a moment. "I knew it, I

just knew it. Me, you can't fool. One look at a man and I can tell everything. What do you want to do, marry her?"

"But I have a wife already."

"What can a wife mean to you? How did you meet her?"

"She was at the theater and someone introduced us. No, I was mind-reading and I told her that she was a widow and the rest of it."

"How did you know that?"

"That's my secret."

"Well, what else?"

"She fell in love with me. She wants to leave everything behind and go abroad with me."

"Just like that?"

"She wants to marry me."

"A Jew?"

"She wants me to convert a little. . . ."

"Just a little, eh?—Why do you have to leave the country?"

Yasha's face grew suddenly grim. "What do I have here? For twenty-five years I've been doing my act and I'm still a pauper. How much longer can I keep walking the tightrope? Ten years at the most. Everyone praises me but nobody wants to pay. In other countries they appreciate somebody like me. There a fellow who knows only a handful of tricks is rich and famous. He performs before royalty, travels about in a fancy carriage. I'd be treated differently even here, in Poland, if my name became famous in Western Europe. Do you understand what I'm saying to you? Here, they imitate everything from abroad. An opera singer can screech like an owl, but if he has sung in Italy, everyone shouts: 'Bravo!' "

"Yes, but you'd have to convert."

"What of it? You cross yourself and they sprinkle you with water. How do I know which God is the right one? No one's been up to Heaven. I don't pray anyhow."

"Once you're a Catholic, you'll pray, all right."

"Abroad, no one pays any attention to it. I'm a magician, not a priest.—You know, there is a new fad now. The lights are put out and you call up the spirits of the dead. You sit around a table with your hands on top of it and the tables rises. All the newspapers are full of it."

"Real spirits?"

"Don't be ridiculous. The medium does it all. He sticks out his foot and raises the table. He clicks his big toe and that means the spirits are sending messages. The wealthiest people attend these seances, especially the women. Let's say someone's son dies and they wish to communicate with him. They give the medium money and he produces the son's ghost."

Zeftel's eyes grew big. "Really?"

"Silly."

"Maybe it's black magic?"

"They don't know any black magic."

"I was told there is a man in Lublin who can show the dead in a black mirror. They say I could see Leibush there."

"Then why don't you go? They'll show you a picture and tell you it's Leibush."

"Well, they do show you something."

"Idiotic," Yasha said, amazed that he should be discussing such matters with someone like Zeftel. "I can show you whomever you like in the mirror, even your grandmother."

"There is no God, is that it?"

"Of course there is, but no one has spoken with Him. How could God speak? If He spoke in Yiddish, the Christians wouldn't understand; if He spoke French, the English would complain. The Torah claims that He spoke in Hebrew but I wasn't there to hear it. As for spirits, they also exist, but no magician can conjure them up."

"And what of the soul? Oh, I'm afraid."

"Afraid of what?"

"At night I lie down and I can't close my eyes: All the dead parade before me. I see how they put Mama into the grave. All white she is . . . Why do we live anyhow? I miss you so much, Yashale! I don't want to be offering advice, but that gentile will drag you down to hell."

Yasha bristled. "Why should she? She loves me."

"It's no good. You can do anything you like but you must remain a Jew. What will become of your wife?"

"What would she do if I were to die? The husband dies and four weeks later the woman rushes to stand under the wedding canopy again. Zeftel, I can be frank with you. There are no secrets between us. I want to have another fling."

"What about me?"

"If I become rich, I'll not forget you either."

"No, you'll forget. The minute you step over

the threshold, you'll have forgotten already. Don't think that I'm jealous. When I first knew you, I tingled. I would have washed your feet and drunk the bathwater. But when I knew you better, I told myself, 'Zeftel, it's a waste—all this trembling.' I'm not an educated woman and don't know much, but I've got a head on my shoulders. I do a lot of thinking and I get all kinds of ideas. When the wind whistles through the chimney I get very moody. You won't believe me, Yashale, but recently I even thought of suicide."

"Why that of all things?"

"Just because I was tired and there was a rope nearby. I saw a hook on the beam. This very hook by the lamp. I climbed up on the footstool and it fit to a hair. Then I began to laugh."

"Why?"

"For no reason at all. You yank the rope and it's all over . . . Yashale, take me to Warsaw."

"What about the furniture?"

"I'll sell everything. Let somebody get a bargain."

"What will you do in Warsaw?"

"Don't worry, I won't sponge off you. I'll go off like that beggar-woman in the story. I'll stop at some door and say, 'Here I stay.' One can do laundry and carry baskets anywhere."

THREE

Yasha had planned to be back at Elzbieta's for supper, but Zeftel would not hear of it. She prepared a favorite dish for him: wide noodles with cheese and cinnamon. As soon as Zeftel unbolted the door and drew the curtains, visitors began to arrive. The women came in to show off the bargains which they had found in the market, and the presents that their men had given them. The older amongst them wore battered slippers, shapeless dresses, soiled head-kerchiefs. They grinned at Yasha with their toothless mouths and coquettishly displayed their own ugliness. The young matrons, in honor of the guest, had dressed up and had covered themselves with trinkets. Although Zeftel supposedly kept their relationship secret, she proudly showed each braggart the string of coral that Yasha had given her. Some of the women tried it on, smirked, winked knowingly. Licentiousness was not the fashion on the hill. The wives of thieves serving in prison remained true for years until their husbands were released. But Zeftel was an outsider—lower than a gypsy. Besides, she was a deserted wife. And Yasha, the magician, had the reputation of being a libertine. The women bobbed their heads, whispered, cast sheep's-eyes at Yasha. His magical powers were well known here. The thieves often claimed that if he joined the brotherhood, his path would be strewn with gold. It was the general opinion on the hill that it was even better to be the wife of a thief than of someone like Yasha, who traveled around with a gentile girl, came home only on holidays and gave his wife nothing but shame and disgrace.

After a while, the men, too, began to drift in. Chaim-Leib, short, broad-shouldered, with a yellow beard, face, and eyes, came in to cadge a Warsaw cigaret. Yasha gave him the whole pack. Zeftel put a bottle of spirits and a platter of onion rolls before Chaim-Leib. He was one of the old guard but already worn out, useless. He had served time in every prison. His ribs had been staved in. A brother of his, Baruch Klotz, a horse-thief, had been boiled alive by peasants. Chaim-Leib thoughtfully puffed on the Warsaw cigaret, drank a tumblerful of vodka, and asked, "What's happening in Warsaw? How is the old Pawiak prison?"

Blind Mechl, a tall, heavy-set individual with the shoulders of a giant, a straight nape, a scar on the forehead, and a torn eye-socket, had brought along a paper-wrapped package. Yasha knew already what it contained: a padlock for him to open. Mechl, himself, was an expert at lock-breaking. He always carried a jimmy and before taking up burglary as a trade, he had been a journeyman locksmith. For years Mechl had been trying to construct a lock that Yasha would not be able to pry. He now sat shyly at the table, waiting patiently for the conversation to come around to locks. Until now he had failed with Yasha for no matter how intricate and artful the lock, Yasha had always managed to spring it within minutes, frequently employing nothing more than a nail or a hairpin. But Mechl would not give up: he kept betting he would construct a "peter" the like of which the angel Gabriel couldn't "jimmy." Every time Mechl visited Lublin he held consultations with the locksmith, Abraham Leibush, as well as with any number of blacksmiths and mechanics. Mechl's room was set up like a tool-shop, with hammers, files, metal saws, all sorts of bars, hooks, drills, pliers, and soldering irons. His wife, Black Bella, claimed Mechl's interest in tools had grown into an obsession. Yasha greeted him with a smile and a wink. Just as Mechl was sure that this time Yasha would fail, so Yasha was convinced that through some inexplicable power he would, with a twist here and a turn there, open the mechanism as if by magic.

Eventually, they were all there: Mendele Katshke, Yosele Deitch, Lazerel Kratzmich. Their current leader was one Berish Visoker, a tiny fellow with shifty eyes, a pointed, bald head, sharp nose and chin, and long arms like an ape. Berish Visoker, like Zeftel, came from Greater Poland. He dressed foppishly, with his colored trousers, yellow shoes, velvet vests, and embroidered shirts. A hat with a feather in it was always on his head. Especially high heels on his boots added to his stature. Berish was so skillful that he could steal a watch from a pickpocket. He knew Russian, Polish, and German, and was on good terms with the authorities, was, in fact, less thief than grafter and intermediary. Years ago he had served a prison term, not for theft but for having cheated a nobleman at a card game known as "Little Chain." Berish Visoker was as sharp at cards as Blind Mechl was at locks. But he was no match for Yasha. Yasha always showed Berish new tricks that baffled him. Even now he had several packs of cards in his pocket, both marked and unmarked. Berish was notoriously restless. He could not stay in a chair. While everyone else sat around the table, he wriggled like a caged animal, or a wolf trying to bite his own tail. He cocked his head and spoke out of the side of his mouth. "When will you become one of us, eh?" he asked Yasha in his nasal tones. "Clasp my hand and join the brotherhood."

"And rot in jail?"

"Keep your wits about you and you skim the cream right off the top."

"Well, you can't be too smart," called out Blind Mechl. "Anybody can get caught."

"All you have to know is how the wind is blowing," Berish Visoker shot back.

Yasha knew well that he must not linger. Elzbieta would be bursting with impatience for him to return. Magda, also, expected him. Bolek despised him, and only sought an excuse such as this to destroy him. But Yasha couldn't just walk out. He had known these people since childhood. They had seen his progress from a bear-trainer's assistant to a star in the Polish theater. The men clapped him on the back, the women flirted with him. They all admired him as a master. He doled our cigars, cigarets. There were also several former sweethearts of his in the crowd, who, although respectably married now and mothers, looked at him coquettishly, grinning reminiscently. Although he had at first been discreet with Zeftel, she herself had revealed their relationship. For such a trollop, a lover was something to advertise.

At first, they gossiped about current events. What was new in the world? When would war start with Turkey again? And what did those rebels want, who threw bombs, tried to assassinate the Czar, and called strikes against the railroads? What was new in Palestine? Who were these heretics who built colonies in the dried-out swamps? Yasha explained everything. He read all the Warsaw newspapers as well as the *Israelita*. He even glanced at the Hebrew gazette although he did not understand the modern expressions. Here in Piask the citizens squatted like toads on a treestump, but out in the world things were happening fast. Prussia had become a powerful nation. The French had annexed parts of Africa—where the black people lived. In England, ships that could cross the ocean in ten days were being built. In America, trains ran right over the rooftops and a building thirty stories high had been erected. Even Warsaw grew larger and more beautiful each year. The wooden sidewalks had been torn up, inside-plumbing installed; Jewish children were permitted to attend the gymnasia and go abroad to study at foreign universities.

The thieves listened, scratching their heads. The women, their faces flushed, traded glances. Yasha told them of the Black Hand Society in America. He related how they sent a note signed with a black hand to a millionaire: Send this many dollars or you'll get a bullet in your head. Even if the millionaire had a thousand bodyguards, if he didn't pay the ransom he was murdered.

Berish Visoker suddenly interrupted, "It can be done here, too."

"And who will get the letter, Treitel the Water-carrier?"

The thieves laughed loudly and relit their burnt-out cigarets.

2

Blind Mechl could not wait. He said, "Yasha, I want to tell you something."

Yasha winked. "I know, I know, show me the bargain."

Mechl unwrapped the paper slowly, revealing a huge lock, complete with clamps and appendages. Yasha instantly grew light-hearted. He began to examine the lock with the crossed eyes and comical mien of bewilderment and mockery which had always brought laughter from a tavern full of peasants as well as from the audience of the Warsaw summer theater, Alhambra. In one second he had become transformed. He hissed, wriggled his nose, even artfully waggled his ears. The women giggled.

"Where did you dig up this contraption?"

"Better show what you can do," Blind Mechl said, half in anger.

"God, Himself, couldn't open such a sealed chamberpot," Yasha jested. "Once you put a peter like this together, it is finished. But if you blindfold me, I'll jimmy it open with my eyes shut. Maybe you'd like to bet on it, eh? Suppose I put up ten rubles to your one."

"Done."

"Put your money where your mouth is," Chaim-Leib shouted.

"We don't need money. I trust him."

"Children, blindfold me!" Yasha said, "but do it so I can't see a thing."

"I'll blindfold you with my apron," said Small Malka, a woman with red hair tied up in back by a kerchief. Her husband was serving time in the Yanov penitentiary. She undid the apron from her waist and, standing behind Yasha, bound his eyes. Meanwhile, she tickled him between the ears with her forefinger. Yasha remained silent.

"What have they put into the mechanism?" he wondered. Although confident as ever, he conceded the possibility of failure. A locksmith had once made a lock for him that no key or jimmy could open. Everything inside had been welded together. Malka folded the alpaca apron several times and knotted it firmly, powerfully, despite her small hands; but, as usual, between the eye and the bridge of the nose there was a space through which he could see. Yasha, nevertheless, did not need to see. He drew from his pocket a thick piece of wire with a sharp point. This was his skeleton key for all locks. He displayed it to the group before turning to the lock. Now he tapped the lock from outside like a doctor tapping his patient with a stethoscope. Still blindfolded, he located the keyhole and inserted the point of the wire. Once within, he worked the wire so that it kept penetrating deeper, reaching to the lock's entrails. For a while he probed and burrowed. He marveled at his own competence. That piece of wire revealed all the secrets, all the wiles that the Lublin experts had incorporated into the lock. Complex as it seemed, it was as childishly simple as the riddles schoolboys ask each other in cheder. If you guessed one, you guessed them all. Yasha could have opened the lock immediately, but he did not wish to shame Blind Mechl. He decided to act out a little scene.

"Say, this *is* a hard nut to crack!" he grumbled.

"What sort of beehive have they braided in there? So many teeth and hooks, a regular machine!" He strained, pushed the wire. He raised his shoulders as if to signify, "I don't have the faintest idea of what's inside this thing!" The crowd grew so quiet that the only sound was Chaim-Leib snorting through his broken, polyp-filled nose. Several of the women began to whisper and giggle, a sign of tension. Now Yasha made the same remark he had made at numerous performances, "A lock is like a woman. Sooner or later it must surrender."

Laughter broke out amongst the women.

"All women aren't the same."

"It's a matter of patience."

"Don't be so sure of yourself," Blind Mechl said in anticipation.

"Stop rushing me, Mechl. You've been fussing with this thing for half a year. You've put everything into it. After all, I'm not Moses."

"It doesn't give, eh?"

"It'll give, it'll give. You only need to squeeze the bellybutton."

And at that moment, the lock sprang open. Laughter, applause, and a general din followed.

"Malka, untie me," Yasha said.

And with trembling fingers Malka untied the apron. The lock lay on the table as if impotent and disgraced. Everyone's eyes were merry, but Blind Mechl's single eye remained grimly earnest.

"You're a warlock or my name isn't Mechl!"

"Sure, I took up black magic in Babylon. I can turn you and Malka here into rabbits."

"Why pick on me? My husband needs a wife, not a rabbit."

"Why not a rabbit? You could jump into his cell through the bars."

Yasha felt ashamed, sitting amongst this unsavory band. If Emilia only knew with whom he associated! She considered him a genius, an exalted artist. They discussed religion, philosophy, the immortality of the soul. He quoted the wise sayings of the Talmud to her. They spoke of Copernicus, Galileo—and here he was with the thieves of Piask. But that's how he was. There was always another role for him to play. He was a maze of personalities—religious and heretical, good and evil, false and sincere. He could love many women at once. Here he was, ready to renounce his religion, yet—when he found a torn page from a holy book he always picked it up and put it to his lips. Everyone was like a lock, each with his own key. Only one such as he, Yasha, could unlock all souls.

"Well, here is your money!"

And Blind Mechl produced a silver ruble from a deep purse. For a moment Yasha considered refusing the ruble, but he realized that this would have been a mortal insult to Mechl, especially now that the band's treasury was so depleted. The brotherhood had a high regard for honor. He could get knifed for refusing. Yasha took the proffered ruble, weighing it in his palm.

"An easy profit."

"Every one of your fingertips should be kissed!" boomed Blind Mechl in the deep voice of a giant. It seemed as if his voice emanated from his thick belly.

"It's a gift from God," Small Malka said. Zeftel's eyes glistened with triumph, her cheeks grew red. Her lips mutely suggested kisses and endearments. Yasha knew he was idolized by all here, both men and women. He was the shining beacon to the citizens of Piask. Chaim-Leib's face seemed yellow as the brass of the samovar Zeftel had placed upon the table.

"If you became one of us, the world would be yours."

"I still believe in the Eighth Commandment."

"Listen to him! He thinks he's a saint!" Berish Visoker sprayed his words. "Everyone steals. What did the Prussians do some time ago? Tore a hunk out of France, then demanded a billion marks besides. They held France by the windpipe. Isn't that stealing?"

"War is war," Chaim-Leib said.

"Whoever can, grabs. That's the way it's always been. The little *goniff* gets the noose, the big *goniff* the fat goose . . . How about a game of cards?"

"You want to play?" Yasha asked, teasingly.

"Did you bring some new hocus-pocus from Warsaw?" Berish Visoker asked. "Let's see you do your stuff!"

"Is this a theater?"

And Yasha took the deck of cards from Berish Visoker. He began to shuffle them very fast. The cards flew into the air, leaped like fish in a net. Suddenly Yasha did something with his hand and the cards fanned out like an accordion.

FOUR

It was restful to be alone with Magda in the wagon again. The summer was in full bloom. The fields grew golden, fruit ripened in the orchards. Intoxicating earth aromas induced lassitude and an ethereal calm. "Oh, God Almighty, You are the magician, not I!" Yasha whispered. "To bring out plants, flowers and colors from a bit of black soil!"

But how had it all come about? How did the stalks of rye know about bearing grain? And how did the wheat know about reproducing itself? No—they didn't know. They did it instinctively. But someone must know. Yasha sat in the driver's seat with Magda and gave the horses free rein. They knew the road by now. All sorts of creatures crossed their path: a field mouse, a squirrel, even a tortoise. Unseen birds sang and trilled. In a forest clearing Yasha spied a flock of gray birds. They were lined up as if about to hold an assembly.

Magda cuddled next to him, silently. It seemed as if her peasant's eyes saw things a city dweller could not see. Yasha was preoccupied also. Towards evening, when the sun set and the wagon trundled along a forest road, he clearly perceived Emilia's face. Like the moon over the pine trees, it moved backwards. The black eyes smiled, the lips moved continuously. He put his arm around Magda and she laid her head on his shoulder, but he was not with her. He was asleep and awake at the same time. He tried to will a sort of decision, but none would come. His fancy grew vivid, and he dreamed this was not a wagon but a train to Italy, in which he rode with Emilia and Halina. He could almost hear the locomotive whistle. Outside the window, cypress trees, palms, mountains, castles, vineyards, orchards of orange and olive trees passed. Everything seemed different: the peasants, their women, the houses, the haystacks. Where have I seen such things? Yasha wondered. In paintings? In the opera? It's as if I'd already experienced all this in an earlier existence.

Customarily he made two stopovers on his trip but he decided now to ride ahead and arrive in Warsaw in the morning. Highwaymen supposedly lurked along the road, but Yasha kept a pistol in his pocket. Riding, he imagined himself performing at European theaters. Ladies in boxes fixed their lorgnettes upon him. Ambassadors, barons, and generals came backstage to pay respects. Now, with a pair of artificial wings he flew over the capitals of the world. Multitudes of people ran through the streets, pointing, shouting and, as he flew, he received messages by carrier pigeon—invitations from rulers, princes, cardinals. In his estate in the south of Italy, Emilia and Halina waited for him. He, Yasha, was no longer a magician, but a divine hypnotist who could control armies, heal the sick, flush criminals, locate buried treasures, and raise sunken ships from the ocean depths. He, Yasha, had become the emperor of the entire world. He ridiculed his fancies but could not banish them. Like locusts they fell upon him: daydreams of harem girls, slaves; tricks that were beyond nature; magic potions, charms, and incantations that unfolded all secrets and bestowed infinite powers. In his imagination he even led the Jews out of exile, gave them back the land of Israel, rebuilt the temple of Jerusalem. He suddenly began to crack his whip as if to dispel the demons which had invaded his thoughts. He needed a clear head now more than ever. He had prepared a series of new and dangerous stunts for his repertoire. One of these involved performing a somersault on the tightrope, a stunt as yet unattempted by any other performer. The important thing was to make up his mind about Emilia. Was he truly prepared to forsake Esther and go to Italy with Emilia? Could he treat Esther so cruelly after her many years of devotion and loyalty? And was he, Yasha, reconciled to converting, becoming a Christian? He had given Emilia his solemn promise, sworn an oath—but was he ready to honor it? And another thing: he could not carry out his plans with Emilia without a large sum of money, at least fifteen thousand rubles. For months now he had been toying with the possibilities of a robbery, but was he indeed capable of becoming a thief? Just recently he had told Chaim-Leib that the Eighth Commandment was holy to him. He, Yasha, had always prided himself on his honesty. And what would Emilia's reaction be if she knew what he intended? What would Esther say? Yes, and his mother and father in the other world? After all, he believed in immortality. A while back, his mother had even saved his life. He had heard her voice caution him, "Move back, Son, move back!" and minutes later a heavy chandelier fell where he had been standing. It would surely have crushed him had he not heeded his dead mother's warning.

He had put off his decision until now. But he could not delay any longer. Emilia was waiting for him to make up his mind. He also had to decide what to do about Wolsky, his impresario who handled all of his engagements. This same Wolsky had elevated him, Yasha, from poverty, had advanced his career. He, Yasha, could not repay Wolsky with evil. As strong as Yasha's love was for Emilia, just as full was it of temptations.

He had to decide this very night, choose between his religion and the cross, between Esther and Emilia, between honesty and crime (a single crime for which, with God's help, he would later make restitution). But his mind would resolve nothing. Instead of attacking the main problem, it dallied, went off on tangents, become frivolous. He could have been the father of grown children by this time, yet he remained the schoolboy who had played with his father's locks and keys and trailed the magicians through the streets of Lublin. He could not even be sure of the extent of his love for Emilia, decide whether the feeling he had was really what is known as love. Would he be able to remain true to her? Already the devil tempted him with all sorts of speculations about Halina, how she would grow up, become enamored of him, become her mother's rival for his affections.

It's true, I *am* depraved, he thought. What was it Father called me? A scoundrel. Lately, his father had appeared in his dreams every night. Just as Yasha closed his eyes, he would see his father. The older man would moralize, warn him, counsel him.

"What are you thinking of?" Magda asked.

"Oh, nothing."

"Is it true that Zeftel the Thief is coming to Warsaw?"

Yasha stirred. "Who said that?"

"Bolek."

"Why didn't you say anything about it until now?"

"I keep quiet about a great many things."

"She is coming but what's that have to do with

me? Her husband's left her and she's starving. She's looking for work as a maid or cook."

"You go to bed with her."

"No."

"You have a girl in Warsaw too."

"You're babbling."

"A widow by the name of Emilia. That's whom you're in such a hurry to see."

Yasha was dumfounded. How could she have learned about Emilia? Had he said something? Yes, he had. He always had to boast, it was his nature. He had even confessed it to Zeftel.

He hesitated a moment. "It is no concern of yours, Magda. My love for you won't change."

"She wants to go off to Italy with you."

"Never mind what she wants. I could as easily forget you as my mother."

He did not know himself if he were telling the truth or lying. Magda remained silent. Once again she laid her head on his shoulder.

2

In the middle of the night it suddenly grew warm as if a nocturnal sun had begun to shine. The moon was overcast. The sky writhed with clouds. All at once thunder and lightning began. In a flash of light the fields were illumined as far as the horizon. The stalks of wheat bowed and the rain struck like a deluge. Before Yasha could collect his thoughts the sheets of water began to flail the wagon like a hailstorm. The tarpaulin tore loose from the frame. The monkey choked off a terrified scream. In less than a minute the highway was mired. Magda clung to Yasha like a dumb creature. Yasha began to lash the horses. The village of Makov was nearby and they would be able to find shelter there.

It was a miracle that the wheels did not leave the road. The horses waded in water nearly up to their posterns. Somehow or other, the wagon rolled into Makov, but he knew of no inn or public house in town. Yasha drove into a synagogue courtyard. The rain ceased and the sky began to clear. Clouds drifted westward, their edges glowing in the rising sun like cinders after a fire. The puddles and gutters ran red as blood. Yasha left the team and wagon in the courtyard and he and Magda walked into the study-house to dry off. It was not right for him to escort a gentile into a house of worship, but it was a matter of life or death now. She had already begun to cough and sneeze.

Outside, day was breaking, but in the prayer-house it was still night. A memorial candle flickered in the *menorah* at the prayer stand. At a lectern sat an old man reciting from a thick prayer-book. Yasha observed that the old man's head was sprinkled with ash. "What is he doing?" Yasha wondered. "Have I already forgotten so much of my heritage?" Yasha nodded to the old man and he nodded back and placed his finger upon his lips to signify that he must not, at this time, speak. Magda sat down on a bench near the stove and Yasha turned to her. There was nothing with which they could wipe themselves. They would just have to wait until everything dried of its own accord. It was warm here. Magda's face glowed in the murk like a pale stain. A puddle had collected beneath her body. Stealthily, Yasha kissed her on the forehead. He looked at the reading-desk with the four pillars, the Holy Ark, the cantor's lectern, the shelves of sacred books. Standing there soaking wet, dripping water and sweat, he tried, by the light of the memorial candle, to read the tablet on the cornice of the Holy Ark supported by the gilded lions: "I am the Lord . . . Thou shalt have no other gods . . . Honor thy father and mother. . . Thou shalt not commit adultery . . . Thou shalt not kill . . . Thou shalt not steal . . . Thou shalt not covet . . ." Now it was dark and all of a sudden the prayer-house was suffused with a purple glow as if from a heavenly lamp. Suddenly, Yasha recalled what the old man was doing: he was still reciting the midnight service. Lamenting the destruction of the temple!

Soon, other Jews began to arrive, mostly older men, bent, with gray beards and feet that could barely scrape along. God in Heaven, how long was it since he, Yasha, had been in a holy temple? Everything seemed new to him: the way the Jews recited the introductory prayers, how they donned the prayer-shawls, kissed the fringed garment, wound the phylacteries, unrolled the thongs. It was all strangely foreign to him, yet familiar. Magda had gone back to the wagon as if fearful of all this intense Jewishness. He, Yasha, chose to remain a moment longer. He was part of this community. Its roots were his roots. He bore its mark upon his flesh. He understood the prayers. One old man said: "God, my soul." A second slowly told the story of how God had tested Abraham, commanded him to offer his son Isaac as a sacrifice. A third intoned: "What are we? What is our life? What is our piety? All the mighty men are as naught before Thee, the men of renown as though they have not been, for most of their works are void, and the days of their lives are vanity before Thee." He recited it all in a lamenting chant and looking all the while at him, Yasha, as if aware of what went on in his mind. Yasha breathed deeply. He smelled tallow, wax, and something else, a blend of putrefaction and spirits of hartshorn, as during the Days of Atonement, when he had been but a lad. A small man with a red beard came up to Yasha.

"You want to pray?" he asked. "I'll fetch you phylacteries and a prayer shawl."

"Thank you, but my wagon is waiting."

"The wagon won't run away."

Yasha gave the man a kopek. On his way out he kissed the *mezuzah*. In the ante-chamber he saw a barrel filled with pages torn from holy books. He rummaged through the barrel and came up with a torn book. An exalted scent arose from the tattered leaves as if, lying there in the barrel, they had continued being read by themselves.

After a while Yasha located an inn. He and Magda had to put on some dry clothes; he had to repair the wagon, grease the axles, rest the team. They had to eat breakfast and catch a few hours' sleep. Since he was traveling with a gentile, Yasha spoke Polish to the innkeeper, posing as a Pole himself. He and Magda sat down at a long, bare table and a Jewess in a head-kerchief, with red eyes and a hairy, pointed chin, served them black bread, cottage cheese, and coffee with chicory. She looked at the prayer-book which Yasha had tucked into his pocket and said, "Where did you get that, Sir?"

Yasha stirred. "Oh, I picked it up near your temple. What is it? A holy book?"

"Let me have it, Sir. You wouldn't understand it anyway. To us, it is sacred."

"I want to look it over."

"How can you? It's in Hebrew."

"I have a friend, a priest. He knows Hebrew."

"The book is torn. Give it to me, Sir!"

"Lay off—," her husband growled from a distance in Yiddish.

"I don't want him walking around with a Jewish book," she replied aggressively.

"What's written here?" Yasha asked. "How to swindle Christians?"

"We swindle nobody, Sir, neither Jews nor Christians. We earn our bread honestly."

A side door opened and a boy walked in, wearing a lint-covered cap and an unbuttoned dressing-gown from under which showed a fringed garment. He had a narrow face and two wide sidelocks like skeins of flax. He had apparently just gotten up as his eyes were still heavy with sleep.

"Grandma, give me milk and water," he said.

"Did you make your ablutions?"

"Yes, I did."

"Did you say your 'I thank Thee'?"

"Yes, I did."

And he wiped his nose on his sleeve.

Yasha continued eating and looked at the boy. "Can I forsake all this?" he asked himself. "This is mine after all, mine . . . Once I looked exactly like that boy." A strange urge came over him to examine as quickly as possible the writing in the torn prayer book. A wave of affection drew him to this grandmother who rose each day with the sun and cooked and baked, swept the house, and served the guests. An almsbox hung on the doorpost. Here she deposited any spare groschen she could scrape together, to help the Jews who wished to go to the Holy Land to die. The atmosphere in this house was alive with Sabbath, holidays, the anticipation of the Messiah, and of the world to come. As the old woman hustled about, she whispered through her whitish lips and nodded her head as if aware of a truth known only to those not deceived by the vanity of worldly things.

3

The arrival in Warsaw was always an event for Yasha. This was where his income came from. It was here that his impresario lived, Miechislaw Wolsky. Posters already plastered on the walls read: "On July first, the summer theater, Alhambra, presents the distinguished circus performer and hypnotist, Yasha Mazur, with a new repertoire of tricks that will astound the esteemed public." Yasha had an apartment here on Freta Street near the Avenue Dluga. Even the mares, Kara and Shiva—Dust and Ashes—revived when they approached Warsaw. It was no longer necessary to urge them on. As soon as the wagon crossed the Praga Bridge it lost itself in the congestion of houses, palaces, omnibuses, carriages, droshkies, shops, cafés. The air smelled of fresh baking, coffee, horse manure, smoke from trains and factories. In front of the castle occupied by the Russian governor-general a military band performed. It must have been some sort of holiday, since every balcony flew Russian flags. The women already wore wide-brimmed straw hats decorated with artificial fruits and flowers. Carefree young men in straw hats and light-colored suits strolled about, twirling their canes. Through the tumult the locomotives whistled and hissed; the railroad couplings clanged. Trains for Petersburg, Moscow, Vienna, Berlin, Vladivostok left from here. After the sobering period following the uprising of 1863, Poland had entered an age of industrial reform. Lodz had expanded with American haste. In Warsaw, wooden sidewalks were ripped up, interior plumbing installed, rails for horse trolleys laid, tall buildings erected, as well as entire courtyards and markets. The theaters offered a new season of drama, comedy, operas, and concerts. Prominent actors and actresses arrived from Paris, Petersburg, Rome, and even distant America. The bookstores featured newly published novels, as well as scientific works, encyclopedias, lexicons, and dictionaries. Yasha breathed deeply. The journey had been wearying but the city exhilarated him. If it's this stimulating here, how much more must it be abroad, he mused. He wanted to run immediately to Emilia but checked himself. He could not very well come sleepy, unshaven, disheveled. Also, he had first to see Miechislaw Wolsky. Yasha had sent him a telegram while still in Lublin.

Yasha had not been in Warsaw recently. He had been touring the provinces. While on the road, he always worried that his apartment would be burglarized. He kept his library there, his antiques, and his collection of billboards, newspaper clippings, and reviews. But, God be praised, the door was still securely locked by two heavy locks and everything within was in order. Layers of dust were everywhere and the air smelled musty. Magda immediately began to tidy up. Wolsky came in a droshky—a Jewish-looking gentile with black eyes, a beaked nose, a high forehead. His artist's cravat perched crookedly on his shirtfront. Yasha received from him numerous offers to perform in Russian and Polish cities. Twirling his black mustache, Wolsky spoke with the fervor of those who depend upon the fame of others for their livelihood. He had even prepared a schedule for Yasha to follow after his summer engagement at the Alhambra had ended. But Yasha realized that Wolsky's bombast was unnecessary. Only the provinces wanted him. No offers had come from Moscow,

Kiev, or Petersburg. His earnings in the provinces were negligible. Even in Warsaw, nothing had changed. The proprietor of the Alhambra had consistently refused to increase Yasha's wage. Praise enough they gave him, but the clowns from abroad were paid more. It was somewhat of a mystery—this obstinacy of the theater-owners. Wolsky's arguments and contentions were useless. Yasha was always among the last to be paid. Emilia was right. As long as he remained in Poland they would treat him like a third-rate performer.

After Wolsky had gone, Yasha lay down in the bedroom. The janitor would tend to the horses, Magda would see that the other animals were fed and watered. All three, the parrot, crow, and monkey were quartered in one room. Scrawny though Magda was, she promptly began to scrub the floor. From generations of peasants she had inherited her strength, along with her servility. Yasha dozed off, awoke, dozed off again. The house was an old one. In the unpaved courtyard below, geese cackled, ducks quacked, roosters crowed, just as in the country. Through the open window, breezes from the Vistula and the Praga forest wafted in. Downstairs, a beggar scratched out a tune on a street-organ and sang an old Warsaw melody. Yasha would have thrown him a coin if his limbs had not felt so numb. He was dreaming and thinking at once. Again to drag himself through the boggy hinterlands? Again to perform in fire-stations? No, he'd had enough of it! His thoughts whirled to the rhythm of the street-organ. He must go away, away, abandon everything. At whatever cost, he must tear himself free of this swamp. If not, someday he, Yasha, would also wander about with a street-organ.

It had just been morning and now it was dusk. Magda brought him a dish of new potatoes with sour milk and parsley. He ate in bed and again placed his head on the pillow. When he opened his eyes once more, it was nighttime. The bedroom was dark, but it could not have been too late, since he could still detect the sound of a cobbler driving tacks into a shoe. No one in the neighborhood had installed gas lamps yet. By the light of naphtha lamps, housewives mended, washed dishes, darned, sewed patches. A drunk argued with his wife while his dog barked at him.

Yasha called to Magda but she had apparently gone out. Only the crow, whom Yasha had taught to speak like a human, answered him. Every time that Yasha returned to Warsaw it was with the anticipation of favorable tidings, but the fates, which are so frequently generous to all sorts of dilettantes and amateurs, were severely sparing with him, Yasha. They never permitted him to get the best of any bargain. On the contrary, everyone took advantage of him. Yasha knew that it was all because of his attitude. He felt inferior and, sensing this, others exploited him. Having surrounded himself with a low class of people, his reward was to be treated like one of them. Emilia was the only miracle in his life, his only hope of salvation from the pit he had dug for himself.

Their introduction had been shrouded in mystery. He had not at first caught her name. He had begun to think of her, had been unable to forget her. His thoughts had rushed on of their own accord. He became inexplicably aware that she was thinking of him as much as he was of her; that she also yearned for and desired him. Through the streets of Warsaw he had roamed like a somnambulist, seeking her in coach-windows, shops, cafés, theater lobbies. On the Marshalkowska Boulevard he had looked for her, on the Nowy Swiat, on the paths of the Saxony Gardens. He stationed himself by a pillar in the Theater Square and waited. One evening, convinced of finding her, he had gone out. He walked the length of the Marshalkowska Boulevard. When he approached a shop-window, there she was, waiting, as if they had previously arranged a rendezvous—dressed in a fur collar and muff, her black eyes focused directly upon him. He moved closer and she smiled, knowingly and enigmatically. He bowed to her and she proffered her hand. And while all this was happening, she blurted, "What an odd coincidence!"

But later she admitted actually having been waiting for him there. She had had a premonition that he had heard her summon him.

4

The affluent householders had already installed telephones, but Emilia could not yet afford such a luxury. Emilia and her daughter, Halina, existed on a meager pension. All that remained from the days when the professor had been alive was the apartment and an old maid-servant, Yadwiga, who for years now had drawn no wages.

Yasha awoke early. He shaved. The apartment contained a wooden tub and Magda filled it with kettles of water. She lathered Yasha with scented soap and massaged him. And as she did she observed slyly, "When one visits a noblewoman, one must smell sweet."

"I'm not visiting any noblewoman, Magda."

"Oh, sure, sure, your Magda is a fool but she can put two and two together."

During breakfast, Yasha's mood suddenly brightened. He spoke only of testing his theory of flight, and the sooner the attempt was made the better. He would also fit her, Magda, with a set of wings. They would soar together like a goose and gander and become as world famous as Montgolfier had been over a hundred years ago. He embraced Magda, kissed her, and assured her that no matter what happened to him he would never forsake her. "Perhaps you may have to be alone for a time while I go abroad but, don't worry, I will send for you. I ask only one thing—trust me." And as he spoke, he looked into her eyes. He smoothed her hair and rubbed her temples. He had such power over her that he could put her to sleep in a minute. In the midst of a heat wave, he could tell her that she was cold and immediately she would begin to shiver. During a frost, he could convince her that she was overheated and her body would flush and perspire. He could prick her with a needle and draw no blood. He had performed innumerable experiments upon her. But he had also evolved a system of mesmerism while she was awake. He would tell her something and it would stick in her brain. He would give her commands weeks and months in advance and she would carry them out later with uncanny promptness. He had already begun to prepare her for the time when he would go away with Emilia. Magda heard him out, smiled tacitly with peasant slyness. She understood all his wiles but at the same time acquiesced, neither capable nor desirous of opposition. At times her mien and grimaces reminded him of the parrot, the monkey, or the crow.

After breakfast, he put on a light suit, kid-leather boots, a hard hat, and tied a black silk tie over his collar. Kissing Magda, he left without a word. He flagged a droshky. Emilia lived on Krolevska Street, opposite the Saxony Gardens. On the way, he ordered the coachman to stop at a florist's where he bought a bouquet of roses. At another shop he purchased a bottle of wine, a pound of sturgeon, a tin of sardines. Emilia often observed jocularly that he came as laden down with presents as Santa Claus on Christmas Eve, but it was already a tradition with him. He knew it for a fact—the mother and daughter had barely enough for necessities. And besides, Halina had weak lungs. It was because of this that her mother wanted to go to southern Italy. Halina had left the boarding-school because money for her tuition had run out. Emilia, herself, sewed and reversed all their dresses, since there was no money left for tailors and seamstresses. In the droshky, holding the packages firmly to keep them from sliding, Yasha looked out at the city which was both strange to him, yet familiar. At one time Warsaw had seemed an unattainable dream. More than anything, he had wished to see his name in print in a Warsaw newspaper or on a theatrical poster. But now he was already trying to free himself of this city which, despite its cosmopolitan pretenses, remained provincial. Only now was it beginning to expand. The droshky rolled between piles of bricks, heaps of sand, mounds of lime. The air, on this June day, smelled of lilac, paint, raw earth, and gutter slops. Gangs of laborers tore the entrails from the streets, dug into the foundations.

On Krolevska Street, the air was clearer. The trees in Saxony Gardens were shedding their last blossoms. Through the fence one could see flower beds, hothouses filled with exotic plants, and a café where young couples ate their second breakfast under the open sky. This was also the season of lotteries, the raffling of prizes for worthy causes. Nursemaids and governesses wheeled infants in baby carriages. Boys in sailor suits rolled their hoops along with small sticks. With colored shovels, tiny girls dressed like fashionable ladies burrowed in sandpiles, digging among pebbles. Others danced in circles. There was a summer theater in the park, too, but Yasha had never performed in it. He had been barred for being a Jew. He paid a higher penalty for his Jewishness than those pious individuals with their beards and sidelocks. In other parts of Europe these restrictions were no longer honored, Emilia had told him. There, an artist was judged simply by his talent.

"Well, we'll see, we'll see," he mumbled to himself. "As fate decrees, so shall it be."

No matter how bold Yasha was when walking the tightrope or mind-reading in the theater, he always lost confidence whenever he came to Emilia's. He was unsure of his appearance, whether his conduct was exemplary enough for a cosmopolite, whether he'd erred in his grammar or etiquette. Was he, perhaps, calling too early in the day? What would he do should he not find Emilia at home? Should he leave the bouquet and the presents, or the flowers only? Don't be so frightened, Yashale, he counseled himself. Nobody is going to eat you, after all . . . she's mad about you, that wench. Fever consumes her. She can hardly wait for you. He puckered his lips and whistled. If he wanted to perform at royal courts he must not be intimidated by an impoverished widow. Who could tell? Perhaps even countesses and princesses would seek his attentions? Women were women, whether in Piask or Paris. . . .

He paid off the coachman, passed through the gate, climbed the marble stairs, and rang the doorbell. Yadwiga opened it promptly—a gray little woman in a white apron and bonnet, her face wrinkled as a fig. He asked for Mrs. Chrabotzky. Was she home? Yadwiga nodded affirmatively, smiled knowingly, took the flowers, the packages, his cane and hat. She opened the door into the drawing-room. The last time he was here had been during a cold spell. Emilia had been sick, her neck enveloped. Now the room was summery. Shafts of sunlight filtered through the curtains, highlighted the rug and the parquet, danced off the vases, the picture frames, the keys of the pianoforte. The rubber-plant in the bucket had sprouted new leaves. On the divan lay a length of material which Emilia was apparently in the process of embroidering, a needle stuck in the cloth. Yasha began to pace to and fro. What a far cry this was from Leibush Lekach's Zeftel!—Still, it was really all the same.

The door opened and Emilia came in. Yasha opened his eyes wide and almost whistled. Until now he had seen her only in black. She had been in mourning for the late professor, Stephan Chrabotzky, and also for the abortive uprising of 1863 and the martyrs who had been tortured and had perished in Siberia. Emilia read Schopenhauer, was enamored of the poetry of Byron, Slowacki, and Leopardi, and idolized the Polish mystics, Norwid and Towianski. She even let Yasha know that she was a Wolowsky on her mother's side and a great-grandchild of the famous Frankist Elisha Shur. Yes, Jewish blood flowed in her veins as it did in most Polish nobility. Now she wore a light, café-au-lait gown. She'd never seemed as beautiful as now: straight, supple, a Polish beauty with high cheekbones, a Slavic nose, but with black Jewish eyes full of wit and passion. Her hair in back was upswept and circled by a wreathlike braid. Her waist was narrow, her bosom high, she seemed a full ten years younger than her actual middle-thirties. Even the down on her upper lip favored her and contributed a sort of female boyishness. Her smile was shy, yet wanton. They had already, in the past, kissed and embraced like lovers. She often confessed that it required all of her self-control to keep herself from complete surrender. But it was her wish to marry in church, to begin their wedded life on a pure basis. He had already promised that, to please her, he would convert to Christianity.

"Thank you for the flowers," she said and extended her hand, not small, but pale and delicate. He lifted it to his lips and kissed it, holding it for a while within his own. Scents of lilac and late spring surrounded them.

"When did you come?" she asked. "I expected you yesterday."

"I was too tired."

"Halina hasn't stopped asking about you. There was something about you yesterday in the *Courier Warshawski*."

"Yes, Wolsky showed it to me."

"A somersault on the tightrope?"

"Yes."

"God in heaven, what people won't try," she cried with astonishment and regret. "Well, it's all a gift, I suppose. You're looking well!" She changed her tone. "Lublin seems to agree with you."

"I rest up there."

"With all the women?"

He did not answer. She said, "You haven't even kissed me yet." And she opened her arms to him.

5

They remained locked in their kiss as if it were a contest to see who would take the first breath. Suddenly she tore herself loose. She always had to make him promise to control himself. She had lived four years already without a man, but it was better to suffer than to act promiscuously. She always observed: God sees all. The souls of the dead are ever present and behold the deeds of their near ones. Emilia had her own religious convictions. The Catholic dogma was to her nothing more than a set of rules. She had read the mystic writing of Svedenborg, Jakob Boehme. With Yasha she often discussed clairvoyance, premonitions, mind-reading, and communication with the spirits of the dead. After Stephan Chrabotzky's death, she conducted seances for a time in her salon, supposedly exchanging greetings with Chrabotzky through table-tipping. Later, she realized that the medium, a woman, was a charlatan. The mysticism had through some strange fashion blended within Emilia with skepticism and a quiet sense of humor. She ridiculed Yadwiga and the Egyptian book of dream interpretations which the servant kept under her pillow—yet she, Emilia, believed in dreams herself. After Chrabotzky's death, several of his colleagues proposed marriage to her, but her dead husband had appeared before her in a dream and urged her to reject them. Once he even materialized before her as she was walking up the stairs at dusk. She revealed to Yasha that she loved him because his character was so like Chrabotzky's and that she had indications that Chrabotzky approved the match. She now took Yasha by both his wrists, guided him to a chair and sat him down as one would a mischievous child.

"Sit. Wait," she said.

"How long must I wait?"

"It all depends on you."

She sat down facing him, in a chaise longue. Her tearing herself away from him had been for her a physical effort. She sat, momentarily flushed as if surprised at her own lust.

They began to converse in the severed phrases of intimates who have been parted and try to bind up the broken threads. Halina had been ill two weeks ago. She, Emilia, had also had the grippe. "I wrote you that, didn't I? Well, I've forgotten . . . Yes, everything is fine now . . . Halina? Gone to the park to read. Very absorbed in books now—but such trash! God, how bad literature has become! Common, cheap . . . Wasn't this May a cold one? Snow, even . . . The theater? No, we went nowhere. Aside from the fact that tickets are exorbitant, the quality of the plays is so absurd . . . Everything translated from the French, and poorly translated at that. The eternal triangle . . . But wouldn't you rather talk about yourself? Where did you wander all these weeks? When you leave everything seems unreal. It all seems like a dream to me. But when a letter comes, the world is all right again. Well, and all of a sudden Halina comes running in all excited—you've been mentioned in the *Courier* . . . What? Some sort of a write-up. Halina is convinced that anyone whose name is mentioned in the newspapers is a demi-god, even if it is because the person has been struck by an omnibus . . . And how are you? You're looking well. You don't appear to have missed us. What do I really know about you? You always were and you still are, an enigma. The more you talk about yourself, the less I can figure you out. You have women all over Poland. You drag yourself around in a covered wagon like a gypsy. It's really amusing. A person with your talent and so unadvanced. Often I think that your entire conduct is a joke on yourself and the world. . . . What's that? About us I certainly couldn't tell you a thing. All our plans are suspended in the air. I'm afraid that everything will drag on like this until we're both old and gray. . . ."

"I've come to you now and we won't be separated again!" he said, amazed at his own words. Until just now he had not yet made a decision.

"What's that?—Well, that's what I've been waiting for. This is what I've wanted to hear!"

And her eyes grew moist. She turned her face aside and he saw her in profile. Presently she rose to tell Yadwiga to serve the coffee. The woman had already brewed it, unbidden. She had ground it herself in a coffee-grinder according to old Polish tradition. The aroma permeated the drawing-room. Yasha was left alone. Well, everything is fate, he mumbled to himself. He was seized by a tremor. With those few words to Emilia, he had just about sealed his destiny. But what would become of Esther now? And Magda? And where would he get the money he needed? And was he truly capable of changing his religion? I cannot live without her! he replied to himself. He was filled suddenly with the impatience of a convict awaiting his release, every hour an eternity. He stood up. Though his heart was heavy, his feet felt uncommonly light. Right now I could turn not one but three somersaults on the tightrope! How could I have put it off this long? Yasha skipped to the window, turned aside the draperies, gazed out at the luxuriant chestnut trees in the Saxony Gardens, at all the schoolboys, young fops, governesses, and couples who strolled along its paths. For example, that young fellow with the flaxen hair and his girl in the straw hat with the cherries! They strutted like two birds, stopped, took another step, moved about in one spot, looked at each other, sniffed one another, played at the games only lovers know. They seemed to be precipitating a tussle or a kind of dance of the sexes. But what was it he saw in her? And how blue the sky was today! Pale blue like the curtain which hung in the temple during the Days of Awe.

Yasha felt a pang of doubt at the comparison. Well, God was God, whether you prayed to Him in the synagogue or in church. Emilia came back. He walked towards her.

"When she brews coffee she smells up the whole house. It's the same when she cooks."

"What will become of *her*?" he asked. "Will we take her along with us to Italy?"

Emilia pondered a moment.

"Are we at that stage already?"

"My mind is made up."

"Well, we'll require a servant too. But it's all idle chatter."

"No, Emilia, it's just as if you were my wife already."

6

The doorbell rang. Emilia excused herself and left Yasha alone once again. He remained still, as if he were in hiding and afraid to reveal his presence to someone who sought him. He had already compromised Emilia, but she still concealed him from her relatives. He had become like one who sees but is himself invisible. He sat there and stared at the furniture, at the rugs. The pendulum in the grandfather clock swung slowly. Golden flecks of sunlight glanced off the prisms of the chandelier, off the album bound in red velvet. From a neighbor's house, piano chords drifted. He had always admired the cleanliness of this apartment, the affluent tidiness. Everything was placed where it belonged. There wasn't a hint of dust anywhere. Those who lived here never seemed to accumulate dirt or anything else superfluous, no disagreeable odors, no disconcerting thoughts.

Yasha listened intently. Emilia had several distant relatives living in town. They frequently dropped in uninvited. Yasha sometimes had had to leave through the kitchen entrance. While he listened, he tried to evaluate his situation. To realize his plans he would need money, at least fifteen thousand rubles. He could only obtain that much money one way. But again, was he prepared for such a step? Being intimate with many women had transformed him into one who lived for the moment, guided himself only by impulse and inspiration. He made plans but everything remained fluid. He spoke of love, but he could not truthfully account to himself what he meant by it, nor what Emilia understood it to be. And during all his transgressions he had always sensed the hand of Providence. Hidden forces propelled him always, even during his performances. But could he expect God to lead him into theft and apostasy? Listening to the notes of the piano, he heard his own thoughts simultaneously. Before every action, a voice within him usually made itself audible, spoke clearly, commanded sternly, proposed all the details. But this time he experienced a sense of anticipation. Something else was scheduled to occur, something was still to be altered. In his notebook he had a list of banks and addresses of wealthy people who kept their money in metal strongboxes, but he had not followed up these possibilities. He had already managed to justify the deed he contemplated, for he had sworn a promise to return everything with interest, once he had won fame abroad, but he had not yet been able to appease his conscience. Fear, disgust, and self-contempt remained. He was descended from people of honor. His grandfathers, on both sides, were famous for their honesty. A great-grandfather once trailed a merchant to Lenczno to pay back a forgotten ten groschen . . .

The door opened and Halina appeared in the doorway: fair, suddenly tall for her fourteen years, with blonde pigtails, light blue eyes, a straight nose, full lips and the transparent paleness of skin peculiar to those afflicted with anemia and weak lungs. She had grown during the short time he had been away, and she seemed ashamed of it. She looked at Yasha, pleased and confused at once. Halina took after her father—she had the mind of a scientist. She yearned to understand everything: each trick that he, Yasha, performed, every word that he spoke to her mother while she, Halina, was present. She was an avid reader, collected insects, could play chess, write poetry. She was studying Italian already . . . For a moment she seemed to hesitate. Then she charged at Yasha with a childish leap and fell into his arms.

"Uncle Yasha!"

She kissed him and let herself be kissed in return.

She promptly besieged him with questions. When had he come? Had he traveled by wagon this time too? Had he seen any wild beasts in the forest? Had he been stopped by highwaymen? How was the monkey? The crow? The parrot?

How were the peacocks in his yard at Lublin? And the snake? The turtle? Would he actually perform a somersault on the wire as announced in the newspapers? Was this possible? Had he missed them—her and Mama? She seemed almost full grown, yet she chattered on like a child. But there was a sense of artificiality as well as playfulness.

"You've shot up like a tree!" Yasha said.

"Everyone refers to my height!" she pouted with childish reproof. "Just as if it were my fault. I lie in bed and I feel myself growing. An imp tugs at my feet. I don't want to grow at all. I should like to remain little always. What shall I do, Uncle Yasha? Is there an exercise to make one remain small? Tell me, Uncle Yasha!" and she kissed his forehead.

So much love! So much love! Yasha mused. Aloud he said, "Yes, there is a way."

"How?"

"We'll put you in the grandfather clock and lock the door. You won't be able to grow taller than the cabinet."

Halina perked up immediately.

"He has a solution for everything! How quickly his mind works! He doesn't have to think at all! How does your brain work, Uncle Yasha?"

"Why don't you take off the lid and look inside? It's just like the mechanism of a clock."

"More clocks? That's all you have on your mind today—clocks. Are you working on a new trick with a clock? Have you read the *Courier*? You're famous! All Warsaw admires you. Why did you stay away so long, Uncle Yasha? I was ill and I called for you every minute. I dreamed about you, too. Mama scolded me because I talked so much about you. She is terribly jealous!" Halina said, blushing at her own words. Just then, Emilia walked in.

"So, your Uncle Yasha is here again. I can't tell you how often she asked about you."

"Don't tell him, Mama, don't tell him. He will become spoiled. He thinks that because he is a great artist and we are insignificant little people he can lord it over us. God is mightier than you, Uncle Yasha. He can perform even finer tricks."

Emilia quickly grew stern. "Do not take the Lord's name in vain. It is no subject for levity."

"I'm not joking, Mother."

"That's the latest fashion: to bring God into every senseless conversation."

Halina seemed lost in thought for a moment. "Mama, I'm simply starved."

"Oh?"

"Yes, if I don't eat something in the next ten minutes, I'll just die."

"Oh, how you carry on. Like a child of six. Tell Yadwiga to give you something to eat."

"And you, Mama, aren't you hungry?"

"No, I manage to survive from one meal to the next."

"But you hardly eat, Mama. A glass of cocoa means breakfast to you. How about you, Uncle Yasha?"

"I could eat an elephant."

"Come on, then, let's eat him together."

Yasha sat down with mother and daughter and they all ate their second breakfast, all the delicacies that Yasha had brought: the sturgeon, the sardines, the swiss cheese. Yadwiga brought coffee with cream. Halina ate with gusto, praising and enjoying every mouthful. "How good this smells! It melts in your mouth!" The crusts of the freshly baked rolls crackled between her teeth. Emilia chewed in a slow ladylike way. Yasha himself ate with enjoyment. He looked forward to these snacks with Emilia and Halina. With Esther, he had little to talk about. She knew nothing beside her housewifely chores and her sewing business. Here, the conversation came easily. It turned to hypnotism. Emilia had often warned Yasha not to discuss this subject before Halina, but he could not very well avoid it. He was advertised in the newspapers as a hypnotist, and Halina was too clever and curious to be dissuaded with a word. Besides, she read adult books. Professor Chrabotzky had left an extensive library. His colleagues from the university and former pupils sent Emilia textbooks and tear-sheets from scientific journals. Halina examined everything. She was familiar with Mesmer, his theories and his trials, had read about Charcot and Janet. The Polish newspapers printed articles about the hypnotist, Feldman, who had caused a sensation in various Polish salons. He had even been permitted to demonstrate his powers in hospitals and private clinics. For the millionth time Halina asked Yasha the same question: How could one person inject his will into another? How was it possible for one person to put another to sleep by looking at him? How could someone be made to shiver with cold in the hottest weather, or in an overheated room?

"I don't know the answer myself," Yasha said. "That's the honest truth."

"But you've done these things yourself."

"Does the spider know how it spins its web?"

"Oh—now he compares himself to a spider! I hate spiders, I despise them! You, Uncle Yasha, I adore."

"You talk too much, Halina," Emilia interrupted.

"I want to know the truth."

"Her father's daughter. She only wants the truth."

"For what other reason are we born, Mama? Why are all the books written? All for truth. Mama, I have a big favor to ask you."

"I know what it is beforehand—and the answer is *no!*"

"Mommy, I beg you on bended knees! Have pity."

"No pity. No!"

What Halina wanted was her mother's permission to have Yasha demonstrate his hypnotism right then and there. Halina was even eager to be hypnotized herself. But Emilia repeatedly denied her daughter's request. One did not trifle with such things. Emilia had read somewhere of a hypnotist who had been unable to arouse his subject. The victim had remained in a trance for days afterwards.

"Come to the theater, Halina, and then you'll see how it's done," Yasha said.

"To tell the truth, I hesitate to take her—such riff-raff go there."

"What must I do, Mother? Sit in the kitchen and pluck chickens?"

"You're still a child."

"Let him hypnotize you, then."

"I don't want any seances in my house!" Emilia said, sharply.

Yasha was silent. They are hypnotized anyway, he thought. Love is based entirely on hypnotism. When I saw her for the first time, I hypnotized her. That is why she was waiting for me that night on Marshalkowska Boulevard. They are all hypnotized: Esther, Magda, Zeftel. I possess a power, a tremendous power. But what is it? And how far does it extend? Would I be able to hypnotize a bank director into opening the vault for me?

He, Yasha, had first heard the word, hypnotism, only a few years before. He had attempted it and had succeeded immediately. He had ordered his subject to sleep and the man had fallen into a heavy slumber. He had ordered a woman to undress and she had begun to take off her clothes. He had told a girl that she would feel no pain and though he had pricked her arm with a pin, she had not cried out, nor had there been any blood. Since then Yasha had witnessed a number of demonstrations by other hypnotists, several indeed by the famous Feldman, but what this power was or how it worked, Yasha could not understand. At times it seemed to him that both hypnotist and subject were indulging in some sort of high-jinks; but nevertheless it was no sham. Perspiration cannot be simulated in cold weather nor a flow of blood prevented when a needle is jabbed into the flesh. Perhaps this was what was once labeled black magic.

"Oh, Mommy, you're so stubborn!" Halina said, munching a sardine on a roll. "Tell me what sort of power this is, Uncle Yasha, before I die of curiosity!"

"It's a force. What is electricity?"

"Yes, what *is* electricity?"

"No one knows. They flash signals here in Warsaw and the electricity carries them in one second to Petersburg or Moscow. The signals go over fields, forests, go hundreds of miles, all in one second. Now there is such a thing as a telephone! and one can hear another's voice through the wires. The time will come when you'll be able to talk from Warsaw to Paris just the way I'm talking to you now."

"But how does it work? Ah, Mama, there is so much to learn! Some people are so wise! How did they become so wise? But it's always men. Why don't women educate themselves?"

"In England there is a woman physician," Yasha said.

"Really? That's funny. I can't help laughing!"

"What's so amusing?" Emilia asked. "Women are people, too."

"Of course. But a woman doctor! How does she dress? Like George Sand?"

"What do you know about George Sand? I'll lock you out of the library!"

"Don't do it, Mommy. I love you, I love you terribly and you're so strict with me. What do I have besides my books? The girls I know are all bores. Uncle Yasha seldom comes to see us. He plays hide-and-seek with us. I can lose myself in books. Why don't the two of you get married?" Halina blurted out suddenly, amazed at her own words. She paled. Emilia blushed to the roots of her hair.

"Are you mad, or what?"

"She is right. We will be married soon," Yasha interrupted. "Everything's been decided. All three of us are going to Italy."

Halina hung her head, shamefaced. She began to toy with the tip of her braid as if to count the hairs. Emilia lowered her eyes. She sat there helpless, ashamed, gratified by Yasha's words. The girl chattered ceaselessly, but this time her foolish prattle had been helpful. He had just then made it official. Emilia lifted her eyes.

"Halina, go to your room!"

FIVE

Usually, Yasha began to rehearse two weeks before the opening. Just this year when he had prepared a new and difficult repertoire, he kept delaying the rehearsals from day to day. The proprietor of the Alhambra had refused to raise Yasha's salary. Wolsky, the impresario, was quietly negotiating with another summer theater, the Palace. Often during the day, when Yasha sat in the Café Lurs, sipping black coffee and leafing through a magazine, he was seized by an odd premonition—a feeling that he would not perform that season. He feared this portent and tried to banish it from his mind, mollify it, erase it—but it kept returning. Would he grow sick?

Was he, God forbid, due to die? Or was it something else altogether? He placed his hands on his forehead, rubbed his scalp, his cheekbones, enveloped himself in a blind darkness. He had wound himself into too many entanglements. He had driven himself into a dilemma. He loved and desired Emilia. He even longed for Halina. But how could he inflict such an outrage against Esther? For so many years she had shown him a rare devotion. She had stood beside him through all his difficulties, helped him in every crisis; her tolerance was the kind that the pious attribute only to God. How could he repay her with a slap? She would not live through the shock, Yasha knew—she would wither and flicker out like a candle. More than once he had seen a person die of heartbreak simply because they no longer had any reason to stay alive. Some of these people had not even been sick when they died. Swiftly and without explanations the Angel of Death performs his magic.

For some time now he had been trying to prepare Magda for his departure. But she was jittery already. Each time he returned from Emilia, Magda looked at him with mute reproach. She had almost ceased speaking to him altogether and had withdrawn like a clam into her shell. In bed, she was frigid, distant, silent. Summers past, the pimples on her face would fade, but this year her complexion was a mass of them. The rash had even spread to her neck and the upper part of her breasts. She had also begun to have accidents.

Plates slipped from her hands. Pots turned over on the hot stove. She had burned her foot, pricked her finger, nearly lost an eye. In this state, how could she be expected to perform somersaults, hand him his clubs and balls to juggle, or spin the barrel on her feet? Even if he, Yasha, managed to go on this season, he would probably have to engage a new assistant at the last minute. Yes, and what of poor Elzbieta? The news of his deserting Magda might kill her.

There was a partial solution to the miserable situation: money. If he could give Esther ten thousand rubles it would temper the blow somewhat. A cash settlement would certainly appease Magda and Elzbieta. In addition, he needed a large sum for himself, Emilia, and Halina. Her plan was to purchase a villa in southern Italy where the climate would benefit Halina's lungs. He, Yasha, would not be able to begin performing right away. He would first have to learn the language, engage an impresario, make contacts. He could not afford to sell his services as cheaply there as he did here in Poland. He would have to begin right at the top. But for all this he needed a backlog of at least thirty thousand lire. Emilia had confessed to him what, actually, he had already known. She owned nothing save a pile of debts which she would have to make good before she could leave town.

Ordinarily Yasha did not smoke. He had weaned himself away from a pipe in the belief that it was bad for the heart and eyes and that it interfered with his sleeping. But now he began to smoke Russian cigarets. He sucked on the tip of a cigaret, sipped black coffee from a saucer, and scanned a magazine. The smoke stung his nostrils, the coffee his palate; the magazine article made no sense. It raved about some Parisian actress, one Fifi, at whose feet all France worshiped. The writer implied that Fifi was a former demimondaine. "Why would all France glorify a tart?" Yasha wondered. Was this France? Was this the Western Europe of which Emilia spoke with such awe? Was this the culture, the art, the aestheticism that the journals wrote about with such fervor? He threw aside the magazine, which was immediately claimed by a white-mustached gentleman. Yasha extinguished his cigaret in the coffee dregs. All his reflections and speculations inevitably led to the one conclusion: he must get his hands on a large sum of money, if not legally, then by theft. But when should he perform this crime? Where? How? Strange that although he had been contemplating this deed for months now, he had never even entered a bank, nor familiarized himself with banking procedure; he had not even determined where the banks stored their money during closing hours, nor the type of safes or locks they employed. He had procrastinated, procrastinated. Whenever he passed a bank, he stepped quickly, averting his face. It was one thing to open a lock on the stage or before the Piask gang, another to steal into a building manned by armed guards. For that, one had to be a born thief.

Yasha tapped his spoon against the saucer to summon the waiter but the man either did not hear, or pretended not to. The café was quite full. There were almost no patrons who, like himself, were alone. Most sat in groups, circles, clusters; the men in morning coats, striped trousers, wide cravats. Some wore pointed beards, some spade beards; some had drooping mustaches, some mustaches that curled. The women wore wide-skirted dresses, and wide-brimmed hats decorated with flowers, fruits, pins, and feathers. The patriots whom the Russians had exiled to Siberia in boxcars after the uprising were dying by the hundreds. They expired from scurvy, consumption, beri-beri, but mainly from ennui and the yearning for the motherland. But the patrons in the café had apparently reconciled themselves to the Russian invader. They talked, shouted, joked, and laughed. The women fell giggling into each other's arms. Outside, a hearse rolled by, but those within ignored it as if death did not concern them. What were they jabbering about with such fervor? Yasha wondered. Why did their eyes gleam so? And that old fellow with the white wedge beard and the mossy pouches under the eyes—why had he pinned a rose in his lapel? He, Yasha, was to all appearances their equal, yet a barrier separated them. But what was it? He never found a clear explanation. Together with his ambition and lust for life, dwelt a sadness, a sense of the vanity of everything, a guilt that could neither be repaid nor forgotten. What was life's purpose if one did not know why one was born nor why one died? What sense did all the fine words about positivism, industrial reform, and progress make when it was all cancelled out in the grave? For all his drive, he, Yasha, was constantly on the brink of melancholy. As soon as he lost his craving for new tricks and new loves, doubts attacked him like locusts. Had he been brought into the world simply to turn a few somersaults and deceive a number of females? On the other hand, could he, Yasha, revere a God whom someone had invented? Could he, Yasha, sit like that Jew with ashes on his head and bewail a temple which had been destroyed two thousand years ago? And would he be able later to kneel and cross himself before that Jesus of Nazareth who, allegedly, had been born of the holy spirit and was no less a personage than God's only son?

The waiter was at the table.

"What does the gentleman wish?"

"To pay," Yasha said.

His words seemed ambiguous—as if he had intended saying: To pay for my deceitful life.

2

In the first act of the play, the husband invited Adam Povolsky to spend the summer with him at his villa, but Adam Povolsky made excuses. He revealed a secret. He had a sweetheart, the young wife of an old nobleman. But the husband was adamant. The sweetheart could wait. He wanted Povolsky, in the course of the vacation, to instruct his daughter on the pianoforte and to give

English lessons to his wife. (French had just about gone out of fashion.)

In the second act, Adam Povolsky carried on affairs with both the mother and the daughter. To get rid of the husband, all three protagonists convinced him that he was arthritic and that he must be off to Pischany to take the mud baths.

In the third act the husband discovered the deception. "I did not have to go to Pischany to wallow in mud," he exclaimed; "I have a morass right here in my house!" He called out Adam Povolsky but now the old nobleman came, the cuckold spouse of Povolsky's inamorata, and he took Povolsky back to his estate. The play ended with a lecture by the old nobleman to Adam Povolsky on the dangers of amorous entanglements.

The farce was adapted from the French. Few plays were put on in Warsaw during the summer but this particular vehicle, *Povolsky's Dilemma*, drew audiences even in the hottest weather. The laughter began with the rising of the curtain and did not cease until the end of the third act. The women muffled their giggles in handkerchiefs while drying the tears caused by uproarious laughter. Occasionally there was a laugh that seemed scarcely human. It cracked like a shot and degenerated into a whinny. Thus one cuckold laughed at another. He slapped his knee and began to topple from his seat. His wife revived him and tried to set him right in his chair. Emilia smiled and fanned herself. The gaslights intensified the heat. Yasha barely maintained an amiable expression. He had seen hundreds of similar farces. The husband was always fatuous, the wife unfaithful, the lover cunning. The moment Yasha stopped smiling, his eyebrows tensed. Who mocked whom here? The same rabble existed everywhere. They danced at weddings and wailed at funerals, swore faithfulness at the altar and corrupted the institution of marriage, wept over a forlorn, fictitious, little orphan and butchered each other in wars, pogroms, and revolutions. He held Emilia's hand but anger burned in him. He could neither desert Esther, convert, nor suddenly turn thief on account of Emilia. He glanced sideways at her. She laughed less than the others, probably to avoid appearing vulgar, but also seemed to enjoy Povolsky's serpentine antics and two-edged bons mots. Who could tell? He probably appealed to her, too. He, Yasha, was short in stature but the farceur was tall and broad-shouldered. In Italy, Yasha would be vocally inept for years to come while Emilia would communicate in French, and quickly learn Italian. While he was roaming about doing performances, risking his neck daily, she would hold a salon, invite guests, seek a match for Halina, perhaps find for herself an Italian Povolsky. They're all the same. Each of them a spider!

No, no! he cried within himself. I won't let myself be trapped. Tomorrow, I'll run away. I'll leave everything behind—Emilia, Wolsky, the Alhambra, the magic, Magda. I've been a magician long enough! I've walked the tightrope too often! He suddenly reminded himself of the new stunt he was scheduled to introduce—the somersault on the tightrope. They would recline on soft cushions while he, pushing forty as he was, would turn somersaults on the wire. And what if he fell and smashed his body? They would put him out on the threshold to beg and not one of his admirers would stoop to fling a groschen into his hat.

He took his hand away from Emilia's. She sought it again but he turned from her in the darkness, surprised at his own rebelliousness. These thoughts were not new to him. He had wrestled with these problems even before he had met Emilia. He lusted after women, yet hated them as a drunkard hates alcohol. And as he planned new stunts, he was plagued by the fear that the old ones were beyond his powers and would cause him an untimely death. He had burdened himself with too heavy a yoke even before Emilia. He supported Magda, Elzbieta, and Bolek. He paid rent for the Warsaw apartment. He roamed for months on end through the provinces, stopping at mean hotels, playing in ice-cold firehouses, traveling dangerous roads. And what did he gain from all this? The humblest farmhand enjoyed more peace of mind and less worry. Esther grumbled frequently that he worked only for the devil.

In some odd way, the farce assisted his ruminations. How much longer would he drift along like this? How many more burdens would he assume? With how many more perils and disasters would he load himself? He was revolted by the actors, the audience, by Emilia, by himself. These important ladies and gentlemen had never acknowledged him, Yasha, nor had he acknowledged them. Artfully, they had fused religion with materialism, connubiality with adultery, Christian love with worldly hate. But he, Yasha, remained a bedeviled spirit. His passions flayed him like whips. Never had he ceased to suffer regret, shame, and the fear of death. He spent agonized nights reckoning his years. How much longer would he remain young? Catastrophically, old age hovered about him. What could be more useless than an elderly magician? Sometimes in bed, unable to close his eyes, long-forgotten passages of the Scriptures would leap to his mind, prayers, his grandmother's wise proverbs, his father's stern moralization. A Yom Kippur tune would start within him:

> To what can man aspire
> When death will quench his fire? . . .

Thoughts of repentance enveloped him. Perhaps there was a God, after all? Perhaps all the holy sayings were true? It just didn't seem credible that the world had created itself or simply evolved out of a fog. Perhaps a Day of Reckoning really waited and a scale where good deeds were weighed against the evil? If it were so, then every minute was precious. If it were so, then he had arranged not one but two hells for himself. One in this world, a second in the other!

But what concrete solution could he now

adopt? Grow a beard and sidelocks? Don a prayershawl and phylacteries and pray thrice daily? Where did it follow that the entire truth was to be found in the Jewish codex? Maybe the answers lay with the Christians, the Mohammedans, or still some other sect? They also had their sacred books, their prophets, all sorts of legends of miracles and revelations. He felt the wrangling of the forces within him, the good and the evil. After a while, he began to daydream of flying apparatuses, of new loves, new adventures, journeys, treasures, discoveries, harems.

The curtain came down at the end of the third act. The applause was deafening. Men began to shout: "Bravo! Bravo!" Someone brought two bouquets of flowers to the stage. The cast clasped hands, took bows, smiled, peered into the box-seats occupied by the wealthy. Could this be the aim of creation? Yasha asked himself. Is this what God wills? Perhaps, it would be better to commit suicide.

"What's wrong?" Emilia asked. "You seem to be in a bad mood today."

"No, it's nothing."

3

It was a just a short distance from the theater to Emilia's house on Krolevska Street, but Yasha hired a droshky for the trip. He ordered the coachman to drive slowly. It had been hot in the theater, but, outside, cool breezes blew in from the Vistula and the Praga forests. Gaslights cast a shadowy glow. The bright sky was brilliant with stars. Simply raising one's eyes heavenward calmed the spirit. Yasha knew little about astronomy but he had read several lay books on the subject. He had even seen Saturn's rings and the mountains of the moon through a telescope. Wherever the truth was to be found, one thing was sure—the sky was vast, limitless. It took thousands of years for the light to travel from the stars before it reached our eyes. Fixed stars, winking and blinking in the heavens, were suns, each with its own planets which were probably worlds themselves. That pale stain up there was perhaps the milky way, a skein of multi-millions of heavenly bodies. Yasha never passed up the astronomical nor other scientific articles in the *Courier Warshawski*. The scientists were constantly making new discoveries. The cosmos was no longer measured in miles but in light years. A mechanism had been invented capable of analyzing the chemical components of the farthest star. Bigger and bigger telescopes were constantly being constructed which revealed the secrets of space. They predicted accurately every eclipse of the moon and sun, the return of every comet. If only I'd applied myself to my education instead of my magic, Yasha mused. But now, it's already too late.

The droshky rode down the Alexander Place parallel to the Saxony Gardens. Yasha breathed deeply. In the darkness the park seemed full of mystery. Tiny flames flared within the depths. Scents wafted from the greenery. Yasha lifted

Emilia's gloved hand and kissed her wrist. He felt love for her once again. He lusted for her body. Her face was shrouded in shadows. Her eyes gleamed like twin jewels, sparkled with gold, with fire, with nocturnal promise. He had bought her a rose on the way to the theater and it now exuded an intoxicating aroma. He lowered his nostrils to the rose and it was as if he breathed in the odor of the universe. If a bit of earth and water can create an aroma like this, creation cannot be bad, he decided. "I must stop brooding about such foolishness."

"What did you say, dear?"

"I said that I love you and that I can't wait until you are mine."

She waited a moment. Her knee touched his through the gown. Something like electricity coursed into him through the silk. He was overcome with desire. A tingle streaked down his spine.

"It's even more difficult for me than for you." She said "thou" to him for the first time in their relationship. She barely managed to breathe the word. He heard it more in his mind than in his ears.

They sat there quietly and the horse walked step by step. The coachman's shoulders drooped as if he were dozing. They both seemed to listen to the lust which moved from her knee to his and back again. Their bodies conversed in a wordless language of their own. "I must have you!" one knee said to the other. He was consumed with an ominous silence as when he walked the tightrope.

Suddenly she bent her head to his. The brim of her straw hat made a roof over his head. Her lips touched his ear.

"I want to bear your child," she whispered.

He embraced her, bit into her lips. His mouth drank, drank. He felt as if he had stopped breathing. Esther had spoken about a child repeatedly, but years had passed since she had last brought up the subject. Magda had also requested a child several times but he had not taken her seriously. He seemed to have forgotten that element of life. But Emilia had not forgotten. She was still young enough to conceive and carry. Perhaps this is the very cause of my torment, he pondered. I am without an heir.

"Yes, a son," he said.

"When?"

And their mouths fused again. They consumed each other in a silent, bestial way. The horse stopped suddenly. The coachman seemed to come awake.

"Gee up!"

They pulled up before Emilia's house and Yasha helped her alight. She did not immediately ring the bell but stood there with him on the sidewalk before the gate. They did not speak.

"Well, it's late." And she pulled the bellcord.

Yasha could determine by the footsteps that it was the janitor's wife, not the janitor, who came to open the gate. The courtyard was dark. Emilia went in and Yasha sidled in behind her. He did it with deftness and spontaneity. Even Emilia was not aware of what had happened. The janitress padded back to her cubicle. He took Emilia's arm in the darkness. She started.

"Who is it?"

"It is I."

"God in heaven, what did you do?" And she giggled in the darkness at his fantastic skill and daring.

They stood there as if silently deliberating.

"No, that is not the way," she whispered.

"I only want to kiss you."

"How will you get into the house? Yadwiga will open the door."

"I'll open it," he said.

He mounted the stairs with her. Several times they stopped to kiss. He made a pass at the door and it swung open. The corridor was dark. A middle-of-the-night stillness emanated from the rooms. He walked into the drawing room, pulling Emilia along with him. She seemed to be holding back. They wrangled silently. He steered her to the divan and she followed like one who is no longer mistress of herself.

"I don't want to begin our life together in sin," she whispered.

"No."

He wanted to undress her and the silken gown began to snap and shoot off sparks. The fire, which he knew to be static electricity, startled him. She was astonished herself. She clasped him by both his wrists, squeezed with such force that it hurt.

"How will you leave?"

"Through the window."

"Halina may waken."

Suddenly she pulled back and said: "No, you must go!"

SIX

The following day Yasha slept late. He dozed until one in the afternoon. Magda's country habits still remained with her. She could not understand how one could stay in bed until midday. But she had long accustomed herself to the fact that Yasha was not like other people. He could eat more and fast longer, he could stay up nights and sleep the whole day through. Waking from profound slumber, he could speak to her as if he had been dissembling. His brow and the veins on his temples would indicate that he was thinking waking thoughts. Who could tell? Perhaps that was how he conceived new stunts? Magda walked about on tiptoe. She served him oat grits with potatoes and mushrooms. He ate and, afterwards, fell asleep again. Magda began to mutter to herself in a peasant jargon: "Snore away your sins, you swine, you cur. Drained himself dry with that scabby duchess." Magda had one remedy for all sorrows—work. Yasha was hard on his clothes and everything needed mending. He lost his buttons, his seams sprang apart, he wore a shirt one day, then cast it aside as if it were lousy. It was always necessary to pick up after him, to wash, polish, sew. His animals also required care: the horses in the stable, the monkey, the parrot, the crow. She was everything to him: a wife, a servant, a stage assistant—and what did she get? Nothing—a crust of bread. Actually, he had nothing himself. Everyone robbed him, swindled him, deceived him. Clever as he was in the theater, hypnotizing and reading minds or when reading his books or papers, he was stupid when it came to practical matters. Also he was ruining his health. He should not go roaming about night after night. Even though he was healthy, he sometimes grew weak as a fly, fell in a faint and lay as if in a seizure.

Magda washed, scrubbed, scoured, dusted. Neighbors dropped in to borrow an onion, a clove of garlic, a drop of milk, a bit of lard with which to brown onions. Magda turned no one away. Compared to these paupers, she was affluent. Besides, she had an unsavory reputation and she was forced to curry favor with her neighbors. She was officially registered with the municipal authorities as a house servant. When the neighbors were at odds with her, they called her strumpet and carrion and suggested she file for the yellow card of a prostitute. Men who were drunk tormented her when she went down to the store or the pump. Youths shouted after her, "Whore for the Jews!"

The belfry-bell of the church of the Holy John rang two o'clock. Magda went to Yasha in the alcove. He was no longer asleep but sitting up in bed and staring.

"Have a nice nap?" she asked.

"Yes, I was tired."

"When do we begin to rehearse? The opening is a week away."

"Yes. I know."

"The posters are everywhere. Your name is in gigantic letters."

"They can all go to hell."

Yasha wanted a bath and Magda promptly began to heat kettles of water for him. She soaped him down in the wooden tub, rinsed him off, massaged him. Magda, like any other woman, longed for a child. She was prepared to bear Yasha an illegitimate one. But he robbed her even of that. He, himself, wanted to be the child. Magda bathed him, petted him, caressed him. He wronged her more than her worst enemy, but when he spent a few hours with her and showed that he needed her, her love for him became more ardent than before.

He asked abruptly. "Do you have any sort of a dress for the summer?"

Instantly her tears began to flow.

"Now you remind yourself?"

"Why didn't you keep after me? You know I'm forgetful."

"I don't badger. I'll leave that to your new lady."

"I'm going to buy you a wardrobe soon. I've told you that you're locked in my heart. Whatever happens, wait for me."

"Yes, I'll wait."

"Take off your clothes. Let's bathe together."

Magda acted shocked at such a suggestion but he held and stripped her. She was not so much ashamed of her nudity as her gaunt body. Her ribs jutted out, her breastbone was flat, almost without breasts, her knees were angular, her arms lean as sticks. The rash had spread from her face to her back. She stood before him, a shame-faced skeleton. He climbed out of the tub and placed her within it. He bathed her, soaped her, fondled her. He tickled her until she had to laugh. Then afterwards he bore her into the alcove and drew the bed-curtains. He now made love to her so often and for such a long period of time that fear gripped her heart. He was clearly a warlock with the strength of the devil.

Lately he had avoided her. For days she had not heard the sound of his voice. Now he spoke to her as he used to. He questioned her about rural customs and she described the various harvest rites. She spoke of the fairies who secrete themselves in the corn and hide from the harvesters' sickles and the flails of the threshers. She told of a female dummy of straw which the boys would cast into the river, of a tree to which the old peasants prayed for rain although the priests had forbidden it, of a wooden rooster kept somewhere in the village elder's attic which, during times of drought, was doused with water as a talisman to bring rain. He heard her out and questioned her.

"Do you believe in God?" he asked.

"Yes, I believe."

"Then why did he create all this? Well, in my trousers pockets are ten rubles. Take them and go to a seamstress."

"I don't like to go through your pockets."

"Go on, take them while they're still there."

She went into the other room where he had hung his trousers and took the ten rubles. When she returned he was once more asleep. She felt like kissing his forehead but she did not want to wake him. Standing in the doorway for a long while, she gazed down at him with the painful awareness that no matter how long she knew him, she would never understand him. He was, and continued to be, an enigma to her, body and soul. Perhaps that was the very reason why she had trembled and clung to him so. Finally, she went to clean up the bath. There was a seamstress in the house, near the second gate. Magda spat on the banknote and tucked it into her bosom. The day had unexpectedly turned happy.

2

He slept the whole summer's day through. It had already rained and the sky had cleared again. He opened his eyes. The alcove was swathed in semi-darkness. He smelled food cooking in the kitchen. Magda was frying potatoes with cutlets and sauerkraut. He had eaten nothing but the oat grits and awoke famished. Dressing quickly, he went into the kitchen. He kissed Magda and ate what was ready: bread with herring milt. He took a half-raw cutlet from the frying pan. Magda scolded him good-naturedly. Then she said: "I wish every day were like this one."

And as she spoke, a scratching was heard at the front door. The knob rattled, Yasha opened the door. An urchin girl stood there, wrapped in a huge shawl. She apparently knew him, for she said: "Panie Yasha, a lady is waiting for you downstairs by the gate."

"What lady?"

"Her name is Zeftel."

"Thank you. Tell her I'll be right down." And he gave the child two groschen.

No sooner did he close the door than Magda clasped both his hands. "No! You shan't go! Your supper's growing cold!"

"I can't let her wait there."

"I know who it is—it's that tart from Piask!"

She held him with such strength that he was forced to shake her loose. Instantly her face contorted, her hair bristled, her eyes flashed green and light as a cat's. He pushed her away and she nearly fell into the water barrel. It was always like this. Whenever he was kind to someone, she wanted to enslave him. He closed the door behind him and heard Magda weep, hiss like a snake, shout something unintelligible after him. He sympathized with her but he couldn't let Zeftel stand out there in the street waiting. He walked down the stairs, breathing the odors of the flats. Children wailed, the sick uttered sighs, girls sang of love. Somewhere up on the roof, cats caterwauled. He stopped for a moment in the dusk and planned a course of action.

I'll give her something and send her away, he decided. My life's complicated enough without her. Just at that second Yasha reminded himself of an appointment that he had with Emilia. He was supposed to eat dinner at her house that very evening. Those had been his parting words just before he had climbed out of her window the night before. How could I have forgotten? he wondered. Lord, I forget everything. I promised to write Esther the minute I reached Warsaw. She's probably half out of her mind with worry. What's wrong with me? Am I sick, or what? He leaned against the bannister as if then and there to take stock of his life. He'd frittered away a day just dozing and dreaming. It was as if he had simply skipped over an entire period of time. There was so much for him to do and think about that he could not allow his thoughts to linger on anything. He should have been planning his opening yet he had not even rehearsed. He never stopped thinking about Emilia but he had not really arrived at any definite decision concerning her. I can't make my mind up about anything, he said to himself, that is what's wrong. What had occurred the day before—Emilia's change of mind at the last moment—had been a blow to him. She had resisted his hypnotic powers. Before he had gone, she had kissed him and again avowed her great love, but her voice had been tinged with a tone of triumph. Maybe it's all for the best that I've forgotten the dinner engagement, he said to himself. Why let her think I'm chasing her? Suddenly he thought: But what if this is the end? Perhaps at this very moment she had stopped loving him or become his enemy?

Absurd thoughts attacked him—he played an inner game of maybes and perhapses, just as he had when he had been a schoolboy and had speculated whether his father was the devil, his teacher a demon, the tutor a werewolf, and everything else merely illusion. The propensities and idiosyncracies of those years remained within him. If no one was about, he would not walk but would hop down the stairs like a bird and run the nail of his forefinger along the plaster wall. He was likewise afraid of the dark, he who, on a dare, had spent a night in the cemetery. Shapes still evolved from the shadows, terrifying faces with bridling manes, pointed beaks, holes instead of eyes. He constantly felt that only the thinnest of barriers separated him from those dark ones who swarmed around him, aiding him and thwarting him, playing all sorts of tricks on him. He, Yasha, had to fight them constantly or else fall from the tightrope, lose the power of speech, grow infirm and impotent.

He went down and saw Zeftel. She was standing before the gate, beneath a lamppost, a shawl draped across her shoulders. The street lamp cast a radiant yellow across her face. She seemed exactly what she was: a provincial woman, freshly arrived in Warsaw. She had arranged her hair in two buns, one on each side, an obvious attempt to appear younger. There hovered about her the transitory air of those who, having torn up their roots, feel alien even to themselves.

"So you're here?" Yasha said.

Zeftel started. "I began to think you weren't coming down."

She made a move as if to kiss him but somehow nothing came of it. A housewife walked by carrying a pail of water from the pump, sighing and mumbling to herself. She jostled against Zeftel, spilling water over her button-top shoes.

"Oh, the devil with her!" Zeftel lifted each foot in turn and wiped it dry with the edge of her shawl.

"When did you arrive?"

She thought the question over as if she had not understood it. The long trip seemed to have confused her.

"I set off and I'm here. What did you think, I took the fare from you for nothing?"

"It was a possibility."

"Piask isn't a town; it's a graveyard. I sold all my stuff. I was cheated. What can you expect of thieves? I was lucky to get out of there alive."

"Where are you staying?"

"I'm with a woman who finds servants work. She promised me a job but so far there's been nothing. The way things are there are more servants than mistresses. I've got to talk something over with you."

"My supper is waiting."

"Yashale, it was just hell, trying to find you. No one knew the street, nor the house number. How can one see the number when it's dark? Until I got that girl to call you, I nearly died. I didn't want to go up to your house. I knew the other one was up there. Two cats in one sack."

"She had just finished cooking. How about waiting another half hour?"

"Come with me now, Yashale. Where can I wait? Every minute there's another drunk. They think every girl is one of those. We'll buy something to eat. All right, you're a big-shot Warsaw magician and I'm only a girl from the country, but, as the saying goes, we are not exactly strangers. Everyone sends his regards: Blind Mechl, Berish Visoker, Chaim-Leib."

"Thanks a lot."

"Thanks for nothing. What do I need with your thanks? I talk to you and you're not even here. Have you forgotten already, or what? Yashale, it's like this," she changed her tone, "I go to this woman agent and she says, 'You came at the wrong time. Everybody is looking for domestic work and all the ladies are away in the country.' I pick up my basket and start to go out when she calls me back. 'Where you running, where?' It seems she lends money to the girls at interest. Anyway, she makes a bed for me on the floor and I lie down. Three cooks are lying next to me, snoring. One makes so much noise I don't close my eyes all night, just lie there and cry. With Leibush after all, I was my own boss. In the morning I was just going out when a man walks in, a dude with a watch on a chain and cuffs with cuff links. 'Who are you?' he asks. So I tell him everything. 'It's like this—my husband deserted me. I don't know where he's gone.' So he keeps asking questions and says, 'I know where your husband is!' 'Where is he?' I shout. Well, to make a long story short, this fellow comes from America, but it seems it's another America. Anyway, Leibush is there. When I hear that, I begin to cry like it was Yom Kippur. 'What are you carrying on for?' he asks. 'It's a pity—your pretty eyes.' He talks so fancy you almost bust and he throws his money around and treats everybody to chocolate bars and halvah. 'Come with me,' he says to me, 'and I'll take you to your husband. He'll either take you back or divorce you.' He's going back in a couple of weeks and he's willing to lend me the ship's fare. But somehow, I'm afraid."

And Zeftel suddenly stopped talking.

Yasha whistled.

"That bird, eh?"

"You know him?"

"I don't have to know him. You know what a pimp is, don't you? He'll drag you off to—God knows where—and stick you in a brothel."

"But he speaks so nicely."

"He knows your husband like I know your great-grandmother."

They strolled towards Dluga Avenue. Zeftel grasped the edge of her shawl.

"What can I do? I've got to find a job. He put me up at his sister's. I spent last night there."

"His sister's, eh? She's his sister like I'm your great-uncle." Yasha was astonished at how quickly he'd adopted Zeftel's tone and jargon. "Most likely a madam, and they split the profits. He'll sell you somewhere—in Buenos Aires or who knows where. You'll rot there alive."

"What are you saying? He even mentioned the name of the city. Where is it again? In America?"

"Wherever it is, it doesn't mean a thing. They come here to deal in flesh, in women—they're white slavers. They wait for dumbbells like you. The newspapers are full of it. Where does this sister live?"

"On Nizka Street."

"Well, let's go over and take a look. Why should he offer to advance you the fare? Can't you understand what kind of fellow this is?"

Zeftel paused.

"Yes, that's why I came to you. But when you're lying on the floor and the bedbugs are eating you alive, you do what you can. At his sister's it's clean. I have a bed to sleep in and linen. She feeds me, too. I offered to pay her but she said, 'Don't worry about it, we'll settle up later.'"

"It's enough. Get out of there unless you want to end up a whore in Buenos Aires."

"What are you talking about? I was a respectable girl. If only Leibush had appreciated me. I'd have made him a good wife. But he spent more time locked up than at home. Three weeks after the wedding he was already in jail. Later he ran away altogether. What could I do? I'm only flesh and blood, after all. All Piask ran after me. His best friends. But I didn't want to waste myself on them. I longed for you. Yashale, I don't want to force myself on you; I have my pride, as the saying goes, but you're here in my heart. After you left I began to long for you. Now that I'm walking next to you, I feel as if I'm flying. You haven't even kissed me yet!" she pouted reprovingly.

"I couldn't back there. Everyone sits at the windows looking out."

"Give me a kiss. I'm still the same Zeftel."

And she held open her shawl for him.

3

That's all I needed! Yasha said to himself. How odd that he had forgotten Zeftel and the fact that he had given her the fare to go to Warsaw. He had forgotten her presence completely. He marveled at his own entanglements, yet took some perverse pleasure from them, as if his life were a storybook in which the situation grows tenser and tenser until one can barely wait to turn the page. Earlier he had felt hungry, but now his hunger had left him. The night was warm, even a trifle humid, but he felt a chill across his back as if he had been sick and had gone outside prematurely. He had to stop himself from trembling. He looked for a droshky, but no droshkies came to Freta Street, and so he steered Zeftel in the direction of Franciskaner Street. I'll get rid of her and go on to Emilia's he decided. Emilia won't know what to think. It was the first time he had broken a promise to her. He was apprehensive lest she become really insulted. Everything was balanced on a hair as it was. He also regretted having run out on Magda and realized suddenly that a change had come over him. There had been times when he had carried on a half-dozen affairs simultaneously without the slightest hitch. He had deceived everyone without a second thought, and had struck out freely when necessary without feeling any qualms of conscience. Now he brooded over the most insignificant trifles, was always seeking to do the right thing. Am I becoming a saint or what? he asked himself. It was hardly worthwhile arguing with Emilia over Zeftel and Magda, and yet that pinpoint in his brain that had the last word ordered him to stay with Zeftel. For some reason he wanted to "take care" of this pimp and his alleged sister.

Freta Street was dark and narrow. But Franciskaner Street was illuminated by gas lamps and the lights from stores which remained open despite the law. Here merchants dealt in leather and dry goods, in prayer books, and feathers. Business was even being transacted in the upstairs apartments, and all sorts of factories and workshops could be glimpsed through the windows. Thread was being wound, paper bags glued, linen and parasols sewn, underwear knitted. From the courtyards came the sound of sawing and hammering, and there was a hum of machinery as at the height of the working day. Bakeries were going full-blast and the chimneys spewed out smoke and cinders. From the broad, slop-drenched gutters rose a familiar stench which was reminiscent of Piask or Lublin. Young men in long gabardines and wearing tousled side-locks walked with Talmudic books under their arms. There was a Yeshivah located here as well as Hasidic study-houses. The few passing droshkies were loaded to capacity with packages, the passengers completely hidden. Only at the corner of Nalevki Street was Yasha able to find an empty droshky. Zeftel reeled as if she were intoxicated, overwhelmed by the clamor and congestion. She climbed into the carriage, catching the fringes of her shawl on something. Once seated, she clutched Yasha's sleeve. As the droshky turned the corner, Zeftel seemed to turn with it. "If someone had told me, today I'd be riding in a droshky with you, I would have thought it was a joke."

"I didn't expect it either."

"It's as light as day here. Light enough to shell peas."

And she squeezed Yasha's arm and drew him to her as if the brightly illuminated thoroughfare had reawakened the love within her.

On Gensha Street night began to close in again. A hearse rolled by, the corpse unaccompanied by a single mourner, destined to enter the grave in darkness. Perhaps someone just like myself, Yasha thought. Up near Dzika Avenue, streetwalkers called out to the passers-by. Yasha pointed. "That's what he wants to make of you."

On Nizka Street it was almost completely dark. The globes of the infrequent lampposts were smoke-stained and murky. The gutters were filled with mud as if it were not summer but just after the Feast of Tabernacles, during the fall rains. Here there were several lumberyards and a few establishments maintained by tombstone carvers. The house where Zeftel was staying was not far from Smotcha Street and the Jewish cemetery. They entered through a door set in a wooden fence. The stairs of the house were on the outside. Yasha and Zeftel entered a pink kitchen, which was illuminated by a naphtha lamp covered with a fringed paper shade. Everything was fringed with paper: the stove, the cupboard, the shelves of dishes. In a chair sat a woman. She had a great sweep of yellow hair, yellow eyes, a beaked nose, a sharp chin. Her feet, in red house slippers, rested on a footstool. A cat dozed nearby. In her hand the woman held a man's sock stretched over a glass as she darned. She raised her eyes in half-surprise.

"Mrs. Miltz, this is the man from Lublin I told you about—the magician."

Mrs. Miltz stuck the needle into the sock.

"She talks about you all the time. The magician did this, the magician did that. You don't look like a magician."

"What do I look like?"

"A musician."

"I did saw away at a fiddle once."

"You did? Well, what's the difference what you do so long as you make, you know what."

And she rubbed her thumb in her palm. Yasha immediately began to talk her language.

"You're not lying. Money is a thief."

"Get her, she just comes to Warsaw and already she goes everywhere." Mrs. Miltz indicated Zeftel. "How did you find him? I was afraid she'd get lost. Why did you ever move to Freta Street?" she addressed Yasha. "Only Gentiles live there."

"Gentiles don't look into strange pots."

"If you cover your pot with a lid, not even a Jew can look in."

"A Jew would lift the lid and take a sniff."

The yellow woman's eyes twinkled.

"As I live and breathe, nobody's fool this," she said half to Zeftel, half to herself. "Have a seat. Zeftel, bring a chair."

"Where is your brother?" Zeftel asked.

The woman raised her yellow eyebrows. "What is it? You want to sign a contract with him?"

"This gentleman wants to speak with him."

"He's in the back room, dressing. He has to go out soon. Why don't you take off your shawl; it's summer, after all, not winter."

After some hesitation, Zeftel removed the shawl.

"He'll have to take a droshky. Some merchants are waiting for him," Mrs. Miltz remarked, as if to herself.

"What does he trade in, cattle?" Yasha asked, astounded at his own words.

"Why cattle of all things? Where he comes from, there is no end of cattle."

"He deals in diamonds," Zeftel interjected.

"I'm an expert with diamonds, too," Yasha boasted. "Take a look at this." And he showed a ring with a large diamond on his little finger. The woman looked at it with amazement and then her expression turned to one of reproof. A bitter smile played about her mouth.

"My brother is a busy man. He has no time for idle talk."

"I want to get down to facts," Yasha said, surprised at his own brazenness.

The door opened and a man entered. He was tall, thick-set, and had yellow hair which was the same shade as the woman's. His nose was wide, his lips thick, and his round jaw was halved by a cleft. His eyes were bulging and yellow. A sickle-shaped scar disfigured his forehead. He wore no jacket, only trousers and a stiff collarless shirt; on his feet were unbuttoned, patent-leather shoes. A broad chest profusely overgrown with yellow hair showed through the gaping shirt front. Yasha saw immediately what kind of a thug this was. There was a smile on the man's face, the smile of the eavesdropper who has kept himself apprised of the conversation. He was all good nature, cunning, confident, a giant who knows himself invincible. Seeing him, the woman spoke, "Herman, this is that magician, Zeftel's friend."

"A magician? All right, so he is," Herman said amiably, his eyes glinting. "A good evening to you," and he gripped Yasha's hand. It was more a show of strength than a handshake. Yasha fell into the spirit of the contest and squeezed as hard as he could. Zeftel seated herself on the edge of the metal bed in which she slept. At last Herman released his grip.

"Where are you from?" Yasha asked.

Herman's protuberant eyes filled with laughter. "Where am I not from? The whole world. Warsaw is Warsaw and Lodz is Lodz! They know me in Berlin and I'm no stranger in London."

"Where are you living now?"

"As it is written in the Scriptures, 'The sky is my chair and the earth is my footstool.'"

"So, you know Scriptures also."

"Oh, you know them, too?"

"I studied them once."

"Where? At a Yeshivah?"

"No, at a study-house, with a tutor."

"So help me God, I was once a student of the Talmud myself," Herman said amiably in a confidential tone. "But that was a long, long time ago. I like eating, and in the Yeshivah you could send your teeth out to storage. I thought it over and decided it was not for me. I went to Berlin to study medicine but the plusquamperfectum of their grammar wouldn't stay in my mind. The German girls appealed to me more. So I continued on to Antwerp and became a diamond polisher, but I saw that the cash was not in polishing but in selling. I like the dice and I believe in the old saying, 'No wrinkles in the belly.' One way or another, I got to Argentina. Lately, there have been a lot of Jews going there. They carry a pack on their shoulders and suddenly they're business men. We call them *quentiniks*, in German they're *hausierer*, in New York peddler, but what the hell's the difference? That agent woman—what's her name again?—has a son in Buenos Aires and he sent his regards to his mother. I met Zeftel at the agency. What is she to you, a sister?"

"No, not a sister."

"For all I care, she can be your aunt."

4

"Herman, you've got to go," the yellowish woman interrupted, "there are businessmen waiting for you."

"Let them wait. I waited plenty for them. Where I come from, no one is in a hurry. The Spaniard says to everything *mañana*—tomor row; he is lazy and wants everything brought to him at home. There are the steppes—they call them *pampas*—where the cattle graze. When the *gaucho*, as they say, gets hungry, he's too lazy to kill a steer; he picks up a hatchet and carves himself a beefsteak from the live animal. He roasts it, hide and all, because he's too lazy even to skin it. He claims it tastes better that way. The Jews out there aren't lazy and that's how they make the *peso*—that's what they call the money. Everything would be fine except that too many men have come and there are too few of Eve's daughters. But without a woman a man is only half a body, as the Talmud says. A girl there is worth her weight in gold. I don't mean that in the bad sense. They get married and that's the end of it.

If the marriage doesn't take, it's a lost cause because divorce is out of the question. It might be a snake you married, you got to stay with it—that's the way the priests want it. So what does a man do? Puts on his walking shoes and is on his way. So the wheel of fortune spins. Rather than have your sister become a maid and wash somebody's drawers, she's better off coming with me and getting what she wants there."

"She isn't my sister."

"And if she isn't, what of it? In Buenos Aires, we don't ask for pedigrees. Genealogy, we say, is only good to put on a gravestone. When you go there it's like being born again. What sort of tricks do you do?"

"All sorts."

"Do you play cards?"

"Occasionally."

"Aboard ship, there's nothing else to do. If it weren't for cards you'd go crazy. It's hot as blazes and when you cross the—what do you call it?—equator, you can suffocate. The sun is straight overhead. At night it gets even hotter. If you go on deck you roast in an oven. So what's left?—cards. On the way here some fellow tried to cheat me. I looked at him and I said, 'Brother, what's that sticking out of your sleeve? The fifth ace?' He'd have liked to jump me but I don't scare easy. Back home everybody carries a gun. If you get too smart you find yourself full of holes. So, like everybody else, I carry a gun. Would you like to have a look at an Argentinian revolver?"

"Why not? I've got a gun, too."

"What do you need it for, your tricks?"

"Possibly."

"Anyhow, he saw he wasn't dealing with some kid. He'd tried to mark the cards but I caught him. Zeftel mentioned you do card tricks. What can you do?"

"Not cheating."

"What then?"

"Fetch me a deck and I'll show you."

"Herman, you've got to go," Mrs. Miltz said impatiently.

"Wait, don't rush me, my business won't run away, and if it does, I don't give a damn. You know what? Let's go in the other room and have a snack."

"I'm not hungry," Yasha lied.

"You don't need to be hungry. The appetite, they say, comes as you eat. Here in Poland, you people don't know how to eat properly. Noodles and chicken soup and chicken soup and noodles. What are noodles anyway?—nothing but water. You only bloat the belly. The Spaniard takes care of a three-pound beefsteak and that puts marrow in your bones. You come to a Spaniard's house and he lies down in the middle of the day and sleeps like a log. It's hot as hell there and flies suck your blood like leeches. In the summer, life begins at night. With us, if somebody has just enough money either to eat or pay for a whore, he chooses the whore. Somehow or other, nobody starves. You like vodka?"

"Occasionally."

"Come on, then, have a glass. Rytza, fetch us

something," Herman said to the yellowish woman. "The Spaniard dearly loves his magic. He'd sell his soul to see a good trick."

The living-room furniture consisted of a table covered with oilcloth, a sofa, and a clothes closet. Suspended from the ceiling was a naphtha lamp which had almost gone out and Herman turned up the wick. Valises, plastered with stickers, and piles of boxes were scattered about the room. Over a chair hung a jacket and also on the chair were a stiff collar and a silver-headed cane. The very air of the place smelt of foreign lands and distant shores. Two photographs, one of a man with a white beard, the other of a woman in a full wig, hung on the wall.

"Have a seat," Herman said. "My sister is about to bring something tempting to eat. She can afford a better apartment but, being accustomed to this place, she doesn't want to move. Back home the houses aren't this big and everything is done right in the courtyard. A *patio*, it's called. The Spaniard hates to climb stairs. He sits outside with the family and drinks a kind of tea—*mate*. Everybody takes a sip through the same straw; it goes from mouth to mouth. Before you acquire the taste, it's like drinking branchwater with licorice milk, but you can get used to anything. In North America, for example, they chew tobacco. One thing you must understand—it's the same world everywhere. They don't eat people in Buenos Aires either. Take a look at me—nobody's eaten me."

"Maybe you've eaten somebody."

"Eh?—That's a good one! You're nobody's fool; the person who keeps his wits about him, skims the gravy right off the top. You come from Piask?"

"No, Lublin."

"Zeftel said you were from Piask."

"You're a thief yourself."

Herman exploded with laughter.

"Say, you're all right. Not everyone from Piask is a thief, no more than everyone from Chelm is a fool. It's only hearsay. On the other hand, who doesn't steal? My mother, may she rest in peace, used to say: 'The honest way is not the easy way.' You can do anything, you only need to know how. Just as I am now, I've already tasted everything. Zeftel tells me you can spring any lock."

"That's true."

"I wouldn't have the patience. Why fool around with a lock when you can smash the door down? What's a door hung on? Nothing but hinges. But that's all in the past. I've become, as the saying goes, a model citizen. I have a wife and children. Zeftel told me her whole story. About her husband deserting her and all the rest of it. If she gets a divorce, she could marry the richest man in South America."

"Who would grant her the divorce—you?"

"What's a divorce—A piece of paper. Everything is paper, my dear man, even money. I mean big money, not pocket change. Those who hold the pen—write. Moses was a man. That's why he wrote that a man could have ten wives, but if a woman looked at another man she had to be

[148]

stoned. If a woman had held the pen she would have written the exact opposite. Do you follow me or not? On Stavka Street there's a scribe who's one of us, and if you give him ten rubles he'll write you a good divorce, signed by witnesses, absolutely legal. But I don't force anybody into anything. I was willing to advance her the ship's fare . . ."

Yasha suddenly raised his brows. "Panie Herman, I'm no simpleton. Leave Zeftel alone. She is not your kind of merchandise."

"What? You can take her with you this very minute. She's already cost me a couple of rubles but I'll write it off as charity."

"Don't do us any favors. How much did she cost you? I'll pay for everything."

"Take it easy, don't get your wind up. Here's the tea."

5

They drank tea and ate cookies and butter-cake. Mrs. Miltz and Zeftel joined them at the table. Herman drank his tea with jam, ate the butter-cake and from time to time took a puff on a fat cigar which rested in a saucer. He offered Yasha a cigar, too, but Yasha declined.

"You can't get a cigar like this in all Warsaw," Herman complained. "This is genuine Havana. None of your substitutes but the real stuff from Cuba. Somebody brought them from there especially for me. In Berlin you'd have to pay two marks for one. I like everything first-class, but you have to pay for everything, and when you pay, already you pay too much. What's a Havana cigar? Leaves, not gold. And what's a good-looking girl? Also flesh and blood. The Spaniard is jealous. You smile at his wife and he goes for his knife, but two blocks away he keeps a mistress and has children by her. After a while, she becomes a frump, too, and he has to go looking for a fresh piece. I read the Polish papers here and I've got to laugh. They write such nonsense! A girl goes out at night to get a jug of milk, along comes a carriage and she's caught inside. Later they take her to Buenos Aires and sell her like a calf in the market. But I've been here weeks and haven't seen any such carriage. And how can you transport such a girl across the border? What about the ship? Nonsense, foolishness. The truth is, they go of their own free will. You go to that district and you meet women from every part of the world. You want a black one—a black one it is; you want a white one—that's what you get. If a Lithuanian from Vilno or Ayshyshok is what you're after, you don't have to go looking, or if you have an urge for the Warsaw product, you'll be accommodated. As for myself, I don't go there. What do I need with it? I've got a wife and children. But the newspapers want readers. It's just as I've been saying, it depends on who holds the pen. I'll tell you one thing: Husbands themselves send their wives into the quarter. And do you know why? Because they're too lazy to go to work themselves. How about some of your tricks? Here's a deck of cards."

"Once you start with the cards you won't go anywhere," the yellowish woman said.

"Tomorrow is another day."

Herman began to shuffle the deck and Yasha saw at once that he was up against a cardsharp. The cards flowed through Herman's hands as if they had a life of their own. So . . . that's the sort of canary you are! Yasha said to himself. Well, we'll soon show you there are some smarter boys around.

Yasha allowed him to perform several tricks: the trick with the three cards, the one with the four sevens, the changed card. Yasha shook his head at this and clicked his tongue, "Tsk, tsk, tsk . . ." He almost said, I was already doing these tricks when I was a little girl.

He reminded himself that it was growing late and that if he still wanted to see Emilia he would have to leave that very minute; nevertheless, he remained seated. Since she is so virtuous, let her wait! a second voice within him said, a spiteful one. Yasha was well aware that his worst enemy was his ennui. To escape it, he had committed all of his follies. It lashed at him like so many whips. Because of it, he had loaded himself down with all sorts of burdens. But now, he did not feel bored. He took the deck from Herman. The fact that Herman left the merchants waiting to spend the time with him indicated to Yasha that the other was afflicted with the same malady as he. It was the disease that bound the underworld to decent society—the card players in a thieves' den to the gamblers at Monte Carlo; the pimp from

Buenos Aires to the drawing-room Don Juan, the cutthroat to the revolutionary terrorist. As Yasha shuffled the cards, he marked them with the edge of his fingernail.

"Pick a card," he said to Herman.

Herman chose the king of clubs.

Deftly Yasha bent the deck.

"Put it back and shuffle the cards."

Herman did as directed.

"Now, I'll pick out the king of clubs for you."

And with the thumb and forefinger he took out the king of clubs.

"Let's just have a peep at your finger-nails."

Yasha showed one trick, Herman another. Herman was apparently familiar with all the tricks. His yellow eyes glistened with the slyness of the expert who had passed as an amateur. He did not have merely one deck in the house, he had a dozen.

"Looks like you've been holding a card up your sleeve," Yasha remarked.

"Cards fascinated me. But it's all over. Dead and buried!"

"You don't play any more?"

"Only a little 'sixty-six' with my Señora."

"Nevertheless, I'd like to show you something."

And Yasha picked up the deck again.

"Choose a suit."

Now Yasha performed some tricks which Herman did not seem to know. He looked at Yasha with a questioning smile. He furrowed his brow, took hold of his nose, held it a while in his large hand with the yellow hair. Mrs. Miltz opened her eyes wide as if incredulous that someone was able to outsmart Herman. Zeftel winked at Yasha, showed him the tip of her tongue. She blew him a kiss.

"Hey there, Rytza, you wouldn't have a carrot, would you?" Herman asked.

"Why a carrot, why not a radish?" she replied, sarcastically.

It was already eleven o'clock but still the men continued to show each other card tricks. Some of the stunts required saucers, cups, boxes, pieces of cardboard, as well as a ring, a watch, a flower pot. The women continued to fetch the necessary equipment. Herman grew overheated. He began to mop the sweat from his brow.

"Together, we could accomplish something."

"What, for instance?"

"We could take on the world."

Rytza brought vodka and the men clinked glasses, said "Prosit!" in cosmopolitan fashion. For Zeftel and herself, Rytza poured sweet brandy. They ate egg-cookies, black bread, swiss cheese. Herman began to speak with a clannish familiarity.

"I see your Zeftel at the agent's. She's pretty and sharp, too, but how was I to know what was what? She says her husband left her; I thought, 'Let him go in peace. I'll help her out somehow.' It was only later she told me about you. She mentioned a magician, but not all magicians are the same. Those who drag around courtyards with street-organs call themselves magicians, too. But you, Panie Yasha, you're an artist! First-class! Tip-top! But I've got a few years on you and I can tell you there isn't much you can do for yourself around here. With your skill you belong in Berlin, in Paris, even New York. London isn't a bad town, either. The Englishman loves to be fooled and he pays for the privilege, as well. Back home in South America, you'd be a God. Zeftel says that you can put people to sleep—how is it called —magnetism? What is this thing, anyway? I've heard of it, I've heard of it."

"Hypnotism."

"You know the thing?"

"Some."

"I've seen it somewhere. The subject really falls asleep?"

"Like a log."

"This means you could put Rothschild to sleep and snatch his money?"

"I'm a magician, not a criminal!"

"Yes, of course, but still . . . How do you do this?"

"I force my will upon the other."

"But how? It's a big world, all right. Always something new coming up. I once had a woman, she did everything I wanted her to. If I wanted her to be sick, she got sick. And if I wanted her to get well, she got well. When I wanted her to die, she closed her eyes."

"Ah, that's too much!" Yasha said, after a while.

"It's the God-damned truth."

"Herman, now you're talking foolishness!" Rytza said.

"She was in my way. Love is fine, but too much love is no good. She wound herself around me like a snake until I couldn't breathe. She was a couple of years older than me and trembled for fear I'd leave her. Once I was walking along the street and she was right on my tail, as usual. I felt smothered and I said, 'I can't go on like this.' 'What do you want?' she asked me, 'That I should die?' 'Just leave me alone,' I said. 'That I can't do,' she said, 'but if you want me to, I'll drop dead.' At the beginning I was afraid, but she made me so wild I felt it was either my life or hers. I began to think that . . ."

"I don't want to hear another word! I don't want to hear another word!" Rytza clapped her hands over her ears.

It was quiet for a time. They could hear the wick in the lamp sucking up the naphtha. Yasha consulted his watch. "Folks, I'm a cooked goose!"

"How late is it?"

"It's already daybreak in the town of Pinchev. Well, I've got to run along. Zeftel, stay for a few days. I'll pay for everything," Yasha said. "These people won't hurt you."

"Sure, sure, we'll settle everything," Rytza said.

"Where are you running to? Where are you running to?" Herman demanded. "Here when it grows a little late, everyone gets panicky. What is there to be afraid of? Back home in Buenos Aires we stay up all night. Winter and summer. When we go to the theater, the play ends around one o'clock. We don't go home afterwards but to a café or restaurant and first we eat a beefsteak and then the real drinking begins. By the time you get home, it's already daytime."

"When do you sleep?" Zeftel asked.

"Who needs sleep? Two hours out of the twenty-four is more than enough."

Yasha rose to take his leave. He thanked them for their hospitality. Rytza looked at him, questioningly, deliberately. It even seemed as if she were giving him a signal. She laid her finger to her lips for an instant.

"Don't be a stranger," she said, "we don't eat people here."

"When will you come?" Herman asked. "I've got something to discuss with you. The two of us have to make some sort of an agreement."

"I'll drop by."

"Don't forget."

Rytza picked up the lamp to light Yasha's passage down the stairs. Zeftel walked at his side. She took his arm. A childish exhilaration came over Yasha. He enjoyed speaking Yiddish, showing tricks in his shirtsleeves. It was like Piask here, but even more exhilarating. Obviously Herman was a white slaver and Rytza his confederate. It defied comprehension but in the few hours that they had known each other, Herman had acted as if he were devoted to Yasha. Rytza, apparently, also looked on him with favor. Who could tell what amorous delights such a woman could serve a man, what bizarre words she might utter in the throes of passion? For a moment, the light from the naphtha lamp lit up the courtyard with its piles of logs and lumber. Then upstairs the door closed and it was dark once more. Zeftel snuggled up to Yasha.

"Could I go some place with you?"

"Where?—Not today."

"Yashale, I love you!"

"Just wait and leave everything to me. Whatever I tell you to do, do it."

"I want to go with you."

"You will be with me. I'll take you along when I go abroad. I'll repay everyone who has been good to me. But be prepared for anything and don't ask any questions. If I tell you to stand on your head, then stand on your head. Do you understand?"

"Yes."

"You'll do as I say?"

"Yes, everything."

"Go back upstairs."

"Where are you off to?"

"There's one more bit of nonsense I have to take care of today."

6

Nizka Street was deserted. There was no chance of hiring a droshky here. He walked on and his tread felt uncommonly light. The street was dark. Over the wooden houses with the spavined roofs hung a suburban sky, thickly seeded with stars. Yasha gazed upward. What, for instance, do they think of someone like me up there? He walked the length of Nizka Street, came out on Dzika Avenue. He had told Zeftel that there was one other item of nonsense of his agenda. But what sort was it? He had slept the whole day and he was now as fresh and alert as if it were morning. A strange desire to visit Emilia came over him. It was complete madness. She was doubtless already asleep by now. Besides, the courtyard gate would be locked. But his climbing out of her window the night before had brought home to him again that doors and gates meant nothing to him. There was a balcony in her apartment. He could scale it in a minute. Emilia complained that she was a poor sleeper. She would hear him. Moreover, he would will her into expecting him and she would open the French doors (if they weren't open anyway). He had a feeling that this day she would not offer further resistance. It was as if he had miraculously put on seven league boots, for here he was on Dzika Avenue; a few minutes more and he was walking down Rimarska Street. He glanced at the bank. The pillars seemed to guard the building like giant watchmen. The gate was shut, all the windows dark. Somewhere nearby were the basement vaults where treasures were stored. But where? The edifice was as huge as a city. To be properly done, the job would require a long winter's night. Then Yasha recalled what Yadwiga, Emilia's servant, had told him about an elderly landowner, one

Kazimierz Zaruski, who had sold his estate years before and now kept his money in an iron safe in his apartment. He lived on Marshalkowska Boulevard, near Prozna Street, alone except for a deaf servant girl who was a friend of Yadwiga. When Yadwiga had told him this story, Yasha had not even bothered to write down the man's address. He had not entertained such notions and certainly none involving a household which Yadwiga visited. But now it all came back to him. I must do something tonight, he said to himself. Tonight I have the power.

From Nizka to Krolevska Street was quite a distance, but Yasha covered the several *versts* in twenty minutes. Warsaw slept, with only here and there a night watchman testing a lock or pounding his staff on the sidewalk as if to reassure himself that no one was tunneling in the ground underneath. They are forever watching but nothing can be kept safe, Yasha said to himself. Neither their women nor their possessions. Who could tell? Maybe at times even Esther was unfaithful to him? His thoughts wandered idly. What if he should sneak into Emilia's bedroom and find her with a lover? Such things did happen. He stood now beneath her window and looked up. The thought of climbing to the balcony, which only a few minutes before he had regarded as not only feasible but as eminently right, seemed, now that he was there, pure absurdity. There was always the possibility that she would awake and, mistaking him for a prowler, raise an outcry. Yadwiga might overhear him or, possibly, Halina. Emilia would certainly never forgive him. The Age of Knighthood was long since past. This was the prosaic nineteenth century. Mentally, Yasha had commanded Emilia to awake and come to the window, but apparently he had not as yet mastered this facet of hypnotism. Even if it should prove effective, the process would be a slow one.

He started down Marshalkowska Boulevard towards Prozna Street. As long as it is inevitable, he said to himself, why not tonight? Evidently, it had been foreordained. How was it called?—predestination? If there was a reason for everything, as the philosophers claimed, and man was merely a machine, then it was as if everything had been written beforehand. He came to Prozna Street. There was only one occupied house on the block; across the street a building was in the process of construction. Piles of bricks lay there, mounds of sand and lime. The inhabited house consisted of a dry-goods store with two apartments, both with balconies, above it. The landowner's apartment obviously faced the front, but which of the two was it? Yasha suddenly knew that it was the one on the right. The windows in the apartment on the left were partially covered by drapes, partially by curtains; the ones on the right had shabby drapes, the kind that would hang in a miser's house. Well, it's now or never! something within Yasha urged. As long as you are here, go on. He can't take his money to the grave with him, anyway. The night won't last forever, the voice cautioned anew. Its intonations were almost that of a preacher.

Climbing the balcony was easy. A bar extended from the door of the dry-goods store and the balcony rested on the heads of three statues. The whole house was studded with figures and decorations. Yasha placed one foot on the bar, took hold of the knee of a goddess, and soon was hanging on the edge of the balcony. He swung his body upwards. It seemed to have grown weightless. He stood for an instant on the balcony and laughed. The impossible was really so possible. Opening the French doors proved more difficult; they were locked from the inside. But he tugged violently on the door and lifted the chain with the skeleton key which he always carried on his person. Better one loud sound, he theorized, than a series of fumbling noises. For a moment he paused to see if there was any outcry. Then he stepped inside and breathed the musty air of the house; here, it was clear, the windows were seldom opened.

Yes, this must be it, he exulted. You can smell the rot and mildew! It was not completely dark inside because of the light of the street lamp. He felt no fear. Yet his heart pounded like a trip hammer. He stood rooted for a moment, astonished at how swiftly thought had become deed. Strange, that the very safe that Yadwiga had described should be right next to him. It stood on end, long and black as a coffin. The powers that control man's destiny had led him directly to Zaruski's hoard.

I mustn't fail, he urged himself. Since I've taken the plunge, I must see it through. He cocked his ears and listened. Somewhere in the adjoining rooms Kazimierz Zaruski and his deaf servant slept. He heard no sound. What would I do if they were to awaken? he asked himself, but he could not supply the answer. He put his hand on the safe and felt the cool metal. Quickly he located the keyhole. He traced it with his forefinger to determine it's type and contour. Then, he reached into his pocket for his skeleton key which he had just had in his hand, but it wasn't there. Undoubtedly he'd tucked it away in another pocket. He began to search his pockets, but the key had vanished. Where could I have put it? The bad luck is starting already! He rummaged some more. Did I drop it on the floor? If so, it had not made a sound. The key had to be somewhere near at hand, but it hid itself from him. Again he thrust his hand into his pockets—again and again. The important thing is not to panic! he cautioned himself. Just imagine that you're doing a performance. Now he searched again, calmly and deliberately, but the skeleton key had disappeared. Demons? he whispered half in jest, half in earnest. He began to feel warm. He was about to break out into a sweat, but he kept back the perspiration and his body remained overheated. Well, I'll just have to find something else. He knelt and unlaced one of his shoes. The shoelaces had metal tips and once Yasha had picked a lock with just such a tip. But no, it's not firm enough to open an iron safe, he decided in the midst of removing the lace. There was probably a corkscrew or a poker in the kitchen, but to grope his way to the kitchen now was to court disaster. No, I must locate the skeleton key! He stooped and only then realized that the floor was covered by a rug. He ran his palm along the rug. Was it possible that the spirits were playing with him? Did such things as spirits really exist? Suddenly, the thought came to him: a safe must have a key, and undoubtedly the old man kept it under his pillow when he slept. Yasha knew what a risky business it would be to try to get the key out from under the old landowner's pillow. He might wake. And what assurance did Yasha have that the key was really there? There were many other possible hiding places in the apartment. But now Yasha was sure that the key lay under Zaruski's pillow. He even visualized the key: the flat head, the teeth underneath. Am I dreaming? Am I going mad? he speculated. But the unseen forces which for years had held sway over him ordered him to go into the bedroom. "It will be easier this way," they prompted. "There is the door."

Yasha got up on his toes. If only the door doesn't squeak, he prayed. It stood half-open. He walked through and found himself in the bedroom. It was darker here than in the other room, for he could not determine exactly where the window was located, could only conjecture, and then his eyes began to adjust to the darkness.

From the murky whirls there began to evolve the contour of a bed, bedding, a head upon a pillow—a naked head with sockets instead of eyes, like that of a skeleton. Yasha froze. Was the old man breathing? He could not hear his breath. Was he awake? Had he just at that moment expired? Was he, possibly, feigning death? Perhaps he lay there ready to rise and attack him? Old men were often extremely powerful. And then the old man suddenly snored. Yasha came closer to the bed. He heard the clang of metal and knew what it was—the skeleton key. Probably it had caught on a button. Now it had fallen to the floor. Had it wakened the old man?

Yasha stood there a moment, prepared to bolt at the first sound. I couldn't kill him! I am no murderer. But the old man had once more fallen into a deep sleep. Yasha leaned over to pick up the skeleton key—he must leave no clues behind him; but again it had disappeared. That bit of wire had engaged him in a game of hide-and-seek. Well, I see it's one of those nights, already. The evil powers have singled me out. Something within him begged him to flee since his luck had deserted him, but, instead, he moved closer to the bed. Try to get hold of his key, he said to himself obstinately.

He ran his hand over the pillow, touched the old man's face unintentionally. He pulled back his hand as if it had been burned. The miser uttered a sigh as though he had only been shamming sleep. Yasha paused. He was prepared for attack, ready to grasp Zaruski by the throat and throttle him. But no, the man was asleep, a thin piping sound coming from his nostrils. Apparently he was dreaming. Now Yasha could see better. He slipped his hand beneath the pillow, convinced that he would touch the key—but there was no key. He raised the old man's head a trifle along with the pillow on which it rested but still he could find no key. This time his instinct had failed him. There was only one course left him. Escape! something within him counseled. Everything has gone wrong! Yet, once more he began to search for the skeleton key on the floor, even though he knew he was inviting disaster. Wagered my last gulden and threw away the ace, he thought, recalling the old Yiddish proverb. The saying had come to him in much the same way as the Scriptures and lessons from cheder popped into his mind in the middle of the night. Sweat suddenly drenched him from head to toe. It was as if a basin of water had been emptied over him. He felt hot and damp as in a steam bath. But he kept looking for the skeleton key. Maybe you should just choke the old bastard! some presence, partly within and partly outside him, suggested, a portion of him which did not have the final say, but was in the habit of offering bad advice and perpetrating cruel jokes upon him just when he most needed all his faculties.

Well, it's a lost cause. I'm going now, he muttered. He rose to his feet and backed out through the half-opened door. How light it was here in comparison to the bedroom! He could see every object. Even the paintings on the walls—the frames, not the canvases. A chest of drawers seemed to rise up from the floor and on it he spied some scissors. Just what I need! He picked up the scissors and went to the safe. The keyhole was now delineated by the light from the street. He probed inside the keyhole with the tip of the scissors, calm once again, listening to the inner workings of the lock. What sort of lock was it? Not English. The blade of the scissors was too wide at the top and he could not probe very deeply. It was evident that the lock was not complicated but there was something in it that Yasha could not make out. It was like a child's puzzle, which if not solved at once eludes one for hours. He needed an instrument that could reach to the lock's vitals.

Suddenly a new idea came to him. He took his notebook from his bosom pocket, tore several pages out of it and twisted them until they formed a stiff cone. Such a tool would not do to pick a lock yet it could penetrate to its bowels. But the cone lacked the solidity and the spring of metal. He found he could not determine anything from it. Well, I'll just have to come back another time. I don't dare wait until daybreak! He glanced at the door leading to the balcony. Failure! A fiasco! For the first time in his life! It had been a terrible night. He was overcome by fear. He knew, deep inside of him, that the misfortune would not be confined to this night alone. That enemy which for years had lurked in ambush within him, whom Yasha had had, each time, to repel with force and cunning, with charms and such incantations as each individual must learn for himself, had now gained the upper hand. Yasha felt its presence—a dybbuk, a satan, an implacable adversary who would disconcert him while he was juggling, push him from the tightrope, make him impotent. Trembling he opened the balcony door. His perspiring body shivered. It was as if winter had suddenly arrived.

8

He was just about to climb down when he heard the sound of voices below. Someone was talking in Russian. It was undoubtedly a passing patrol. Quickly he drew back his head. Perhaps he'd been seen on his way up? The patrol might be waiting for him. He stood there in the darkness and listened. If they know about me, I am trapped. —But no, no one could have seen him. He had looked in all directions before making the ascent. The patrol had just happened along. He still could not forgive himself for having failed so miserably. Perhaps I should look for my skeleton key again? he thought. He walked back into the bedroom, a gambler who has lost everything, and is no longer afraid to take a chance. At the open door he stopped, horrified. The old man lay in bed, his face completely covered with blood. There was blood on the pillow case, the bedspread, the old man's nightshirt. God Almighty, what's happened? Has he been killed? Have I, thought Yasha, had the bad luck to rob a house where there has been a murder?—But I just now

heard him breathe! Is there a killer here? Yasha
stood numb with fear. And then he laughed. It
wasn't blood at all, merely the light of the rising
sun. The window faced the East.

Once more he began his search for the key, but
there on the floor it remained night. The darkness enveloped everything. Yasha groped about
aimlessly. A weariness came over him; he felt a
weakness in his knees and his head ached.
Though he was awake his mind began to weave
dreams—fanciful threads which escaped capture,
for no sooner did he reach out for them than they
unraveled. Well, there's no chance of finding it
now. The old man may wake any second. A notion that the miser was cunningly shamming
sleep returned to him. He was about to rise when
his fingers brushed against the skeleton key.
Anyway no trace of him would remain now.
Quietly he retreated to the front room, which
daylight had also entered. The walls had become
a paper-like gray. Ashy flecks hovered in the air.
He approached the safe on shaky legs, fitted the
skeleton key into the keyhole, and began to
probe. But his will, strength, and ambition had
been spent. His brain was heavy with sleep. He no
longer had the ability to spring this antiquated
lock. It was obviously a neighborhood job, put together by an ordinary locksmith. If I had some
wax I could at least take an impression of this
contraption. He stood there bereft of passion, not
certain which was the more astonishing—his earlier greed or his present indifference. He fumbled
a moment longer. He heard a snort, and realized

that it had come from his own nose. The skeleton key had caught on something and he could turn it neither to one side nor the other. He became reconciled to abandoning it there, then with one try he freed it.

He stepped out onto the balcony. The patrol had disappeared. The street was deserted. Though the street lights were still lit the darkness above the rooftops was no longer that of night but more the gloom of an overcast sky, or the murkiness of twilight. The air was cool and moist. Birds had begun to twitter. Now is the moment, he said to himself with a sort of resolution and with a sense that the words possessed a double meaning. He began to descend but his feet lacked their usual sureness. He wished to support them upon the shoulders of a statue but they fell short of the goal. For a moment he hung from the edge of the balcony feeling that he was about to doze off—suspended in air. But then he wedged his foot in a depression in the wall.—Just don't jump, he warned himself, but, even as the thought came to him, he dropped and knew at once that he had landed too violently on his left foot.—That's all I need now, a week before the opening! He stood on the sidewalk testing the foot and only then did he feel the pain. Just then he heard shouting. The voice sounded aged, rasping and alarmed. Was it the landowner? He looked up but the cries were coming from the street. He saw a watchman with a white beard running toward him, brandishing a stout cudgel. The man began to blow a whistle. He had apparently spied Yasha descending from the balcony. Yasha forgot about his injured foot; he ran swiftly and easily. The police would arrive at any second. He did not know himself in which direction he was fleeing. Judging from his speed one would have thought his foot was uninjured, but as he ran he felt a drawing in his left foot, a piercing pain below the ankle around the toes. He had either torn a ligament or broken a bone.

Where am I now?—He had sped down Prozna Street and had come into Grzybow Place. He heard no more shouting or whistling, but he still had to hide somewhere, for the police might approach from another direction. He hastened towards Gnoyne Street. Here the gutter was strewn with mud and manure. Moreover, it was dark, as if the sun had not yet risen in this neighborhood. The light of the street lamps glared and Yasha stumbled against the shaft of an unhitched wagon. This part of the city was a hodge-podge of loading yards, markets, and bakeries. The smell of smoke, oil, grease, was everywhere. He was nearly run down by a meat-wagon. So close did the horses come to him that he smelled the fetor of their muzzles. The teamster cursed him. A janitor waved his broom at him with righteous indignation. Yasha stepped up onto the sidewalk and saw the courtyard of a synagogue. The gate stood open. An elderly Jew entered, prayer-shawl bag under his arm. Yasha darted inside.—Here they will not search!

He walked past a synagogue which was, to all appearances, shut (no light could be seen through the arched windows), and came to a study-house. In the yard stood crates filled with loose pages torn from holy books. The smell of urine was overpowering. Yasha opened the door at what appeared to be both study and poorhouse. The light of a single memorial candle flickering near the cantor's lectern showed him rows of men lying on benches, some barefoot, some wearing battered old shoes, some covered with rags, others half-naked. The air stank of tallow, dust, and wax.—No, they will not search here, he repeated to himself. He moved to an empty bench and sat down. He sat there in a daze and rested his damaged foot. Bits of manure clung to his shoes and trousers. He would have shaken them loose but in this holy place that would have been a desecration. For a moment he listened to the snoring of the beggars, incredulous at what had happened. His gaze moved toward the door and he listened for the footsteps of the police coming to arrest him. It seemed to him that he heard hoofbeats, an approaching trooper, but all the while he knew it was merely his imagination. At last there came a rusty voice crying out, "Up! Up! Up with your lazy carcasses!" The beadle had arrived. The figures began to sit up, rise, stretch, yawn. A match was struck by the beadle and his red beard was momentarily illuminated. He walked over to a table and lit a naphtha lamp.

At that very moment it occurred to Yasha what sort of lock was on Zaruski's safe and how it could be opened.

9

One by one the derelicts shuffled outside. Slowly
the worshipers began to assemble. In the early
morning light the naphtha lamp seemed pallid.
Inside the room it was neither dark nor light; a
sort of pre-day twilight prevailed. Some of the
worshipers had already begun to recite the introductory prayers, others simply paced back and
forth. The nebulous figures reminded Yasha that
corpses were said to pray during the night in synagogues. These shadows followed a fluctuating
course. They droned with an unearthly chant.
Who were they? Why did they rise so early?
Yasha wondered. When did they sleep? He sat
there like one who had had a severe blow on his
head yet knew that his senses were addled. He
was awake but something within him slept the
deep sleep of midnight. He rested and examined
his left foot. Pain coursed through it, stabbing
thrusts and a drawing sensation which com-
menced at the big toe and traveled up past the
ankle as far as the knee. Yasha reminded himself
of Magda. What would he tell her when he came
home? In the years that they were together, he
had often been cruel to her, but he knew somehow that this time she would be hurt more than
ever before. He could be sure that he could not
give an opening performance if his foot were damaged, but he kept from thinking about that. He
stared off somewhere in the direction of the cornice of the Holy Ark, recognizing the tablet with

the Ten Commandments. He recalled that only last night (or was it still the same day?) he had told Herman he was a magician, not a thief. But soon afterwards, he had gone off to commit a burglary. He felt dull and confused, unable any longer to understand his own actions. The men put on their prayer shawls and their phylacteries, they affixed the thongs and cloaked their heads, and he watched them with astonishment as if he, Yasha, were a gentile who had never witnessed this before. The first quorum had already assembled to say the prayers. Young men in sidelocks, skullcaps, and sashes sat down at the tables to begin studying the Talmud. They bobbed their heads, gesticulated, grimaced. For a long while the congregation was silent. They were reciting the Eighteen Benedictions. Soon the cantor began to intone the high Eighteen Benedictions. Every one of his words sounded to Yasha strangely alien yet strangely familiar: "Blessed art Thou, Oh Lord our God and God of our fathers, God of Abraham, God of Jacob, and God of Isaac . . . Who bestowest lovingkindness and possessest all things. Thou sustainest the living with lovingkindness, quickenest the dead with great mercy, supportest the falling, healest the sick, loosest the bound, and keepest thy faith to them that sleep in the dust."

Yasha translated the Hebrew words and considered each one. Is it truly so? he questioned himself. Is God really that good? He was too weak to answer himself. For a while he heard the cantor no longer. He was half dozing, although his eyes remained open. Presently he roused himself, hearing the cantor say, "And to Jerusalem, Thy City, return in mercy and dwell therein as Thou hast spoken . . ."

Well, they've been saying this for two thousand years already, Yasha thought, but Jerusalem is still a wilderness. They'll undoubtedly keep on saying it for another two thousand years, nay, ten thousand.

The red-bearded beadle approached. "If you would like to pray I'll fetch you a prayer shawl and phylacteries. It will cost you one kopeck."

Yasha wanted to refuse but he immediately thrust his hand into his pocket and took out a coin. The beadle offered change, but Yasha said, "Keep it."

"Thank you."

Yasha felt an urge to run. He had not worn phylacteries in—God knows how many—years. He had never put on a prayer shawl. But before he even made the attempt to rise, the beadle was back with the prayer shawl and phylacteries. He offered a prayer book, as well.

"Do you have to say Kaddish?"

"Kaddish?—No."

He did not have the strength to rise. It was as if he had been shorn of all his powers. He was also afraid. Perhaps the police were waiting for him outside? The prayer shawl bag lay next to him on the bench. Deliberately, Yasha took out the prayer shawl. He fingered the phylacteries within. It seemed to him that everyone was looking at him and waiting to see what he would do. In his stupor it appeared to him that everything depended on what he would now do with the prayer shawl and phylacteries. If he did not handle them properly, it would be proof that he was hiding from the police . . . . He began to put on the prayer shawl. He looked for the spot where the embroidery was supposed to be, or a stripe which indicated the section meant to be worn over the head, but he could find neither embroidery nor stripe. He fumbled with the ritual fringes. One fringe even lashed him across the eye. He was filled with an adolescent shame and fear. They were laughing at him. The entire assemblage was giggling behind his back. He put on the prayer shawl as best he could but it slid off his shoulders. He took out the phylacteries and could not determine which one was for the head and which for the arm. And which should one put on first? He sought clarification in the prayer book, but the print blurred before his eyes. Fiery sparks began to sway before him. I just hope I don't faint, he cautioned himself. He felt nausea. He began to plead with God: Father in Heaven, take pity on me! Everything else, but not this! He shook off the faintness. Taking out a handkerchief, he spat into it. The sparks continued to dip before his eyes, rising and falling in seesaw motion. Some were red, some green, some blue. There was a clanging in his ears as if bells were ringing. An old man walked over to him and said, "Here, let me help you. Remove the sleeve. From the left arm, not the right . . ."

Which is my left hand? Yasha asked himself.

He began to pull the sleeve from his left arm and the prayer shawl again fell from his shoulders. A group gathered around him. If Emilia were here to witness this! he thought suddenly. He was now not Yasha the magician but some fumbling lout whom others assist and make the butt of their scorn. Well, it's come, God's punishment! he said to himself in his anxiety.

He was overcome with regret and humility. Only now did he realize what he had attempted and how Heaven had thwarted him. It came over him like a revelation. He permitted the men to do with him as they pleased, as one who's suffered a fracture and lets others bandage it for him. The old man wound the thongs around Yasha's arm. He recited the blessing and Yasha repeated it after him, like a little boy. Telling Yasha to lower his head, he fixed upon it the proper phylactery. He wound the thongs around Yasha's fingers in such fashion as to form the Hebrew letters *Shadai*.

"It must be a long time since you've prayed," a young man observed.

"Very long."

"Well, it is never too late."

And the same group of Jews, who but a moment before had watched him with a sort of adult derision, now looked upon him with curiosity, respect, and affection. Yasha distinctly sensed the love which flowed from their persons to him. They are Jews, my brethren, he said to himself. They know that I am a sinner, yet they forgive me. Again he felt shame, not because he had been clumsy, but because he had betrayed this fraternity, befouled it, stood ready to cast it aside. What's the matter with me? After all, I'm descended from generations of God-fearing Jews. My great-grandfather was a martyr for the holy name. He remembered his father who, on his deathbed, had summoned Yasha to his side and said, "Promise me that you will remain a Jew."

And he had taken his, Yasha's, hand and held it until he entered his death throes.

How could I have forgotten this? How?

The circle of Jews had dispersed and Yasha stood alone in the prayer shawl and phylacteries, prayer book in hand. He felt his left foot draw, tear, but he continued his prayers, translating the Hebrew words to himself, "Blessed be He who spake and the world existed, blessed be He who was the maker of the world in the beginning. Blessed be He who speaketh and doeth. Blessed be He who decreeth and performeth. Blessed be He who hath mercy upon the earth and payeth a good reward to them that fear Him."

Oddly enough he now believed these words: God had created the world. He does have compassion for His creatures. He does reward those who fear Him. And as Yasha intoned these words, he reflected upon his own lot. For years he had shunned the synagogues. All of a sudden, in the course of days, he had twice strayed into houses of worship; the first time on the road when he had been caught in the storm, and now again for the second time. For years he had picked the most complex locks with ease, and now a simple lock which any common safe-cracker could have sprung in a minute had stumped him. Hundreds of times he had leaped from great heights without injury, and this time he had damaged his foot jumping from a low balcony. It was obvious that those in heaven did not intend to have him turn to crime, desert Esther, convert. Maybe even his deceased parents had interceded in his behalf. Again Yasha raised his gaze to the cornice of the Holy Ark. He had broken or contemplated breaking each of the Ten Commandments! How near he had come to strangling old Zaruski! He had even lusted for Halina, already woven a net in readiness to ensnare her. He had plumbed the very depths of iniquity. How had this come about? And when? He was by nature good-hearted. In the winter he scattered crumbs outside to feed the birds. He seldom passed a begger without offering alms. He bore eternal hate against swindlers, bankrupts, charlatans. He had always prided himself on being honest and ethical.

He stood there with bent knees and was aghast at the extent of his degradations and, what was perhaps worse, his lack of insight. He had fretted and worried and ignored the very essence of the problem. He had reduced others to dirt and did not see—pretended not to see—how he himself kept sinking deeper in the mud. Only a thread restrained him from the final plunge into the bottomless pit. But the forces which are compassionate towards man had conspired that he now stand in prayer shawl and phylacteries, prayer

book in hand, amongst a group of honest Jews.
He chanted "Hear O Israel" and cupped his eyes
with his hand. He recited the Eighteen Benedictions, contemplating every word. The long-forgotten childhood devotion returned now, a faith
that demanded no proof, an awe of God, a sense
of remorse over one's transgressions. What had
he learned from the worldly books? That the
world had created itself. That the sun, the moon,
the earth, the animals, man, had come out of
mist. But where had the mist come from? And
how could a mist create a man with lungs, with a
heart, a stomach, brain? They ridiculed the faithful who attribute everything to God, yet they
themselves attributed all sorts of wisdom and
powers to an unseeing nature which was unaware
of its own existence. From the phylacteries
Yasha sensed a radiance that reached into his
brain, unlocked compartments there, illuminated the dark places, unraveled the knots. All
the prayers said the same: There was a God Who
sees, Who hears, Who takes pity on man, Who
contains His wrath, Who forgives sin, Who wants
men to repent. Who punishes evil deeds, Who re-
wards good deeds in this world and—what was
even more—in the other.

Yes, that there were other worlds, Yasha had
always felt. He could almost see them.

I must be a Jew! he said to himself. A Jew like
all the others!

SEVEN

When Yasha went outside again, Gnoyne Street was filled with sunlight, with dray-wagons, horses, out-of-town merchants and factors, vendors of both sexes, hawking all sorts of wares. "Smoked herring!" they cried, "Fresh bagels!" "Hot eggs!" "Chick peas with sugar beans!" "Potato patties!" Through the gates rolled wagons stocked with lumber, flour, crates, barrels, goods covered by mats, sheets, and sacks. The shops dealt in oil, vinegar, green soap, axlegrease. Yasha stood at the synagogue gate and looked ahead of him. The very Jews who a moment previously had worshiped with such fervor and had chanted, "Let the great name be blessed for ever, Amen," had dispersed, each to his own store, factory, or workshop. Some were employers, some employees, some masters, some handymen. It now seemed to Yasha that the street and the synagogue denied each other. If one were true, then the other was certainly false. He understood that this was the voice of evil having its say, but the piety, which had consumed him as he stood in the prayer shawl and phylacteries in the prayer-house, began to cool now and evaporate. He had decided to fast this day as if it were the Day of Atonement, but the hunger which gnawed at him had to be appeased. His foot ached. His temples throbbed. His earlier complaints against religion reasserted themselves. Why all the excitement? something within him demanded. What proof is there that a God exists Who hears your prayers? There are innumerable religions in the world, and each contradicts the other. It's true you weren't able to open Zaruski's safe and you hurt your foot into the bargain, but what does that prove? That you're unnerved, exhausted, light-headed . . . Yasha remembered that while praying he had made all sorts of resolutions and had sworn the most exacting vows, but in the few minutes he had been standing here, all their substance had vanished. Could he really live the way his father had? Could he actually forsake his magic, romantic attachments, his newspapers and books, his fashionable clothes? The vows he had made in the study-house now sounded excessive, like the phrases one whispers to a woman in the throes of passion. He raised his eyes toward the pallid sky.

If You want me to serve You, Oh God, reveal Yourself, perform a miracle, let Your voice be heard, give me some sign, he said, under his breath. Just then Yasha saw a cripple approaching. He was a small man and his head, cocked to one side, appeared to be trying to tear itself loose from his neck. So also with his gnarled hands—they seemed about to crack from his wrists even while he was collecting alms. Apparently his legs had only one goal: to grow more twisted. His beard had the same contorted look and was in the act of tearing itself from his chin. Each finger was bent in a different direction, plucking, it seemed, an unseen fruit from an unseen tree. He moved in an unearthly jig, one foot in front of him, the other scraping and shuffling behind. A twisted tongue trailed from his twisted mouth, issuing between twisted teeth. Yasha took out a silver coin and sought to place it in the beggar's hand but found himself hampered by the odd contortions of the man. Another magician! he thought, and felt a revulsion, an urge to flee. He wished to throw the coin to the other as quickly as possible, but the cripple, apparently, had his own game—pushing closer, he sought to touch Yasha, like a leper determined to infect someone with his leprosy. Fiery sparks again flashed before Yasha's eyes, as if they were constantly present and only needed the opportunity to reveal themselves. He cast the coin at the beggar's feet. He wanted to run but his own feet began to tremble and twitch as if imitating the cripple's.

He spied a soup kitchen and walked inside. The

floor was sprinkled with sawdust. Although it was still early, the patrons were already dining: chicken soup with noodles, fritters, stuffed derma, sweetbreads, carrot stew. The odor of food made Yasha nauseous. I mustn't eat this kind of food so early in the morning, he admonished himself. He looked back as if about to walk out but a stout woman blocked his path. "Don't run away, young man, no one is going to bite you here; our meat is freshly killed and strictly kosher."

What connection can there be between God and killing? Yasha wondered. The woman pulled up a chair and he sat down at a long table, which he shared with the other diners.

"A glass of vodka with an egg cookie?" she suggested. "Or chopped liver with white bread? Chicken soup with buckwheat?"

"Bring me whatever you please."

"Oh? You can be sure I won't poison you."

She fetched a bottle of vodka, a tumbler, a basket of egg cookies. Yasha picked up the bottle but his hand was trembling and he spilled some of the vodka on the tablecloth. Some of his fellow patrons began to shout, half in warning, half in jest. They were provincial Jews wearing patched gabardines and unbuttoned undergarments faded from the sun. One had a burst of black whiskers extending up to his eyes. Another's beard was red—like a rooster's wattles. A little further down the table sat a Jew wearing a fringed garment and a skullcap. He reminded Yasha of the teacher who had first taught him the Pentateuch. Maybe it is actually he? Yasha thought. No, he would most certainly be dead by now. Perhaps it is his son? Earlier he had felt happy being in the company of devout Jews but now he was ill at ease sitting among them. Does one say a benediction over the vodka? he wondered. He moved his lips. When he took a sip from the tumbler the bitterness cut into him; darkness swam before his eyes. His throat burned. He reached for an egg cookie but wasn't able to break off a piece. What's the matter with me? Am I sick? What is it? He felt hostile and ashamed. When the proprietress brought him liver with the white bread he knew that he should make his ablutions, but there were no facilities for washing here. He bit off a piece of the bread and the man in the fringed garment asked, "How about making your ablutions?"

"He has, already," the fellow with the black beard answered sarcastically.

Yasha sat silent, amazed at how his earlier affection had been transformed into vexation, pride, and a desire to be alone. He looked away from the others and they soon began talking about their own affairs. They discussed everything at once: commerce, Hasidism, saintly miracles.—So many miracles, yet so much poverty, sickness, epidemics, Yasha reflected. He ate the chicken soup with groats and chased away the flies. His foot continued to ache. He felt his stomach growing bloated.

What should I do now, he asked himself. See a doctor? And how could a doctor help? They have only one remedy—put on a cast. Iodine I can smear on myself. But what if it doesn't get better? You can hardly turn somersaults on the tightrope with such a foot. The more Yasha considered his situation, the graver it appeared. He was nearly penniless—injured, how could he earn his living! What could he tell Emilia? She must be frantic at his not showing up the day before. And what explanation would he make to Magda when he returned home? Where could he say he had spent the night? What was a man worth if his entire existence depended upon a foot—even his love? Now was the time to kill himself.

He paid his bill and left. Again he saw the cripple. The man was still spinning and twisting as if seeking to bore his head into an invisible wall. Doesn't he ever grow tired? Yasha thought. How can a merciful God permit a human being to suffer such torment? A wish to see Emilia rose in Yasha. He longed for her company, needed to talk to her. But he could not go to her as he was, dirty and unshaven, the cuffs of his trousers spotted with manure. He hailed a droshky and asked to be driven to Freta Street. He rested his head against the wall of the cab and tried to doze off. Let me imagine myself dead and riding to my own funeral, he thought. Through his shut eyelids he could see the daylight, pink here, cool and shaded there. He listened to the sounds coming from the streets and inhaled the acrid odors. He had to hold on with both hands to keep from falling. No, I must change. This is no life! he said to himself. I don't have a moment's peace of mind any more. I must give up magic and women. One God, one wife, like everyone else . . .

From time to time he opened his eyes slightly to see where he was. They were passing the square on which the bank stood, and the building which the day before had appeared so still and foreboding was crowded with soldiers and civilians. A wagon-load of money rolled in, escorted by armed guards sitting on the outside. When Yasha again peered through his lids he saw the new synagogue on Tlomacka Street, where the reformed Jews worshiped and the rabbis preached in Polish instead of Yiddish.

They are religious, too, Yasha reflected, but they wouldn't allow paupers to worship in there. The next time he looked he saw the old Polish arsenal the Russians had converted into a prison. Behind its bars sat Yasha's counterparts. He dismounted at Freta Street and climbed the stairs to his house. Now for the first time he felt the extent of his injury. He was forced to lean his weight on his uninjured foot and drag the other behind him. Each time that he lifted the foot he felt a sharp pain somewhere near his heel. He rapped on the door but Magda did not open it. He knocked louder. Was she as angry as that? Had she killed herself? He pounded with his fist and waited. He did not have his key with him and he placed his ear to the door; he heard the parrot screaming. Then he remembered the skeleton key. It would still be in his pocket but he felt a revulsion for this object which had so humiliated him. Nevertheless, he took it out and opened the door. No one was inside. The beds were made but it was impossible to tell whether they had been slept in the night before. Yasha went into the room where the animals were kept. His appearance excited them. Each seemed to be trying in its own language to say something to him. Every cage had food and water in it, so it was not that they were hungry or thirsty. The windows were open to let in the air and the sun. "Yasha! Yasha! Yasha!" the parrot shrieked, then snapped its crooked beak and looked askance with a sort of vain querulousness. It seemed to Yasha as if the bird were trying to say, "You're only hurting yourself, not me. I can always earn my few grains." The monkey leaped up and down, and the tiny face with the flattened nose and the wrinkled brown eyes was filled with the sorrow and anxiety of the man in the story book, who is a victim of a magic spell which has caused him to grow bestial. It seemed to Yasha that the monkey asked, "Haven't you learned yet that all is vanity?" The crow tried to speak but only a human-like cawing and a sort of mimicry came from its throat. Yasha fancied that the bird scolded, mocked, moralized.

He reminded himself of the mares. They were in a stall in the court. Anthony, the janitor, was tending to them but Yasha now longed to see them—Kara and Shiva—Dust and Ashes. He had wronged them, too. On a day like this they should have been grazing in a green pasture, not standing in a hot stall.

He went back to the bedroom and lay down on

the bed, fully dressed. He intended to remove his shoes and apply cold water to his foot, but he was too weary to do it. He closed his eyes and lay there as if in a trance.

2

Only when he awoke did he realize how deeply he had slept. He opened his eyes and did not know who he was, where he was, nor what had happened to him. Someone was pounding on the front door, and although Yasha heard the knocking, it did not occur to him to open the door. His foot hurt him badly, but he could not remember the reason for the pain. Everything within him seemed paralyzed but he knew that memory would soon return and he lay there, amazed at his rigidity. Again he heard the knocking and this time he understood that he must open the door. He recalled what had happened. Was this Magda? But she had a key! For a moment he lay there, his limbs numb. Then he summoned up strength enough to rise and walk to the door. He was barely able to move his left foot. Apparently the foot had abscessed for his shoe felt tight, the foot hot. He opened the door. Wolsky stood there in a light-colored suit, white shoes, and a straw hat. He appeared sallow, wrinkled, as if he had not slept. The black, semitic eyes gazed at Yasha with a sort of knowing mockery, as if aware of what Yasha had been up to the night before. Yasha promptly lost his patience.

"What's the matter? What are you laughing at?"

"I'm not laughing. I have a telegram from Ekaterinoslav."

And he took a telegram out of his pocket. Yasha noticed that Wolsky's fingers were tobacco-stained. He took the telegram and read it. It was an offer from an Ekaterinoslav theater for twelve performances. They guaranteed a respectable fee. The director demanded immediate confirmation. Yasha and Wolsky walked into the other room. Yasha sought not to drag his foot.

"Where is Magda?"

"Out marketing."

"How come you're dressed?"

"What do you want me to be, naked?"

"You don't wear a suit and tie so early in the morning. And who tore your pants?"

Yasha seemed to have lost his power of speech. "Where are they ripped?"

"Right here. Besides you're all dirty. Were you in a fight or something?"

Yasha had not realized until now that his pants were torn at the knees and stained with lime as well. He hesitated a moment. "I was attacked by hoodlums."

"When? Where?"

"Last night, on Gensha Street."

"What were you doing on Gensha Street?"

"I went to visit someone."

"What hoodlums? How did they tear your pants?"

"They were trying to rob me."

"What time was that?"

"One in the morning."

"You promised me you'd go to bed early. Instead you stay up to all hours and get into street brawls. Kindly take a couple of steps."

Yasha bristled.

"You're neither my father nor my guardian."

"No. But you do have a name and a reputation to maintain. I've devoted myself to you as though I were your father. The moment you opened the door I could tell you were limping. Roll up your trouser leg, please, or, better still, take off your pants altogether. You'll gain nothing by deceiving me."

"Yes, I fought back."

"You were probably drunk."

"Sure, and I also killed a few people."

"Ha! Only a week before the opening. You've finally got a name. If you appear in Ekaterinoslav, all of Russia will be open to you. Instead, you roam around, God knows where, in the middle of the night. Lift your trousers higher. Your underwear, too."

Yasha did as he was bid. Beneath his left knee was a bruise, black and blue, with a large area of torn skin. There was blood on his underpants. Wolsky looked on with mute reproof.

"What did they do to you?"

"They kicked me."

"The pants are stained with lime. And what's that down there? Horse manure?"

Yasha kept silent.

"Why didn't you put something on it? Cold water at least?"

Yasha did not answer.

"Where's Magda? She never goes out at this time."

"Panie Wolsky, you're not a prosecutor nor am I, as yet, in the witness stand. Don't cross-examine me!"

"No, I'm not your father nor a prosecutor, but I *am* responsible for you. I don't wish to insult you but it's me in whom the confidence is placed, not you. When you came to me you were an ordinary magician, who performed in market-places for a few groschen. I pulled you out of the gutter. Now that we're on the brink of success, you go ahead and get drunk or the devil knows what. Last week already, you should have been rehearsing but you didn't even show up at the theater. Posters are plastered all over Warsaw announcing that you are beyond any magician that has ever been, but you smash your leg and don't even call a doctor. You haven't taken your clothes off since yesterday. You probably jumped out of some window," Wolsky said with a change of tone.

A shudder ran down Yasha's back.

"Why a window?"

"Undoubtedly escaping from some married woman. The husband probably showed up unexpectedly. We know all about those matters. I'm an old hand at that game. Get undressed and go to bed. You're fooling no one but yourself. I'll call a doctor. It's all over the newspapers about you performing a somersault on the tightrope. It's the talk of the town. All of a sudden you do a thing like this. If you should fail now, everything is finished."

"It'll heal by the time I open."

"Maybe it will and maybe it won't. Get undressed. Since it was a jump, I'd like to examine the whole leg."

"What time is it?"

"Ten after eleven."

Yasha wanted to say something else but at that moment he heard a key turning in the lock of the door. It was Magda. She came in and Yasha's eyes opened wide. She was wearing her Sunday dress, last year's straw hat with the flowers and cherries, and high-button shoes. She resembled a country woman off to the city to go into service. Overnight she had grown thinner, swarthier, older. Sores and lesions covered her face. Seeing Wolsky, she was taken by surprise and began to retreat toward the door. Wolsky took off his hat. The hair on his scalp lay like a wrinkled wig. He nodded. His black eyes darted from Yasha to Magda with fatherly concern. His lower lip hung loose in bewilderment.

3

"Panna Magda," Wolsky resumed after a moment, in the tone of one who preaches morality but does so reluctantly. "We two made an agreement that you would look after him. He is a child.

Artists are like little children and sometimes a lot worse. See what he has done to himself!"

"I beg you, Panie Wolsky, say no more!" Yasha interrupted.

Magda did not answer but looked silently at Yasha's bare foot and the wound.

"Where did you go so early in the morning?" Yasha asked. He quickly realized that these words gave away the fact that he hadn't spent the night at home, but it was too late to recall them. Magda started. Her green eyes grew light and malevolent as an angry cat's.

"I'll give you a full account later."

"What's going on between you two?" Wolsky asked, like an elderly kinsman. He did not wait for an answer but continued, "Well, I'll have to fetch a doctor. Apply cold compresses. Maybe you have some iodine in the house? If not, I'll bring some from the apothecary."

"Panie Wolsky, I don't want a doctor!" Yasha said sternly.

"Why not? You have six days until the opening. People have already bought tickets in advance. Half the theater is sold out."

"I'll be ready for the opening."

"That foot won't heal by itself that quickly. Why are you so afraid of a doctor?"

"There's somewhere I have to go today. I'll see the doctor later."

"Where do you have to go? You can't walk around with a foot like that."

"He has to run off to one of his whores!" Magda hissed. Her mouth trembled, her eyes looked off somewhere. It was the first time that Magda—the silent, the bashful—had said anything like that, and in front of a stranger. The words came out in rural accents and, although not loud, were shrill as a scream. Wolsky grimaced as if he had swallowed something.

"I have no wish to mix in your affairs. Nor even if I wished to, do I have the right. But, there is a time for everything. We've waited for years for this day. This is your chance: you'll become famous. Don't, as the saying goes, put aside your gun an hour before victory."

"I'm throwing away nothing!"

"I beg you. Let me get a doctor."

"No."

"Well, no is no. I've been an impresario nearly thirty years and I've seen how artists commit suicide. Scramble up the mountain for years but just when the summit is in view, fall and smash themselves. Why this should be, I don't know. Perhaps they have a taste for the gutter. What shall I tell Kuzarski? He asked about you. There's a conspiracy against you in the theater. And how shall I answer the director in Ekaterinoslav? I must reply to his telegram."

"I'll give you an answer tomorrow."

"When tomorrow? What will you know tomorrow you don't know now? And what's the point in you two wrangling? You've got to work together. You've got to rehearse just like every other year. If anything, this year more. Unless what you want is to please your enemies and fail with a vengeance."

"Everything will be all right."

"Well, as it is fated, so it will be. When shall I return?"

"Tomorrow."

"I'll be here tomorrow morning, but do something for your foot. Take a step—let's see. You're limping! You can't fool me. You either sprained or fractured something. Soak it in hot water. If I were in your shoes I wouldn't wait until tomorrow. The doctor might order you to put the foot in a cast. What will you do then? The rabble will storm the theater. You know what the clientele of a summer theater is. It's not the opera where the manager comes out before the curtain and announces to the honorable guests that the prima donna has a sore throat. Here they immediately start throwing rotten eggs and stones."

"I've told you, everything will be all right."

"Well, let's hope so. At times I regret not being in the herring business."

And Wolsky bowed to both Yasha and Magda. He mumbled something in the hall. Then he went out, slamming the door.

A Christian and he wails like a Jew, Yasha said to himself. He had an impulse to laugh and looked out of the corners of his eyes at Magda. She had not spent the night at home, he decided. She'd been wandering about. But where had she been? Was she capable of this sort of revenge? Jealousy and disgust mingled in him. He had an impulse to seize her by the hair and drag her along the floor. Where were you? Where? Where? Where? he wanted to say. But he restrained himself. He imagined that each second the rash on her face grew worse. He unclenched his fist, lowered his head, stared down at his naked leg. He looked angrily at Magda.

"Fetch me cold water from the pump."

"Get it yourself."

And she burst out crying. She fled from the room, slamming the door so violently that the windowpanes rattled.

I guess I'll lie down for another half-hour, Yasha said to himself.

He returned to the bedroom and stretched out on the bed. His leg had stiffened and he could barely extend it. He lay there looking out at the sky through the window. High above him a bird was in flight. It seemed as small as a berry. What would happen to such a creature should it injure its leg or wing? For it there would be only one way out—death. It was the same with man. Death was the broom which swept away all evil, all madness, all filth. He closed his eyes. His foot throbbed, pinched. He wanted to remove the shoe but the shoelace had become knotted. The swelling had grown! He felt the flesh on his toes becoming puffy and sponge-like. The foot might well become gangrenous. Perhaps it would have to be amputated. No! Rather death! Well, my seven years of good fortune are over! They are not to be trusted! he exclaimed, not knowing whether he meant women or gentiles, or a combination of both. Undoubtedly, the devil dwells in Emilia also. His mind became vacant and he lay in that warm fatigue that precedes sleep. He dreamed that it was Passover, after the Seder, and that his father was saying, "Isn't that funny? I've lost a groschen!" "Papa, what are you saying? It's Passover!" "Oh, the ceremonial wine has made me drunk."

The dream lasted only a few seconds. He awoke with a start, and the door opened as Magda came in carrying a basin of water and a napkin to be used as a compress. She glared at him spitefully.

"Magda, I love you," he said.

"Scum! Whoremaster! Assassin!" She burst into tears again.

4

Yasha was well aware that what he contemplated was pure madness, but he had to go and see Emilia. He was like a subject who has been hypnotized and must fulfill his master's commands. Emilia was expecting him, and her expectation drew him like a magnet. Magda had gone off somewhere again. He knew that now was the moment to go. The following day might be too late. He rose resolving to ignore his foot; he needed a shave, a bath, a change of clothes. I must talk everything over with her, he said to himself; I can't leave her hanging in mid-air. When he went to shave he found his razor had vanished. Magda had a habit of hiding things. Each time she cleaned up, something else was missing. She was capable of concealing a tie in the stove, slippers under a pillow. Always the peasant! Yasha thought. He put on a fresh shirt but a cuff link fell from the sleeve and disappeared. Apparently it had rolled under the wardrobe, but he was unable to bend. He had other cuff links somewhere, but where? Magda even tucked money away in odd places where it would turn up months afterwards. Yasha stretched out on the floor and began to search under the wardrobe with his cane, but this effort produced only stabbing pains in his foot. Then his stomach began to ache also. The devils are starting already, he muttered to himself. Now there's nothing but bad luck.

Magda had returned and had removed her Sunday dress. He could see she had been shopping for she held a basket from which protruded the legs of a chicken.

"Where are you going? I was just about to prepare lunch."

"Prepare it for yourself."

"Running back to your Piask whore?"

"I'll go where I please."

"We're finished. I'm going home today. You dirty Jew!"

She seemed afraid of her own words; her mouth agape, she stood with her hand raised as if to avert a blow. Yasha blanched. "Well, that's the end!"

"Yes, the end. You bring out the devil in me!"

And she threw down her basket and intoned a peasant dirge as if she had been scourged. The chicken lay there, its bloody neck aloft, ringed by onions, beets, potatoes. Magda fled into the kitchen and then Yasha heard a rattling sound as if she were vomiting or strangling. He had risen to his feet, still gripping the cane he had used in his search for the cuff link. For some inexplicable reason he righted the chicken and covered its torn neck with a beet. He continued to search for the cuff link. He wanted to go into the kitchen to see what Magda was up to but he restrained himself. In a little while Emilia will undoubtedly call me the same name, he thought. Yes, everything is collapsing like a house of cards.

He dressed himself somehow. When he passed the corridor he heard through the closed door Magda scraping a pot with a whisk. He hobbled down the stairs, feeling pain with each step. He barely managed to reach the barber shop but there was no one on the premises. He called out, stamped his sound foot, pounded on the wall, but no one came. They just leave everything and go off! he grumbled to himself. That's Poland for you. And still they complain that the country is torn to pieces. Probably ran off to play cards, the bum! Well, I'll just have to go to her unshaven. Let her see the state I'm in. He stood waiting for a droshky, but none came. That's the kind of country this is, he mumbled; all they can do is rebel every few years and rattle the chains.

He managed to get to the Avenue Dluga, found a barber shop and walked in. The barber was busy cutting a customer's hair. "When a barrel is filled with cabbage, you can't stuff any more in," the barber was saying. "Cabbage isn't like flax; it can't be squeezed together. When the barrel's full, it's full. With dough, dear sir, it's even worse.

I'm reminded of something that happened to a woman who wanted to bake a cake for her mother. She kneaded the dough, added the yeast, and all the other things. At the last minute she decided to bring the dough to her mother's house in Praga and bake it there, because the flue in her stove was blocked or the stove smoked or something like that. So she packed the dough in a basket, covered it with a cloth, and took the omnibus. It was warm in the omnibus and the dough began to rise. It crept out of the basket as if it were alive. She tried to stuff it back but dough is something that won't be pushed. When she squeezed from one side it billowed out the other. The cover flew off. The basket swelled, and bang! it burst. Anyway, I *think* it burst."

"Is dough that strong?" the man in the chair asked.

"Of course it is. A real commotion started in the omnibus. There were several smart alecks on board and. . . ."

"She must have put a lot of yeast in that dough."

"It wasn't so much the yeast as the heat. It was a hot summer day and. . . ."

Why do they go on like that? Besides, he's a liar; the basket would never have burst, Yasha thought. But my shoe will! My foot's abscessing. And why doesn't he acknowledge my presence? Maybe I'm one who sees but isn't seen!

"Is there a long wait?" he asked.

"Till I'm finished, sir," the barber said, mingling courtesy with derision. "I have just one pair of hands. I just can't cut hair with my feet and, if I could, what would I stand on? My head, perhaps? What do you think, Panie Miechislaw?"

"You're absolutely right," his customer replied. He was a short, big-headed man with a straight nape and blond, spiky hair which reminded Yasha of a pig's bristle. The man turned and looked at Yasha with contempt. His eyes were a watery blue, small and deeply set. Evidently the barber and his customer had formed an alliance.

Nevertheless he waited until the barber had finished with his customer and the tips of the man's mustache had been waxed. Suddenly the barber underwent a transformation and began to chat familiarly with Yasha.

"Lovely day, isn't it? Summer, real summer! I like the summer. What good is the winter? Frost and catarrh! Sometimes it is too hot in the summer and one sweats, but that's no tragedy. Yesterday I swam in the Vistula and someone drowned before my very eyes."

"In the bathhouse?"

"He wanted to show off and swam from the men's to the women's bathhouse. They wouldn't have let him in anyhow because the women bathe naked. So what was the sense of the whole thing? Is it worth while to give one's life for a joke? When they pulled him out he looked asleep. I couldn't believe he was dead. And for what purpose this sacrifice? Just to make an impression."

"Yes, people are mad."

I must decide everything today, Yasha said to himself in the droshky. Today is my Day of Reckoning. He closed his eyes, to devote himself exclusively to his thoughts. But he passed street after street without reaching a decision. Again, blindly, he heard the sounds of the city, inhaled its smells. Coachmen shouted, whips cracked, children caroused. From courtyards and bazaars warm breezes blew, rank with manure, fried onions, the sewage, and the odors of the slaughterhouse. Laborers were ripping up the wooden sidewalks, changing round cobblestones to square ones, installing gas street lights, digging ditches for sewers and telephone lines. The bowels of the city were being rearranged. Sometimes when Yasha opened his eyes it seemed to him that the droshky was about to sink into the sandy depths. The earth seemed about to collapse, toppling the buildings; all Warsaw appeared on the verge of suffering the fate of Sodom and Gomorrah. How could he decide anything now? The droshky rolled past the synagogue on Gnoyne Street. When was I here? he asked himself in confusion. Was it today? Yesterday? The two days blended into one. His praying there in prayer shawl and phylacteries, the piety which had possessed him, were alien now, dreamlike. What sort of power possessed me? My nerves must be completely shattered! The droshky pulled up to Emilia's house and Yasha handed the driver a gulden instead of the usual twenty-groschen fare. The coachman offered him change but Yasha waved it away. He's a pauper, he thought, let him keep the extra ten groschen. Every good deed would boost his standing with heaven.

Slowly he mounted the steps, his foot now causing him less discomfort. He rang the bell and Yadwiga answered the door. She smiled and said confidentially, "The mistress is expecting you, has been since yesterday."

"What's new around here?"

"Not a thing. Oh yes, there was something! Pan Yasha may remember my telling him about old Zaruski and his deaf servant-maid, the one who's my friend. Well, they had a robbery there yesterday."

Yasha's mouth became dry. "Did they steal the treasure?"

"No, the thief got panicky and ran away. Leaped from the balcony. The night watchman saw him. Don't ask what's going on over there! The old man raised a terrible fuss! It was just awful! He wanted to discharge my friend. The police came. My friend cried her heart out. Thirty years—thirty years in one household!"

She said all this with a sort of perverse pleasure. Her friend's misfortune gave Yadwiga some sort of inner satisfaction. Her eyes sparkled with a malice that Yasha had not seen in her before.

"Yes, there are no lack of thieves in Warsaw."

"Ah, there's that fortune to tempt them. Kindly go into the drawing room. I'll announce you to the Mistress!"

It seemed to Yasha that Yadwiga had grown younger. She did not walk now but almost skipped along. He went into the drawing room and seated himself on the sofa. They mustn't notice anything wrong with my foot. If they do, I'll claim that I fell. Or perhaps it would be better for me to mention it right off. It would seem less suspicious that way. Yasha had expected Emilia to come running to him immediately, but she took longer than usual. She's repaying me for last night, he thought. At last he heard footsteps. Emilia opened the door and Yasha saw that she was once again dressed in a brightly colored gown, this one evidently new. He rose but did not go immediately to her.

"What a marvelous dress!"

"Do you like it?"

"It's splendid! Turn around, let me see it from the back!"

Emilia did as she was told and Yasha availed himself of the moment to limp closer to her.

"Yes, exquisite!"

She turned to face him.

"I was afraid it wouldn't please you. What happened to you yesterday? I didn't sleep at all last night because of you."

"What did you do, then, if you didn't sleep?"

"What can you do at such a time? I read, I walked about. Really, I was most concerned about you. I thought that you'd already . . ." Emilia broke off.

How could she have been reading when there was no light in her bedroom? Yasha thought. He wanted to confront her with this but restrained himself, aware that by such a confrontation he would give himself away. She studied him, her face expressing curiosity, resentment, devotion. Through some imperceptible power (or omen) he knew that she regretted having repulsed him the other night, and that she was now prepared to rectify her error. She wrinkled her brow as if attempting to fathom his thoughts. He studied her and it seemed to him that she had aged—not by days but by years, as sometimes happens to a person who has suffered a grave illness or a deep sorrow.

"Something bad happened yesterday," he said.

Her face blanched. "What?"

"While I was rehearsing, I fell and injured my foot."

"I sometimes wonder that you survive at all," she said reproachfully. "You undertake the superhuman. Even if you are blessed with talent, you don't have to squander it, especially at the wages you are paid. They don't appreciate you at all."

"Yes, I do give too much. But that's my nature."

"Well, it's both a curse and a blessing . . . Have you seen a doctor?"

"Not yet."

"What are you waiting for? You're opening in a few days!"

"Yes, I know that."

"Sit down. I knew there was something wrong. You were supposed to come and you didn't. I didn't know why, but I couldn't sleep. I woke at one o'clock and didn't shut my eyes again. I had this odd sensation that you were in danger . . ." she suddenly addressed him with the familiar *thou*. "I told myself that my fears were ridiculous. I didn't want to be superstitious but I couldn't rid myself of that feeling. When did it happen? At what time did you fall?"

"As a matter of fact, it was during the night."

"At one o'clock?"

"Around then."

"I knew it! Although I can't imagine how. I sat up in bed and for no reason at all began to pray for you. Halina woke up, too, and came in. There's something about that girl which defies explanation. There's a strange sort of bond between us. When I can't sleep, she can't either, although I am very careful not to make any noise. What happened? Was it a jump?"

"Yes, I jumped."

"You must see a doctor immediately and if he says not to perform you must listen to him. You can't trifle with such things, especially in your case."

"The theater will go bankrupt."

"Let it. No one is immune to accidents. If only we were already together, I would take care of you. You don't look at all well. Did you get a haircut?"

"No."

"You look as if you'd had a haircut. I know you'll think this ridiculous but for days I've had a premonition of this. You mustn't worry, I foresaw no great tragedy, but there was certainly something. I tried to keep my spirits up. When I had no word from you this morning I felt simply desperate. I even thought of going to your place. How can such things be explained?"

"You can't explain anything."

"May I see your foot?"

"Later, not now."

"All right, dearest. But there is something important I must discuss with you."

"What is it? Tell me."

"We must make some definite plans. Perhaps what I'm saying is in bad taste, but we are neither of us children any more. It's come to the point where I cannot endure this waiting any longer, this feeling of everything being up in the air. The situation is making me ill. I'm not an irresponsible person by nature. I must know exactly where I stand. Halina must resume her schooling; she cannot afford to lose another semester. You make thousands of promises but everything remains as before. Now that you've revealed our intentions to Halina, she gives me no peace. She's a clever girl, but a child remains a child. I know I shouldn't be speaking like this to you when you're in pain, but I can't impress upon you too strongly just what I've been going through. In addition to everything else, I long for you terribly. The moment we say goodbye and I close the door, my torment begins. I feel strangely insecure as if I were on an ice-floe which might crack at any moment and cast me into the water. I start to believe that I've grown vulgar and have lost all shame."

And Emilia ceased her flow of words. She stood there, her head bowed, trembling, her eyes cast down as if she were ashamed to her very core.

"Do you mean physically?" Yasha asked after some hesitation.

"Everything together."

"Well, we'll decide everything.".

6

"You tell me each time that we'll decide. Is there so much that needs deciding? If we intend to go, I must give up my apartment and sell the furniture. I might get something for it, although it isn't worth much any more. But maybe we can send it on to Italy. Those are the practical things that we must do. Nothing will come from just talking. We should also apply for passports because the Russians make everything difficult. We should determine the exact week and day of our departure. There's also the matter of finances. I haven't discussed this with you previously because the subject is extremely distasteful to me. Whenever I have to speak of it the blood rushes to my face," (her face indeed reddened), "but we can accomplish nothing without it. We also spoke of your—well, you did promise to assume the Christian faith—I know that these things are mere formalities, one does not acquire faith by being sprinkled with water. But without it, we cannot marry. I'm saying all this to you on the assumption that your promises were given in good faith. If they were not, why continue the farce? We're no longer children."

And Emilia stopped talking.

"You know I meant every word I said."

"I know nothing. What do I know about you, anyway? There are times when I feel I don't even know myself. When I used to hear of this sort of thing I always blamed the other woman. You do have a wife, after all, although God knows you're not faithful to her and your whole conduct, generally, is that of a man who is footloose. I am sinning, too, but I am true to my church. From the Catholic point of view, when someone is converted to our faith he is reborn and all his prior relationships are nullified. I neither know your wife nor do I want to. Another thing, yours is a childless marriage. A marriage without children is like only half a marriage. I am not young any more, either, but I can still have a baby and I would like to bear your children. You'll laugh, but even Halina spoke of it. She once said, 'When you marry Uncle Yasha I should like a little brother.' A man with your talents must not die without leaving an heir. Mazur is a good Polish name."

Yasha was sitting on the sofa, Emilia opposite him in a chaise longue. He looked at her and she looked back at him. He realized suddenly that he could put things off no longer. The words that he had to say must be uttered this very instant. But he had not yet determined what to say or how to act.

"Emilia, there's something I must tell you," he began.

"Say it, I'm listening."

"Emilia, I have no money. My entire fortune consists of the house in Lublin, but I cannot take that from her."

Emilia considered this for a moment.

"Why didn't you say anything before this? Your manner implied that money was not the problem."

"I always felt that I could get it at the last minute. If the opening proved successful, there was always the possibility that I could perform abroad. There are always foreign theater owners here—"

"You'll pardon me, but our plan was something else altogether. How could you be sure you'd find employment in Italy? They might sign you for France or the United States. It would be strange if we were married and you had to be in one place and Halina and I in another. She must remain for a time in Southern Italy. A winter in England, for example, would kill her. Besides, you planned to take a year off and study European languages. If you travel about Europe without knowing the languages, they will treat you no better than they do here in Poland. You're forgetting everything that we decided. We planned to buy a house with a garden near Naples. That was our plan. I don't mean to reprove you in any way but if you wish to better your situation you must follow a precise plan. This business of living from day to day, extempore, as you theatrical people put it, has brought you nothing but trouble. You've admitted that yourself."

"Yes, it's true, but I must get my hands on some money. How much would all this cost? I mean, what's the very minimum?"

"We've gone over all that already. We would need at least fifteen thousand rubles. Anything over would be that much better."

"I'll just have to get the money."

"How? As far as I know it doesn't rain rubles in Warsaw. It was my impression that you'd already accumulated the required capital."

"No, I have nothing."

"Well, that's that. You mustn't think my feelings towards you have changed because of this. But our plans obviously cannot remain the same. I've already notified some of the people close to me that I'm about to go abroad. Halina can't remain at home forever. A girl her age must go to school. Besides, you and I cannot be together here. It would be senseless for both of us. You have a family and who knows what else. As it is I'm losing sleep because of the sympathy I feel for your wife, but if I were to leave the country, she would seem remote. To steal a husband from a wife and take a chance that she might come crying to me would be too much!"

And she shook her head negatively, to stress her refusal. She shuddered at the same time.

"I'll get the money."

"How? Will you rob a bank?"

Halina entered.

"Ah, Uncle Yasha!"

Emilia looked up.

"How many times have I told you to knock before you come in. You're not a three-year-old."

"If I've interrupted anything, I'll go."

"You didn't interrupt a thing," Yasha said. "What a lovely dress you're wearing!"

"What's so nice about it? A dress I've outgrown. But it's white and I adore white. I should like our house in Italy to be white. Why can't the roof be white too? Oh, it would be gorgeous—a house with a white roof!"

"Perhaps you'd like the chimney-sweep to be all in white, too?" Yasha teased.

"Why not? It's possible to make soot white. I read that when a new Pope is chosen, white smoke comes out of the chimney at the Vatican, and if the smoke is white, the soot can be white as well."

"Yes, everything will be arranged for you, but right now go back to your room. We are in the midst of discussing things!" Emilia said.

"What are you talking about? Don't frown so, Mother, I'm leaving right away. I'm terribly thirsty but that isn't important. Before I go there's only one thing that I want to say—you seem in a bad humor, Uncle Yasha. What's wrong?"

"I've lost a boatload of sour milk."

"What? What sort of comic expression is that?"

"It's a Yiddish saying!"

"I should like to know Yiddish. I would like to know all the languages: Chinese, Tataric, Turkish. It's said that animals have a language of their own, too. I once passed Grzybow Place and the Jews looked so funny with their long caftans and black beards. What's a Jew?"

"I've told you to get out of here!" Emilia's voice rose.

Halina turned to go just as there was a knock on the door. Yadwiga stood at the threshold.

"There's a man here. He wishes to speak with the Mistress."

"A man? Who is he? What does he want?"

"I don't know."

"Why didn't you ask his name?"

"He wouldn't say. He looks like he's from the Post Office or something."

"Well, another pest. One second. I'll go out to see him." And Emilia went out into the corridor.

"Who can that be?" Halina asked. "I took a book out of the school library and lost it. Actually, I didn't lose it at all, it fell into the sewer and I was too disgusted to pick it up. I was afraid to bring it home because if Mama saw me with such a filthy book she would scold me terribly. She is good, but very bad, too. Lately, she's been acting strangely. She doesn't sleep nights, and when she can't sleep, I can't sleep either. I get in bed with her and we lie there and talk like two lost souls. Occasionally she sits at a little table, puts her hands on it and waits for the table to predict her future. Oh, she is funny sometimes, but I love her madly. In the middle of the night she is so good. At times I wish it were always in the middle of the night and that you, Uncle Yasha, were together with us and we all passed the time together. Maybe you'd like to hypnotize me now? I feel a strong desire to be hypnotized."

"What do you need it for?"

"Oh, just because! Life is so dreary."

7

"Your mother doesn't want me to, and I won't do something she opposes."

"Just make it last until she returns."

"It doesn't happen that quickly, anyway you are hypnotized."

"What ever do you mean?"

"Ah, you are compelled to love me. You will always love me. You will never forget me."

"That's true. Never! I should like to talk nonsense. May I talk nonsense? So long as Mama is out of the room?"

"Yes, go on."

"Why isn't everybody like you, Uncle Yasha? Everyone else is so pompous and full of self-importance. I love Mama, I love her terribly but there are times when I hate her. When she gets into a bad mood she takes it out on me. 'Don't go here! Don't stand there!' Once I broke a flower pot quite unintentionally, and she didn't speak to me the whole day. That night I dreamt that an omnibus—horses, conductor, passengers and all—was driving through our apartment. I was puzzled in my dream. Why would an omnibus ride through our apartment? Where were all the people bound? And how had the omnibus got through the doorway. But it just simply rode by and made stops, and I thought: When Mama comes home and sees this she will raise a terrible fuss! I had to laugh and I woke up laughing. I must laugh now too at that foolish dream. But is it my fault? I dream about you, too, Uncle Yasha, but since you are mean and won't hypnotize me, I shan't tell you about the dream."

"What do you dream about me?"

"I won't tell you. My dreams are all either comical or just plain crazy. You're liable to think I'm mad. It's just awful the thoughts that come to me. I want to drive them away, but I can't."

"What kind of thoughts?"

"I can't tell you that."

"You don't have to hide anything from me. I love you."

"Oh, you only say so. Actually, you are my enemy. Maybe you are even a devil who's assumed human form? Perhaps you have horns and a tail like the Baba Yaga?"

"Yes, I do have horns."

And Yasha put two fingers up to his head.

"Don't do that, it frightens me. I'm an awful coward. At night I'm simply terrified. I'm afraid of ghosts, evil spirits, all that sort of thing. A neighbor of ours had a six-year-old daughter, Janinka. A pretty child with blonde curls and blue eyes like a cherub. All of a sudden she caught scarlet fever and died. Mama didn't want me to find out, but I knew everything. I even saw through the window how they carried out her coffin—a tiny coffin decorated with flowers. Oh, death is horrible. I don't think about it during the day, but when it gets dark, I begin to think about it."

Emilia came in. She looked from Yasha to Halina and remarked, "Well, aren't *you* a fine pair?"

"Who was the stranger?" Yasha inquired, surprised at his audacity.

"If I told you, you would laugh—although it's no laughing matter. We have an acquaintance who lives close by, a wealthy old man named Zaruski, a usurer, a miser. He is actually not even an acquaintance but Yadwiga is friendly with his servant and because of that, he's begun to greet me. Last night someone broke into his house. The thief came by way of the balcony and a night watchman saw him descend. The watchman chased him but the man got away. He didn't manage to open the safe. It now seems he left a notebook with the addresses of other apartments he planned to rob and my address was included among them. A detective was just here to warn me. I told him plainly, 'There isn't much he can steal here.' Isn't that strange?"

Yasha's palate became dry.

"Why would he leave a list of addresses behind?"

"He apparently lost it."

"Well, you will have to be careful."

"How can anyone be careful? Warsaw has become a nest of thieves. Halina, go to your room!"

Halina rose, languorously. "All right, I'm going. What we talked about must remain a secret!" she said to Yasha.

"Yes, an eternal secret."

"Well, I'll be going. What other choice have I if I'm driven out. But you're not leaving yet, Uncle Yasha?"

"No, I'll stay awhile."

"Goodbye!"

"Goodbye!"

"Au revoir."

"Au revoir."

"Arrivederci!"

"Hurry up!" Emilia snapped.

"Well . . . I'm going," and Halina walked out.

"What secrets does she have with you?" Emilia asked, half in jest.

"Momentous secrets."

"There are times when I regret not having had a son instead of a daughter. A boy isn't home as much nor does he mix into his mother's affairs. I love her but sometimes she upsets me. You must keep in mind that she's a child, not a grownup."

"I speak to her as to a child."

"That's odd about that thief. Couldn't he find a richer household than mine? Where do people obtain their information? They evidently go through the gates and read the directories. But I'm afraid of thieves. A thief can easily be a murderer, too. The front door has a padlock, but the door leading to the balcony has only a chain."

"You're on the second floor. That's too high for prowlers."

"True. How did you know that Zaruski lived on the first floor?"

"Because I am the thief," Yasha said hoarsely,

shocked himself at the words he uttered. His throat contracted. Darkness rose before his eyes, and again he saw the fiery sparks. It was as if a dybbuk had spoken within him. A tingle zigzagged down his spine. Once more he felt the nausea which precedes fainting.

Emilia paused a moment. "Well, it's a good idea. Since you can climb down from the windows, you should be able to climb up a balcony."

"I can, indeed."

"What's that? I didn't hear you."

"I said, 'I can, indeed.'"

"Well, why didn't you open the safe? Once you begin something, you ought to finish it."

"Sometimes you can't."

"Why are you speaking so softly? I can't make out what you are saying."

"I said, 'Sometimes you can't.'"

"'If one can't, one shouldn't try,' according to the old proverb. Funny, just a short while ago I was thinking that thieves could break into his apartment. Everyone knows he keeps his money on the premises. Sooner or later, it *must* be stolen. That's the fate of all misers. Well, but the accumulation of wealth is in itself a passion."

"A sort of passion."

"What's the difference? In the absolute sense perhaps all passions are either totally foolish, or completely wise. What do any of us know?"

"No, we know nothing."

They were both quiet. And now at last she broke the silence.

"What's the matter with you? I must take a look at your foot!"

"Not now, not now."

"Why not now? How *did* you fall, tell me."

She doesn't believe me, she thinks I'm joking, Yasha thought. Well, everything's lost anyway. He looked at Emilia but he saw her as if through a mist. It was dark in the room; the windows faced to the north and were overhung by wine-colored drapes. A strange indifference came over him, the sort of indifference that comes when one is about to commit a crime or risk one's life. He knew that what he was about to say would destroy everything, but he did not care.

He heard himself saying, "I hurt my foot jumping from Zaruski's balcony."

Emilia raised her brows. "Really, this is hardly the time for jokes."

"It's the absolute truth."

8

In the silence that followed, he could hear the chirping of the birds on the other side of the window. Well, the worst is over, he said to himself. He understood his objective, now—to put a finish to the whole affair. He had taken upon himself too heavy a burden. He needed to cut himself loose from everything. He glanced towards the door as if prepared to flee without a parting word. He did not lower his eyes but looked squarely at Emilia, not with pride but with the fear of one who cannot allow himself the luxury of fear.

Emilia looked back at him, not angrily, but with that sort of curiosity mixed with scorn which one feels seeing the futility of all one's endeavor. She looked as if she were restraining herself from laughter.

"Really, I don't believe . . ."

"Yes, it's the truth. I was in front of your house last night. I even wanted to call up to you."

"But instead you went there?"

"I didn't want to wake Halina and Yadwiga."

"I'm hoping that you are only teasing me. You know I'm gullible. Easily taken in."

"No, I'm not teasing. I heard Yadwiga speak of him and I thought this would be a solution to our problem. But I panicked. I'm apparently not cut out for that sort of thing."

"You've come to confess to me, is that it?"

"You asked me."

"What did I ask?—But it's all the same, all the same. If this isn't one of your games, I can only pity you. That is, both of us. If it is a joke, I have only contempt for you."

"I didn't come here to play games."

"Who can tell what you would or wouldn't do? You are, obviously, not a normal person."

"No."

"I just read of a woman who let herself be seduced by a madman."

"You are the woman."

Emilia's eyes narrowed. "That is my lot. Stephan, may he rest in peace, was likewise a psychopath. Of another type. Apparently I'm drawn to that kind of man."

"You mustn't blame yourself. You are the noblest woman I ever met."

"Whom have you met? You stem from offal and you are offal. Pardon my harsh words, but I am only stating a fact. The blame is mine alone. I was aware of everything, actually you concealed nothing, but in the Greek drama there is a sort of fate—no, it has another name—wherein a person sees everything that will befall him but must fulfill his destiny nevertheless. He sees the pit but falls into it anyhow."

"You are not yet in the pit."

"I cannot be deeper in the pit than I am. If you had one spark of manhood in you, you would have spared me this final disgrace. You could have gone and never come back. I wouldn't have sent an emissary after you. At least I would have had a memory."

"I'm sorry."

"Don't be sorry. You told me you were married. You even admitted that Magda was your mistress. You also told me that you are an atheist or however you put it. If I could accept all this, there's no reason for me to fear a thief. It's only amusing that you should prove such an inept thief." And Emilia emitted a sort of chuckle.

"I might still prove to be a good one."

"Thank you for the promise. I just don't know what to tell Halina." Emilia changed her tone. "I hope you realize you must go away and never return. And you must not write, either. As far as I'm concerned, you're dead. I, too, am dead. But the dead have their milieu, also."

"Yes, I'll go. Rest assured that I will never . . ." And Yasha made a motion as if to rise.

"Wait! I see that you can't even get up. What have you done to yourself? Sprained your ankle? Fractured your foot?"

"I did something to it."

"Whatever it was, you won't perform any more this season. Possibly, you've crippled yourself for life. You must have some sort of covenant with God since he punished you directly on the spot."

"I'm just a bungler."

Emilia covered her face with her hands. She bent her head. She appeared to be considering something deeply. She even massaged her forehead with her fingertips. When she removed her hands, Yasha saw, to his amazement, a transformed face. In so few seconds, Emilia had changed. Pouches had appeared beneath her eyes. She resembled someone who had just awakened from a short, deep sleep. Even her hair was disarranged. He detected wrinkles in her forehead and white in her hair. As if this were a fairy tale, she had cast off some spell which had kept her eternally young. Her voice, too, had grown dull and listless. She looked at him with confusion.

"Why did you leave behind the list of addresses? And why my address of all things? Is it conceivable that . . ." and Emilia did not go on.

"I left behind no addresses."

"The detective didn't make up the story."

"I don't know. I swear before God I don't know."

"Don't swear to God. You most certainly did make a list and it fell out of your pocket. It's decent of you not to have excluded me." And she smiled wearily, the sort of smile one sometimes exhibits in the face of tragedy.

"Really, it's a mystery! I'm beginning to doubt my own reason."

"Yes, you are a sick person!"

At that moment what had happened all came back to him. He had ripped pages from his notebook and from them had fashioned a cone with which to probe the keyhole. He had apparently left the cone behind and the list had included Emilia's address. Who could tell what other addresses had been there? In that second he realized that leaving the pages had been tantamount to informing upon himself. Wolsky's address might easily have been among them, as well as addresses of impresarios, actors, theater owners, and firms from which he purchased equipment. It was not improbable that his own address was included, since he liked to amuse himself at times by writing his street and number and festooning it with hairs, appendages, tails, and flourishes. He felt no fear but something within him laughed. His very first crime and he had denounced himself. He belonged with those incompetents who steal nothing but leave enough clues to lead the police directly to them. The police and the courts dealt mercilessly with such fools. He remembered what Emilia had said about those who see the pit but nevertheless fall into it. He felt ashamed of his clumsiness. This means I dare not go home. They'll learn my address in Lublin as well. Yes, and this foot in the bargain . . .

"Well," he said, "I shan't trouble you any longer. It's all up with us." And he rose to go.

Emilia got up also.

"Where are you going? You haven't murdered anyone!"

"Forgive me if you can."

And Yasha began to limp towards the door. She began to move as if to block his path.

"Do go and see a doctor."

"Yes, thank you."

It seemed as if she wanted to say something else to him, but he quickly backed into the hallway, grabbed his hat and coat, and let himself out.

Emilia shouted something after him, but he slammed the door and, injured foot and all, began to race down the stairs.

EIGHT

Yasha remained standing for a while at the courtyard gate. Was a police agent waiting for him just outside? Suddenly, he remembered the skeleton key. No, it was not in the suit he had on. It was in the one he had worn the day before. But if his house had been searched, then the key had been discovered.—Well, it doesn't matter now. Let them lock me up! Tomorrow's newspapers will be full of me, anyhow. What will Esther say when she finds out? The Piask gang will be delighted; they will consider it a fine irony. And what about Herman? And Zeftel? And Magda—not to mention her brother! And how about Wolsky? The crowd at the Alhambra? Anyway, I'll be taken to the prison hospital. He could feel the swelling in his foot pressing on his shoe. And I've lost Emilia, as well, he said to himself. He walked through the gate but no policeman was waiting. Perhaps the man was lurking across the street? Yasha thought of entering the Saxony Gardens but he did not do so; Emilia, peering through her window, might see him. He walked in the direction of Graniczna Street, came out on Gnoyne Street again, and saw, in a watchmaker's window, that it was only ten minutes to four. God in heaven, how long this day was! It seemed like a year! He felt he must sit and he had the notion to enter the study-house again. He turned into the courtyard of the synagogue. What's happened to me, he marveled. Suddenly I've become a real synagogue Jew! In the synagogue the evening services were in progress. A Lithuanian Jew was intoning the Eighteen Benedictions. The worshipers were dressed in short coats and stiff hats. Yasha smiled. He was descended from Polish Hasidim. In Lublin there were scarcely any Lithuanian Jews but here in Warsaw there were many. They dressed differently, talked differently, prayed differently. Although it was a hot day, a chill which the sun could not dissipate came from the synagogue. He heard the cantor chant, "And to Jerusalem, Thy city, return in mercy and dwell therein as Thou hast spoken."

So? They wish to return to Jerusalem too? Yasha said to himself. From early childhood he had considered Lithuanian Jews half-Jews, an alien sect. He could barely understand their Yiddish. He saw that there were clean-shaven men among the congregation. What was the point in shaving the beard, then praying, he asked himself. Perhaps they use scissors—that would constitute a lesser sin. But as long as one believed in God and the Torah, why compromise? If there was a God and His Law was true, then He must be served night and day. How long did one survive in this rotten world? Yasha went to the study-house. It was filled with people. Men studied the Talmud. The sunlight filtered through the windows and cast oblique pillars of dust. Young men with lengthy sidelocks swayed over volumes of the Talmud, shouted, chanted, prodded one another, gesticulated. One grimaced as if his stomach ached, a second wagged his thumb, a third twirled the fringes of his sash. Their shirts were grimy, their collars loosened. Some had lost their teeth prematurely. One's beard grew in black tufts—a tuft here, a tuft there. The beard of another small fellow was as red as fire, his head shaven, and from his skull hung yellow sidelocks, long as braids. Yasha heard him cry: They sued him for wheat and he admitted barley.

Can God will it thus? Yasha asked himself. All this business about wheat and barley. This knowledge concerns only commerce. He reminded himself of the cry of the anti-semite: The Talmud only teaches the Jew to be a swindler.

This fellow probably has a little shop somewhere. If he doesn't have one now, he will someday. Yasha found an empty bench near the bookshelves. It felt good to sit down. He closed his eyes and listened to the sounds of the Torah.

Shrill adolescent voices mingled with the hoarse, rattling accents of the old. The voices shouted, mumbled, chanted, enunciated single words. Yasha recalled what Wolsky had said to him once over a glass of vodka: that he, Wolsky, was no anti-semite, but that the Jew in Poland had created a bit of Bagdad in the midst of Europe. Even the Chinese and Arabs, according to Wolsky, were civilized in comparison to the Jew. On the other hand, the Jews who wore short cloaks and shaved their beards were either eager to Russianize Poland or were revolutionaries. Quite often they were both exploiting and stirring up the working classes at the same time. They were radicals, Freemasons, atheists, internationalists, seeking to seize, dominate, and befoul everything.

A silence descended upon Yasha. He could be considered one of these beardless Jews, but he found them more alien than the pious sort. From childhood on he had been surrounded by religious people. Even Esther kept a Jewish home with a kosher kitchen. Such a breed was perhaps too Asiatic, as the enlightened Jews claimed, but at least they had a faith and a spiritual homeland, a history, and a hope. In addition to their laws governing commerce, they had their Hasidic literature, and they studied their cabala and books of ethics. But what did the assimilated Jews have? Nothing of their own. In one place they spoke Polish, in another Russian, in still others, German and French. They sat around in the Café Lurs, or the Café Semodeni, or the Café

Strassburger, drinking coffee, smoking cigarets, reading a variety of newspapers and magazines, and telling jokes which elicited the kind of laughter that Yasha always found unpleasant. They carried on their politics, forever planning revolutions and strikes, although the victims of these activities were always the poor Jews, their own brethren. As for their women, they gallivanted in diamonds and ostrich-plumes, arousing Christian envy.

It was odd but no sooner did Yasha find himself in a House of Prayer than he began taking stock of his soul. True, he had alienated himself from the pious but he had not gone over to the camp of the assimilated. He had lost everything: Emilia, his career, his health, his home. Emilia's words returned to him, "You must have some sort of a covenant with God since he punishes you so promptly." Yes, Heaven kept a sharp lookout over him. Possibly it was because he had never stopped believing. But what did they want of him? Earlier that day he had known what was required—that he keep to the path of righteousness as had his father before him and his father's father before that. Now he was again a prey to doubts. Why did God need these capotes, these sidelocks, these skullcaps, these sashes? How many more generations would wrangle over the Talmud? How many more restrictions would the Jew put on himself? How much longer would they wait for the Messiah, they who had already waited two thousand years? God was one thing, these man-made dogmas another. But was one able to serve God without dogmas? How had he, Yasha, come to be in his present predicament? He most certainly would not have been involved in all these love affairs and other escapades if he had put on a fringed garment and had prayed thrice daily. A religion was like an army—to operate it required discipline. An abstract faith inevitably led to sin. The prayer house was like a barracks; there God's soldiers were mustered.

Yasha could remain there no longer. He felt hot and yet he was shivering. Obviously, he had a fever. He decided to go home. Let them arrest me, if they wish! he thought. He was reconciled to draining the cup to the last bitter dregs.

Before leaving the study-house he took down a book from the shelves at random; opening it to the middle he consulted it as his father had been in the practice of doing whenever he was uncertain of his proper course of action. The volume, he discovered, was the *Eternal Paths* by Rabbi Leib of Praga. On the right-hand page was a verse from Scripture: "He closeth his eyes not to see evil," along with the Talmudic interpretation, "Such a man is one who does not look at women while they stand at their washing." Laboriously Yasha translated the Hebrew words. He understood what they were getting at—there must be discipline. If a man did not look, he did not lust, and if he did not lust, he did not sin. But, if one broke the discipline and did look, one ended by violating the Seventh Commandment. He had opened the book and found a text concerning the very problem which was uppermost in his mind.

He put the book back; a few moments later he took it down again and kissed it. This book, at least, required something of him, Yasha. It marked out a course of action, albeit a difficult one. But mere worldly writing demanded nothing. For all such authors cared, he could kill, steal, fornicate, destroy himself and others. He had often met literary men in cafés and theaters; they busied themselves kissing women's hands, bestowing compliments upon all and sundry; were constantly ranting against publishers and critics.

He hailed a droshky and ordered the coachman to drive him to Freta Street. He knew that Magda would make a scene but he mentally rehearsed the words he would say to her: Magda dear, I am dead. Take everything I own—my gold watch and diamond ring, my few rubles—and go home. If you can, forgive me.

2

In the droshky Yasha felt a fear he had never previously experienced. He was afraid of something but did not know what it was. The weather was hot yet he felt cold. He trembled all over. His fingers had become white and shrunken, the tips shriveled like those of a mortally-ill person, or of a corpse. It was as if his heart were being crushed by a giant fist. What's wrong with me, he asked himself. Has my last hour come? Do I fear being arrested? Do I long for Emilia? He continued to tremble and was seized by a cramp; he could scarcely breathe. So desperate was his condition that he began to console himself. Well, not everything is lost yet. I can live without a leg. And perhaps I may find some solution. Even if I'm arrested, how long will they keep me in prison? After all, I only attempted burglary—I didn't do anything. He leaned against the back of the seat. He wanted to put up his coat collar but he was too embarrassed to do so on such a hot day. But he did put his fingers inside his coat to warm them. What is it? Can it be gangrene? he asked himself. He wanted to untie the lace on his shoe but when he bent over he almost fell from the seat. The driver evidently guessed that something was wrong with his passenger and kept turning around. The pedestrians were also looking at him, Yasha noticed. Some even stopped to stare. "What's wrong?" the coachman anxiously asked. "Shall I stop?"

"No, drive on."

"Shouldn't I take you to a druggist?"

"No, thank you."

The droshky stopped more often than it moved, impeded by draywagons loaded with lumber and sacks of flour and by huge moving vans. The dray horses stomped their thick legs on the cobblestones and the stones gave off sparks. At one spot they rode by, a horse had collapsed. For the third time that day Yasha passed the bank on Rimarska Street. This time he did not even glance at the building. He had given up his interest in banks and money. Now he felt not only dread, but digust at himself. So strong was the sensation that it produced nausea. Maybe something's happened to Esther, he thought suddenly. He remembered a dream he had had, but just as the dream began to take shape, it slipped from him without leaving a trace. What could it have been? A beast? A verse from the Scriptures? A corpse? There were times when he was tormented nightly by dreams. He dreamed of funerals, monsters, witches, lepers. He would awaken drenched with sweat. But these weeks he had dreamed little. He would fall asleep, exhausted. More than once he had awakened in the same position in which he had fallen asleep. Yet he had known that the night had not been dreamless. Asleep, he led another life, a separate existence. From time to time he would recollect some dream of flying or some such stunt contrary to nature, something childishly preposterous, based on a child's misunderstandings or perhaps even on some verbal or grammatical error. So fantastically absurd would the dream have been that the brain, when not asleep, simply could not sustain it. He would remember and forget it at the very same instant.

As soon as he got out of the droshky, he became calm. Slowly, he mounted the stairs, supporting himself on the banister. He had neither his house key nor his skeleton key with him. If Magda was not at home, he would be forced to wait in the hall. However, the janitor, Anthony, had a key. Before knocking, Yasha listened at the door. There was no sound. He began to knock but no sooner had he touched the knob than the door swung open. When he walked into the front room he beheld a horrible sight. Magda was hanging from the ceiling, an overturned chair beneath her. He knew immediately that she was dead. Instead of crying out or hurrying to cut her down, he just stood there and gaped. She had only a petticoat on; her feet were naked and had turned blue. He could not see her face, only her neck with the bun of hair. To him she looked like an oversized doll. He wanted to move, to go and cut her down but he continued to stand there as though helpless. Where was there a knife? He must summon help, he knew, but he felt ashamed to face the neighbors. At last he threw open the door and cried out, "Help!"

His cry had not been very loud and no one responded. He sought to increase the volume but could not. A childish urge to flee almost overcame him, but instead he opened the door of a neighboring apartment and called, "You must help me. Something terrible has happened!"

The apartment was full of barefoot, half-naked children. Near the kitchen stood a stout flaxen-haired gentile woman who turned her sweat-stained face to him. She had been in the act of peeling an onion. Seeing him, she asked, "What's the matter?"

"Come! I need help! Magda. . . ." And he could not speak further.

The woman followed him into his apartment and immediately began to moan. She gripped his shoulders. "Cut her down! Cut her down!" she commanded.

He wanted to do as she bid but the woman clung to him, shrieking into his ear, still holding the paring knife and the onion. Yasha's ear was almost sliced off. Soon, other occupants of the house rushed in. Yasha saw one of them fumble with the rope, lift Magda up, loosening the noose and passing it over her head. All this time he stood immobile. Now they were busy attempting to resuscitate her, rotating her arms, pulling her hair, dousing her with water. Each minute more people came in. The janitor and his wife were already there. Someone ran to fetch a policeman. Yasha could not see Magda's face, only the slack body which yielded to all treatment with the unresisting flaccidity of the dead. A woman pinched the corpse's cheeks and then crossed herself. Two old hags threw themselves into each other's arms, appeared to be conspiring silently. Only then did Yasha become aware that there was no sound from the other room. He walked into the room and found all three animals dead. Apparently Magda had strangled them. The monkey lay with eyes open. The crow, enclosed in its cage, looked as if it had been stuffed. The parrot was on its side, a drop of dry blood on its beak. Why had she done this? No doubt to prevent the creatures from crying out. Yasha tugged at someone's sleeve to show what had happened. The policeman was already in the apartment. He pulled out his notebook and wrote down what Yasha told him.

There were other arrivals: a physician, a civilian official, another policeman. Yasha expected to be arrested momentarily. He wanted to be taken to prison but the officials left, their only admonition being that the corpse was not to be touched. And now the rest of the men left and returned to their jobs—one was a cobbler, another a cooper. Only two women remained: the stout woman who had been peeling the onion and a white-haired crone with a face sprinkled with warts. The body had been placed on one of the beds and now the stout woman turned to Yasha: "She'll have to be laid out, you know. She was a Catholic."

"Do whatever's necessary."

"We must notify the parish. The Russians will want to perform an autopsy."

Then at length they left Yasha alone. He wanted to go to Magda in the bedroom but was afraid, his childhood fear of the dead returning. He threw open the windows as if to keep in touch with the courtyard, and left the front door ajar. He dared not see the animals again, though he wished to, afraid of their silence also. The stillness of death hung over the apartment, a silence pregnant with strangled screams. But in the corridor there was still a buzzing, voices whispering. Yasha stood in the center of the room and looked through the window at the pale blue sky, where a bird soared. Suddenly, he heard music. A street musician had come into the courtyard. He was playing an old Polish melody, a ballad of a girl who had been abandoned by her lover. Children gathered about the musician and, oddly enough, Yasha was grateful to the organ-grinder. His tune had banished death's silence. As long as he played, Yasha could face Magda.

He did not approach the bed immediately but remained standing at the threshold of the room. The women had covered the dead girl's face with a shawl. He hesitated a moment and then walked over and raised the shawl. He did not find Magda but an image molded of some lifeless substance, wax or paraffin—nose, mouth, features all unfamiliar. Only the high cheekbones retained some resemblance. The ears were white as bone, the eyelids were puckered, as though the eyeballs beneath had already withered. On the throat was a bluish-brown bruise from the rope. Her lips were silent and yet she was screaming—a cry such as no mortal could long endure. Swollen and cracked, the mouth shouted, Look what you have done to me! Look! Look! Yasha wanted to cover her face but his hands were paralyzed and he could not move. Presumably, this was the same Magda who had quarreled with him that very morning, had later brought him a pot of water from the pump; but that other Magda could be asked forgiveness and mollified. This one, lying here limp on the bed, had passed into eternity, cutting herself off from good or evil. She had transcended the abyss that could not be spanned by a bridge. Yasha touched her forehead. It felt neither cold nor warm but beyond temperature. Then Yasha raised one of her eyelids. The pupil seemed that of a living person, but it stared at nothing; it was not even looking into itself.

A hearse arrived and Magda was carried out. A huge fellow in a blue apron and wearing an oilskin cap which only partially concealed a shock of yellow hair, took her in one hand as though she were a chicken, dropped her on a stretcher, and covered her with a gunny sack. He shouted something to Yasha and handed him a document. He was assisted by a short man with a curly mustache, who likewise seemed angry at something. The assistant stank of whiskey and the odor made Yasha think of a drink. The pain and the fear had become unendurable. He listened to the two men descend the stairs. The sound of whispering came from the other side of the door. Generally, the relatives hid the corpse from the officials, seeking to avoid an autopsy. Yasha realized he should have made some sort of arrangements with a priest, but everything had happened too quickly. He had just hung around, doing nothing. The neighbors were talking about him, he knew, astounded at his odd behavior. He had not even accompanied Magda's body to the hearse; a childish shame had overwhelmed him. If there had not been people to face, he would have left, but he waited for the crowd to disperse. By this time, the apartment was almost dark. He stood staring at a spot on the door latch, feeling hemmed in on all sides by uncanny forces. Behind him the silence rustled and snorted. He was afraid to turn his head. Some shadowy form lurked nearby, ready to leap upon him and attack him with tooth and claw—something monstrous and nameless. He had been familiar with this presence from childhood. It revealed itself to him in nightmares. It was, he assured himself, a figment of his imagination, but nevertheless he could not deny its existence. He held his breath. Such terror could be endured only a few seconds.

Outside the noises had ceased and Yasha rushed to the door. He tried to pull it open but it wouldn't move. Won't they let me out? he wondered in terror. He tugged at the knob and all at once the door swung open as if blown by a gust of wind. He saw a dark form scamper away; he had nearly killed a cat. Sweat drenched his clothes. Slamming the door behind him, he dashed down the stairs as though pursued. He saw the janitor standing alone in the courtyard and he waited until the man retired to his cubicle. Yasha's heart did not beat now so much as flutter. His scalp prickled. Something was crawling down his spine. He did not feel the same terror as before, but he knew he would never return to that apartment.

The janitor closed the door to his room and Yasha sprinted through the gate. Now once again he felt the dull ache in his foot. He kept close to the walls, his greatest wish being not to be seen, or at least not to be conscious of others watching him. He reached Franciskaner Street and hurriedly turned the corner, like a boy playing truant from cheder. The events of the past twenty-four hours seemed to have made him a child again, a frightened, guilty schoolboy, plagued by fears he could not divulge and by entanglements no stranger could understand. At the same time he had the sobriety of maturity—of one who dreams and knows that he dreams.

Get drunk? Was there a tavern nearby? There were several on Freta Street but there everyone knew him. On the other hand, Franciskaner was inhabited only by Jews; here, there was no drinking. He remembered that there was a bar on Bugay Street somewhere, but how could you get there without passing Freta Street? He walked to Nowiniarska Street and came out on a street called Bolesc.* That should be the name of all streets, he said to himself. The whole world is one great agony. He had passed Bugay Street and he doubled on his tracks. Streetwalkers were already standing under the lampposts and around gates, although it was not yet evening; but none of them motioned to him. Am I so repulsive that even they aren't interested? he wondered. A tall laborer wearing a checked jacket, blue cap, and low boots, approached. He had a narrow, sunken face which had been half-eaten away and, in place of a nose, a black plaster on a string. A dwarf of a prostitute, who scarcely came up to the man's waist, walked up to him and led him off. Yasha could see his legs shaking. The girl could not have been more than fifteen. What is he afraid of? something within Yasha asked, laughingly. Syphilis?

Yasha reached Bugay Street but the tavern he remembered having been there had disappeared.

* Bolesc means pain in Polish

Had it been closed? He wanted to ask of some passerby, but he was ashamed to. What's the matter with me? Why should I feel the shame of a goat in a cabbage patch? he asked himself. All the while he was searching for the tavern, he knew it was somewhere close by, eluding him. Just because he was so anxious not to be seen, everyone was gaping at him. Can they know me here? he wondered. Can some of them have been to the Alhambra? No, it's not possible. They were whispering about him, laughing in his face. A small dog growled and snapped at his trousers. He was ashamed to drive away so small a creature, but the dog foamed with rage and yelped so loudly it scarcely seemed small at all. The devil who was exacting revenge upon Yasha apparently was not yet satisfied. He kept adding annoyance to annoyance. Then, suddenly, Yasha saw the tavern. He was standing right next to it. As if they had all had a hand in the joke, suddenly everyone began to laugh.

Now he no longer even wished to go into the place; he would have preferred another but he felt he could not turn around and walk away. It would indicate surrender. He went up the three steps, opened the door, and was hit by a blast of heat and steam. The stench of vodka and beer mingled with something else which was oily and musty. Someone was playing an accordion and there was a great scurrying about, swaying, clapping of hands, and dancing. Apparently here it was like one big family. His eyes became misty and for a moment he could not see. He searched for a table but there were none, not even benches. He felt blinded and as if a cane or a rope had been placed in his path to trip him. Somehow, he managed to reach the bar but could not break through the crowd of drinkers and, anyway, the bartender had walked to the other side of the bar. Yasha put his hand into his pants pocket looking for a handkerchief but he could not find one. He could move neither forward nor backward. It was as if he had been caught in a trap. Heavy beads of perspiration dripped from his forehead. His desire to drink had, in one instant, been transformed into disgust. The nausea returned and again fiery sparks danced before his eyes: two large sparks, almost as big as coals.

"What do you want?" someone asked from behind the bar.

"Me?" Yasha replied.

"Who else?"

"I'd like a glass of tea," and he, himself, was astounded at his words. The other hesitated.

"This is not a tea-room!"

"Make it vodka."

"Glass or bottle?"

"Bottle."

"Quart or pint?"

"Pint."

"Forty or sixty?"

"Sixty."

Surprisingly, no one laughed.

"Anything to eat?"

"Might as well."

"A salted roll?"

"That'll do."

"Sit down; I'll bring your order."

"Where do you sit?"

"Where do you think?"

Then Yasha spied a table. It was like demonstrations in hypnotism which he had read about in magazines and more than once had conducted himself.

4

He sat down at the table and only then sensed how weary he was. He could no longer stand the shoe on his left foot; he put his hand under the table and tried to undo the lace. He recalled a passage from the Pentateuch: "Behold, I am at the point of dying, and what profit shall this birthright give me?"

Suddenly, the fear, anxiety, embarrassment left him. He no longer cared whether he was stared at or mocked. He was unable to untangle the shoelace and he pulled at it so vigorously that he tore it. He removed the shoe and the sock gave off a noxious heat.—Yes, it's getting gangrenous, gangrenous . . . I'll join her soon! And as he felt his foot it swelled as the dough of which the barber had spoken earlier that day. What time does this place close, I wonder? Not early. He desired to do only one thing—sit and rest. He closed his eyes and enveloped himself in the darkness of his being. Where was Magda now? What was being done to her? They must have already dissected her body. Students learning anatomy. He slumped as though from the burden of the horror.

What would her mother say? Her brother? So much punishment at one blow!

Someone brought him a bottle of vodka and a glass, along with a basket of salted rolls. Yasha poured himself half a glassful of the vodka and drank it down quickly, as if it were medicine. His nose burned and so did his throat and eyes. Maybe I should rub my foot with it, he thought. Alcohol is supposed to help this sort of thing. He poured some of the vodka into his hand, stooped, and massaged it into his ankle. Well, anyway, it's too late! Then he drank another glassful. The alcohol went to his head but it did not make him feel better. He imagined Magda's head being cut from her body, her stomach being split open. And only a few hours before she'd brought a chicken from the market, to prepare for his supper. Why did she do it? Why? something within him screamed. He had left her before. She had known all his secrets. She had been tolerant of him. It was almost unbelievable that at this time yesterday he had been in good health, planning to perform somersaults on the tightrope, and with Magda and Emilia still his. Catastrophe had struck him as it had Job. One misstep and he had lost everything . . . everything . . .

There was only one way out now—it was time to see what lay on the other side of the curtain. But how? Throw himself into the Vistula? But it would be dreadful for Esther. No, he could not leave her a deserted wife. The very least he could do was arrange for her to remarry . . . He could scarcely keep himself from vomiting. Yes, Death was his master. Life had cast him to the winds.

He held the bottle in his hand but could drink no more. He sat there, blind, his lids shut. The accordion did not stop playing the old Polish mazurka. The din in the tavern became ever louder. He had already resolved to die but, nevertheless, he needed a place to spend this night. Something still required thinking out. But where could he go with his injured foot? If it were only day! By now, everything had shut down. A hotel? Which one? And how could he go there with his foot in this condition? He was unlikely to find a droshky in the neighborhood. He wanted to put his shoe on, but it had vanished. He felt around for it with his toe but it wasn't there. Had someone stolen it? He opened his eyes and saw all about him in the tavern wild eyes and flushed faces. Hands waved, bodies reeled, feeble arms sought to do battle; there was much kissing and embracing. The waiters, dressed in grimy aprons, came and went, bringing food and vodka. The accordionist played, his black hair and thin mustache almost touching his instrument, his eyes screwed up tight, his expression rapturous. His body was bent close to the floor which was sprinkled with sawdust. Evidently, there was another room in the tavern, for the sound of a piano could be heard. A curl of steam circled the naphtha lamp. Opposite Yasha sat a huge man, his skin pockmarked; he had a long mustache, a short pimpled nose, and a scar cut into his forehead. He kept grimacing at Yasha. His watery, crossed eyes rolled in exaltation, the ecstasy of one on the brink of madness.

Yasha touched his shoe and stooped to get it. He tried to put it on but it would no longer fit. This made him think of the story he had learned in cheder about Nero who, hearing of his father's death, found his shoes had become too small for him; for, as it is written, "A good report maketh the bones fat." How far away all that seemed now: his teacher, Reb Moshe Godle, the children, that volume of the Talmud containing the story of the destruction of the temple which is studied before the ninth day of Ab.—Well, I can't sit here until they close! I must find a place to sleep.

He forced the shoe onto his foot but kept it unlaced, then tried to get his waiter's attention by tapping his glass against the bottle. The giant across the way from him laughed and Yasha saw a set of broken teeth. It was as if he and Yasha were involved in some great joke together. How can a man like that live? Yasha asked himself. Is he drunk or mad? Does he have anyone at all in the world? Does he work? Perhaps what I'm going through now has already happened to him. Saliva dropped from the giant's mouth; he was laughing so hard his eyes were tearing. Yet he was someone's father, husband, brother, son. Savagery was stamped upon his features. He was still in that primeval forest from which mankind was evolved. Such men die laughing, Yasha said to himself. And then finally the waiter came. Yasha paid his bill and got to his feet. He could barely walk. Each step he took was agony.

It was very late but, nevertheless, Bugay Street remained crowded. There were women seated upon the stoops, upon stools, upon boxes. Several shoemakers had moved their benches outside and hammered by candlelight. Even the children were still awake. A sulfurous breeze blew from the Vistula. Foul odors rose from the sewers. Above the rooftops the sky glowed as if reflecting some distant fire. Yasha looked for a droshky but soon realized he would spend the whole night waiting for one. He started off down Celna Street, continued on Swietojanska Street, and came out on Castle Place. He could move only a few steps at a time. He was overwhelmed by heat, nauseated. At every gate, at every lamp-post stood groups of prostitutes. All about him drunkards reeled along as though seeking some-one to fall against. A woman sat at an open door underneath a balcony. She had tousled hair and eyes which were aflame with the joy of madness, and in her arms she clutched a basket stuffed with rags. Yasha bent his head; he belched and tasted an unfamiliar bitterness. I know, it's the world! Every second or third house contained a corpse. Throngs of people roamed about the streets, slept on benches, lay on the banks of the Vistula in the midst of filth. The city was sur-rounded by cemeteries, prisons, hospitals, insane asylums. In every street and alley lurked murder-ers, thieves, degenerates. Policemen were every-where in sight.

Yasha saw a droshky and motioned at it but the driver, after looking him over, drove on. Another droshky appeared but did not stop, either. The third droshky that came along did stop, though somewhat tentatively. Yasha climbed in.

"Take me to a hotel?"

"Which?"

"Any one. Just a hotel."

"How about the Cracowsky?"

"All right—the Cracowsky."

The coachman cracked his whip and the droshky trundled off, down Podwal Street, into Mead Street, into New Senator Street. Theater Square was still crowded, filled with carriages. Apparently, there had been a special performance of the opera. Men shouted, women laughed. Not one among all these people knew that someone called Magda had hanged herself, nor that a magician from Lublin was racked by pain. The laughter and carousing will go on until they too turn to dust, Yasha said to himself. It seemed odd to him now that he had devoted his every waking thought to entertaining this rabble. What was I after? To have these dancers upon graves spare me some of their applause? Was that why I became a thief and murderer?

The droshky pulled up at the Cracowsky Hotel and at that very instant Yasha realized that the trip had been useless—he did not have his identification papers with him.

5

Yasha paid the coachman and told him to wait. He sought to coax the room clerk into renting him a room although he was without credentials, but the dwarf-like individual behind the desk was adamant.

"It can't be done. Strictly forbidden."

"Suppose a man loses his papers? Must he die?"

The clerk shrugged his shoulders. "I have my orders."

Judgments, they do not know them—something within Yasha quoted for him. Thus had his father labeled the Russian laws.

Yasha walked outside in time to see the droshky pulling away; someone had outbid him for the vehicle. He sat down on the doorstep of a neighboring building. This was the second consecutive night he had wandered about. Things are moving swiftly, he thought; tomorrow night, perhaps, I'll be sleeping in my grave. There were streetwalkers here also. Across the way from him he saw a woman dressed in black, wearing long earrings. She looked almost like a middle-aged housewife but she gave him the glance of a prostitute. Evidently, she was one of the unregistered ones, those who offer themselves in courtyards or doorways. She looked directly at him, as though trying to hypnotize him; her gaze clung to him in entreaty. She seemed to be saying, Since we are in the same fix, why not be so together? The light of the streetlamp bathed her in yellow and Yasha could see the wrinkles on her face, the lines in her forehead, the rouge she had smeared over her cheekbones, the mascara around her large, dark eyes. He lacked even the strength for sympathy—

all he could feel was amazement. So this is the way the powers that be operate, he thought; they play with a man and then cast him aside as offal. But why him in particular? Why this woman? How was she worse than those pampered ladies who sat in the boxes at the opera and looked down at the audience through their lorgnettes? Was everything chance? If so, then chance was God. But what was chance? Was the universe chance? If the universe was not, could only a part of it be chance?

He saw a droshky coming and beckoned to the driver. The droshky stopped and he climbed in. The woman across the way watched him reproachfully. Her eyes seemed to be saying to Yasha: Will you forsake me also? The coachman turned his head but Yasha could not think of what to tell him. He wanted to go to a hospital but he heard himself saying, "Nizka Street."

"What number?"

"I don't remember the number. I'll direct you."

"All right."

He knew that it was madness to visit the yellowish woman and her brother—the pimp from Buenos Aires—at this time of night, but he had no alternative. Wolsky had a wife and children; Yasha realized he could not barge in on him in this condition. Maybe I should wake Emilia? he thought. No; even Zeftel won't be pleased to see me. He played with the notion of catching a train to Lublin but decided against it. He must arrange Magda's funeral. He could not just abandon the corpse and run. Anyway, the police undoubtedly knew that it was he who had broken into Zaruski's house the night before. It would be better to be arrested here in Warsaw than in Lublin. At least Esther would be spared the sight. Besides, Bolek was waiting in Piask. Had he not warned Yasha years ago that he would kill him? The best solution would be to leave the country. Maybe go to Argentina. But not with his foot the way it was . . .

The droshky traveled along Tlomacka Street, Leshno Street, and then on to Iron Street. There it turned into Smotcha Street. Yasha did not doze off, but sat hunched up as though chilled by a fever. Now, he was more concerned about the impropriety of visiting Zeftel at this hour and about the shame of exposing his situation to her and her hosts, than with sorrow for Magda or the fear of losing his foot. He took a comb from his pocket and ran it through his hair. He adjusted his tie. The thought of his financial predicament frightened him. A funeral would cost several hundred rubles and he had nothing. He could sell his team of horses but the police were after him and would arrest him the moment he set foot in the apartment on Freta Street. The wisest course would be to surrender to the police. He would receive everything he needed: a place to sleep, medical attention. Yes, that is the only solution, he told himself. But how should he go about it? Stop a policeman? Ask to be driven to the police station? Crowded as the other streets had been with officers of the law, now there was not a single one about. The street was deserted, all the gates locked, all the windows shut. He thought of telling the driver to take him to the nearest police headquarters but he was too ashamed to do so. He would think me mad, Yasha decided. Just the fact that I limped made him suspicious. Overwhelmed though he was by anxiety, Yasha could not rid himself of his pride and vanity.—The best solution of all is death! I'll put an end to it. And perhaps this very night!

He suddenly grew calmer, his decision made. It was as if he had stopped thinking. The droshky turned into Nizka Street and headed back in an easterly direction towards the Vistula, but Yasha could not remember which was the house. He was certain it had had a boarded fence with a gate but no such courtyard was to be seen. The coachman brought the droshky to a halt.

"Maybe it's nearer Okopova Street."

"Yes, maybe."

"I can't turn around."

"Suppose I get out here and find it myself," Yasha said, aware that this was stupidity; each step he took was an effort.

"If you wish."

He paid and climbed down. His injured leg had fallen asleep at the knee joint. Only when the droshky drove off did Yasha realize how dark it was here. There were only a few smoky streetlamps, placed at a great distance from each other. The street was unpaved, a mass of pits and mounds. Yasha looked about him but could see nothing. It was as if this were a street in some country village. Possibly this wasn't even Nizka

Street? Could it be Mila or Stavka Street? He
looked for matches even though he knew there
were none in his pocket. He limped toward Okopova Street. His coming here had been madness.
End everything? How did one do it? You couldn't
hang or poison yourself in the middle of the
street. Go to the Vistula?—but that was versts
away. A breeze blew from the cemetery. Suddenly, he wanted to laugh. Had anyone ever been in
such a dilemma? He hobbled as far as Okopova
Street but the house he wanted had vanished. He
raised his eyes and saw a black sky, dense with
stars, interested only in its heavenly business.
Who was concerned about a magician on earth
who had allowed himself to be trapped? Yasha
limped to the cemetery. These lives were done,
their accounts settled. If he could find an open
gate and an open grave, he would lie down in it,
conduct a proper Jewish funeral for himself.

What else remained for him?

6

But nevertheless he returned the way he had
come. He had become accustomed to the pain in
his foot. Let it tear, let it burn, let it abscess! He
reached Smotcha Street and continued on. Suddenly he saw the house. There it was: the fence,
the entrance. He touched the gate and it swung
open, revealing the stairs which led to Herman's
sister's apartment. The occupants were up;
lamplight streamed through the window. Well,
fate does not wish me to die yet! He was ashamed

to enter uninvited, limping, disheveled, but told himself, encouragingly: after all, such things have happened before. They won't throw me out. Even if they do, Zeftel will go with me. She loves me. The lamplight shining in the darkness returned him to life. They'll do something for my foot. Perhaps it can be saved. He considered calling out to Zeftel so as to prepare them for his arrival, but decided that this would be foolish. Limping to the stairs, he began to climb. He made as much noise as he could so as to announce himself. He had already prepared his opening remark: An unexpected visitor! A very strange thing happened. But those inside were apparently too engrossed in what they were doing to notice what was going on outside. Well, one lives through everything, Yasha comforted himself. What was engraven on that goldsmith's ring?— "This too shall pass." He knocked lightly on the door but there was no answer. They were in the other room, he decided. He knocked louder but there was no sound of footsteps. He stood there, shamed, humbled, prepared to surrender the vestige of pride he had left. Let this serve as an atonement for my sins, the voice within him uttered. He knocked three more times, very loudly, but still no one came. He waited and listened. Are they asleep, or what? He turned the knob and the door opened. A lamp was burning in the kitchen. Zeftel lay on the iron bed and, beside her, was Herman. They were both asleep. Herman was snoring deeply and sonorously. All the interior voices in Yasha became silent. He stood there gaping and then moved to the side for fear one of the pair should open his eyes. Now a shame he had never felt before came over him—a shame not for the couple but for himself, the humiliation of one who realizes that despite all his wisdom and experience, he has remained a fool.

Later, he could not recall how long he stood there: a minute? several minutes? Zeftel lay facing the wall, one breast bared, her hair in disarray, as if completely crushed by Herman's enormous bulk. Herman was not quite naked—he wore some sort of undershirt of foreign manufacture. Perhaps most remarkable of all was that the flimsy bed supported all that weight. There was a lifelessness about the faces and, had Herman not been snoring, Yasha would have thought the couple had been murdered. Two spent figures, two wornout puppets, they lay under a blanket. Where is the sister? Yasha asked himself. And why had they left the lamp burning? He wondered, and even as he did so wondered why he was wondering. He felt sorrow, emptiness, a sense of powerlessness. It was not unlike the feeling he had experienced a few hours earlier when he had discovered Magda dead. Twice in one day there had been unveiled to him things which are best concealed. He had looked on the faces of death and lechery and had seen that they were the same. And even as he stood there staring, he knew that he was undergoing some sort of transformation, that he would never again be the Yasha he had been. The last twenty-four hours were unlike any previous day he had experienced. They summed up all his previous existence, and in summing it up had put a seal upon it. He had seen the hand of God. He had reached the end of the road.

EPILOGUE

Three years had gone by. In Esther's front room she and two seamstresses were noisily putting the finishing touches to a wedding gown. The dress was so voluminous and had so long a train that it occupied the entire work table. Esther and the girls bustled about like dwarves constructing a suit of armor for a giant. One girl basted, the other sewed on tape. Esther, wielding an iron, pressed out the wrinkles between the flounces, constantly testing the iron with her finger. From time to time, she sprayed water from a jug on the spot she was about to press. Although she did not perspire easily, even in hot weather, her forehead was beaded with drops of sweat. What could be worse than burning a hole in a wedding gown?

One brown stain and all the work would have been for nothing. Nevertheless, Esther's black eyes twinkled. Despite her small hand and her narrow wrist, she handled the iron firmly. She was not one to scorch a dress.

Every now and again, she glanced out of the window that looked into the courtyard. The small brick structure or, as Esther thought of it—prison—had stood there for more than a year, but she still had not become accustomed to it. At times she would forget momentarily what had happened and would imagine it was the Feast of the Tabernacles—that an arbor had been erected outside. Generally she kept the curtain of this particular window drawn, but today she needed the daylight. The three years had aged Esther. The skin under her eyes had webbed and her broadening face had acquired an over-ripe, ruddy color. Her head, as always, was kerchiefed, but now those hairs that could be seen were gray rather than black. Only her eyes remained youthful and glistened like black cherries. For three years she had carried within her a heavy heart. It was no less heavy today but nevertheless she joked with her assistants, exchanged with them the usual trade banter about the bride and groom. The girls glanced at each other knowingly; theirs was no longer an ordinary workshop. Not for one moment was it possible to ignore the presence of the small, doorless house with its tiny window, behind which sat Yasha the Penitent— as he was now known.

The first appearance of this phenomenon had

created great excitement in the town. The Rabbi, Reb Abraham Eiger, had summoned Yasha to him and had cautioned him against doing what he planned. True, a hermit in Lithuania had had himself bricked up, but pious Jews were opposed to that sort of thing. The world had been created for the exercise of free will and the sons of Adam must constantly choose between good and evil. Why seal one's self in stone? The meaning of life was freedom and the abstinence from evil. Man deprived of free will was like a corpse. But Yasha was not so easily dissuaded. In the year and a half that he had been doing penance he had learned much. He had engaged a tutor to instruct him in the Mishnah, the Agadahs of the Talmud, the Midrash, even the Zohar, and produced for the Rabbi a variety of prototypes—saints who had had themselves put under restraint for fear they would be unable to resist temptation. Had not a holy man put out his eyes so that he might not look at his Roman mistress? Had not a Jew in Shebreshin sworn himself to silence for fear of uttering a word of slander? Had not a musician from Kovle feigned blindness for thirty years to avoid gazing upon another man's wife? Harsh laws were merely fences to restrain a man from sin. The young men who were present at Yasha's debates with the Rabbi still discussed them. It was hard to believe that in a year and a half this charlatan, this libertine, had absorbed so much of the Torah. The Rabbi disputed with him as with an equal. Yasha had remained firm in his resolve.

Finally, the Rabbi had placed his hand upon Yasha's head and had blessed him.

"Your actions are intended for the glory of Heaven. May the Almighty help you!"

And he had presented Yasha with a copper candlestick so that he might light a candle at night or on overcast days.

In the taverns of Piask and Lublin there had been much wagering on how long Yasha would endure his living grave. Some had estimated a week, others a month. As for the municipal authorities, they had debated the legality of Yasha's actions. Even the Governor had been kept informed. Yasha had calmly seated himself in a chair and Esther's house had been overrun by hundreds of observers as the masons worked. Children had climbed trees and had sat perched on rooftops. Pious Jews had come forward to speak with Yasha and discuss his motives, and equally pious matrons had attempted to dissuade him from his course. Esther also had wept and entreated until her voice was hoarse. Then, escorted by a group of women, she had gone to the cemetery to ascertain by measuring graves what length in candles she must give to charity. Her hope had been that such a gift would influence the spirits of saints to intercede with her husband and force him to reverse his decision. He must not leave her a deserted wife, albeit one who had her spouse so close at hand. But neither the sage admonitions, nor the laments, nor the warnings, had been of any avail. The walls of the small house had grown higher hour by hour. Yasha had allowed himself a space only four cubits long and four cubits wide. He had grown a beard and side-locks and had put on a wide fringed garment, a long gabardine, and a velvet skull cap. As the ma-sons worked, he had sat, book in hand, mumbling prayers. There had not even been sufficient room inside for a bed. His possessions consisted of a straw pallet, a chair, a tiny table, a pelisse with which to cover himself, the copper candlestick which the Rabbi had given him, a water jug, a few holy books, and a shovel with which to bury his excrement. The higher the walls had grown, the louder had become the laments. Yasha had cried out to the women, "Why all this wailing? I'm not dead yet."

"If only you were," Esther had called back in bitterness.

So vast and tumultuous had the crowd become that the police had ridden in on horseback and dispersed them. The town Natchalnik had com-manded the laborers to work day and night to put an end to the excitement. It had taken the ma-sons forty-eight hours to complete their task. The building had a shingled roof and a window which could be shuttered from the inside. Curios-ity-seekers had continued to come until the rains began to fall, and then the number had de-creased. All day the shutters of the small window remained closed. Esther had the fence around the house repaired to keep off strangers. Soon it became clear that those who had wagered that Yasha would not stay immured more than a week or a month had lost their bets. A winter passed, a summer, than another winter, but Yasha the Magician, now known as Reb Jacob the Penitent, remained in his self-ordained prison. Thrice daily Esther brought him food: bread with groats, potatoes in their skins, cold water. Thrice daily he left off his meditations and, for her sake, spoke with her for a few minutes.

2

Outside it was a sunny, hot day, but Yasha's cell was dark and cool, even though shafts of sunlight and warm breezes did manage to penetrate the shuttered window. Every now and again, Yasha would open the shutters and a butterfly or a bumblebee would fly in. Sounds came to him: the chirping of birds, the lowing of a cow, the cry of a child. There was no need for him to light a candle this midday. He sat in his chair at the small table, perusing the Two Tablets of the Covenant. That winter he had lived through days when he had wished to tear down the walls and free himself from the cold and dampness. He had developed a rasping cough. His limbs had been racked with pain. He had urinated too frequently. At night he had huddled in all his clothes under the pelisse and blanket which Esther had thrust in through the window, yet he had been unable to get warm. From the ground had risen a gnawing frost that chilled him to the bone. Often he had felt that he was already in his grave, and at times he had even wished for death. Now it was again summer. To the right of his cell grew an apple tree and he heard the rustle of its leaves. A swallow had built its nest among the branches and bustled about all day, bringing in its bill stalks and grubs for its young. Yasha managed to force his head through the window and saw before him the fields, the blue sky, the roof of the synagogue, the spire of a church. A few bricks removed and he could—he knew—wriggle through the window. But the thought that he could fight his way to freedom at any moment he chose stifled his desire to leave his cell. He knew quite well that on the other side of the wall lurked unrest, lust, the fear of coming day.

As long as he sat there, he was protected against the graver transgressions. Even his worries were different from those outside. It was as if he had become again a foetus in his mother's womb and once more the light referred to in the Talmud shone from his head, the while an angel taught him the Torah. He was free of all needs. His food cost only a few groschen a day. He required neither clothing, nor wine, nor money. When he recalled his expenses during the time he lived in Warsaw or traveled in the provinces, he laughed to himself. No matter how much he had earned in those days it had not been enough. He had kept a whole menagerie of animals. He had required closetsful of clothes. He had constantly driven himself into new expenditures and had been in debt to Wolsky; had borrowed money on interest from usurers in Warsaw and Lublin. Ceaselessly, he had been signing promissory notes, seeking out endorsers, purchasing gifts, and been in everyone's debt. Wallowing in his passions, he had found himself in a net which kept drawing tighter about him. Performing on the tightrope had not even been enough. He had kept trying to invent more and more daring stunts which were certain to destroy him. He had turned to theft—only a small mischance had prevented him from going to an actual prison. Here, in his solitude, all externalities fell away like the husks which the cabalists call the evil spirits. He had cut through the net as if with a knife. With one stroke, he had canceled all his accounts. Esther managed to earn her own living. He had settled all his debts; had given Elzbieta and her son, Bolek, the team and wagon; had left Wolsky the furniture from his Freta Street apartment, along with his equipment, costumes, and other paraphernalia. Now Yasha possessed nothing but the shirt upon his back. Yes, but was this sufficient to cleanse him of his sins? Could he atone for the evil he had done simply by reducing his burden?

Only here, in the stillness of his cell, could Yasha meditate upon the extent of his wickedness: the number of souls he had committed to torture, to madness, to death. He was no highwayman plying his trade in the forests but, nevertheless, he had murdered. What difference did it make to the victim how one killed? He could absolve himself before a mortal judge (one who was himself evil), but the Creator could neither be bought off nor deceived. He, Yasha, had destroyed, not innocently but with purpose. Magda cried out to him from the grave. Nor was this the

only horror he was guilty of. Now he acknowledged them all. Even if he remained in his cell for
a hundred years he could not atone for all his iniquity. Repentance alone did not cancel out such
mortal sin. One could only gain absolution by
begging forgiveness and receiving it from the victim himself. If one owed even half a groschen to
someone who lived on the other side of the world,
he must locate his creditor and settle the account. So it was written in the holy books. And
each day Yasha remembered some additional evil
for which he had been responsible. He had violat-
ed every law of the Torah, had broken nearly
every Commandment. And yet, while doing these
things, had considered himself an upright man,
capable of accusing others. How did the little discomfort he now suffered balance against the an-
guish he had caused? He was still alive, in more or
less good health. Even his foot had healed without crippling him. The true punishment, he
knew, would be given only in the other world;
there must be an accounting for every deed,
every word, every thought. Only one consolation
remained: that God was merciful and compassionate and that, in the final reckoning, good
must triumph over evil. But what was evil? He
had studied the literature of the cabala with his
instructors for three years: already he was aware
that evil was merely God's diminishing of Himself to create the world, so that he might be called
Creator and have mercy toward His creatures. As
a king must have his subjects, so a Creator must
create, so a benefactor have his beneficiaries. To

this extent, the Lord of the Universe had to depend upon His children. But, it was not enough to guide them with His merciful hand. They had to learn to cleave to the path of righteousness by themselves, of their own free will. The celestial worlds were awaiting this. Angel and seraph longed for the sons of Adam to be righteous, to pray with humility, give with compassion. Indeed, each good act improved the Universe, every word of the Torah braided crowns for the Godhead. Conversely, the most insignificant transgression reverberated in the most ethereal worlds, delaying the day of deliverance.

There were times, even here in his cell, when Yasha's faith wavered. As he read the sacred books, nagging thoughts came to him: How can I be sure that these speak the truth? Perhaps there is no God? The Torah may be the invention of man? Possibly I torture myself in vain? Vividly, he heard the Evil Spirit debate with him, remind him of past delights, advise him to begin again his debauchery. Yasha had to circumvent him each time differently. When pressed too hard he would seemingly agree with his opponent that he must return to the world, but then would postpone the moment of freedom. Other times he would reply in rebuttal: Let us say for the sake of argument, Satan, that God does not exist, but that the words spoken in His name are nevertheless correct. If a man's lot depends on another's misfortune, then there is good fortune for no one. If there is no God, man must behave like God. On one occasion Yasha demanded of Satan: Well, then, who created the world? Where do I come from? and you? Who makes the snow fall, the wind blow, my lungs take in air, my brain think? Where did the earth come from, the sun, the moon, the stars? This world with its eternal wisdom had to be the creation of some hand. We can perceive God's wisdom—why not then believe that behind this wisdom is concealed the mercy of the creator?

Entire days and nights were consumed by such disputes, driving Yasha to the brink of madness. Now and again Belial would withdraw and Yasha's faith would be restored and he would actually see God, feel His hand. He would begin to understand why goodness was necessary, would savor the sweetness of prayer, the delicious taste of the Torah. It would become clearer to him, day by day, that the Holy books he studied led to virtue and eternal life, that they pointed the way to the purpose of creation, while that which lay behind him was evil—all scorn, theft, murder. There was no middle road. A single step away from God plunged one into the deepest abyss.

3

The holy books cautioned Yasha not to let down his guard for an instant. Satan's attack never abates. Temptations are offered one after the other. Even as a man lies on his deathbed, Samael comes before him and attempts to win him to idolatry. It was true, Yasha discovered. For now, Esther began to seek him out almost hourly, rapping upon the shutter, lamenting, and assailing him with all her troubles. At night she would rouse him from sleep and attempt to kiss him. There was no feminine wile that leads to sin and makes of learning a mockery that she did not employ. As if this were not enough, men and women began to visit him as though he were a thaumaturgic rabbi. They sought his advice, begged him to intercede on their behalf. Yasha pleaded that he be left in peace, since he was no rabbi, not even the son of a rabbi, only an ordinary man, and, in addition, a sinner, but to no avail. Women stole into the courtyard, pounded on the shutter, even tried to smash it down by force. They wailed and shrieked and, when thwarted, cursed him. Esther complained that they disturbed her work. Yasha was overcome by fear. He had anticipated everything but not this. He, himself, was in need of advice. According to the law, was it right for him to deny the people and cause them sorrow? Was not this, itself, a display of arrogance? But could one such as he listen to their petitions like a rabbi? Both courses were wrong. After much consideration and many wretched nights Yasha decided to write to the Lublin rabbi. He composed his letter in Yiddish, including all the particulars and promised to abide by the Rabbi's decision. The Rabbi did not take long to reply. His answer, likewise written in Yiddish, commanded Yasha to receive those who came for two hours each day, but to accept no redemption money. The Rabbi wrote: "He to whom Jews come in audience is a rabbi."

And so Yasha now received people daily from two until four in the afternoon. So as to avoid confusion, Esther wrote numbers on cardboard and distributed them, as it was done in the offices of busy physicians. But even this did not help. Those who had an invalid at home, or who had recently suffered some tragedy, demanded to be admitted first. Others sought to bribe Esther with money and presents. Before long there was talk in the city of the miracles performed by Yasha the Penitent. He only had to make a wish, it was rumored, and the sick grew well; it was said that a conscript had been pulled right out of the hands of the Russians, that a mute had regained speech, and a blind man his sight. Yasha was now addressed by the women as Holy Rabbi, Holy Saint. Against his wishes, they showered his cell with banknotes and coins which he ordered distributed to the poor. Young Hasidim, who feared lest Yasha acquire some of the adherents of their own rabbis, mocked him and composed a lampoon listing all his former sins. A copy of it was sent to Esther.

No, the temptations never ceased. Yasha had withdrawn from the world but, through the tiny window which he had left to admit air and light, evil talk, slander, wrath, and false flattery came. It became clear to Yasha why the ancient saints had chosen exile and had never slept twice in the same place; had feigned blindness and deafness and muteness. One could not serve God amongst other men, even though separated by brick walls. He considered putting a pack upon his back and, with staff in hand, striking out for the unknown, but this he knew would cause Esther unendurable grief. Who could tell? She might even become ill from sorrow. He had noted how her health was failing. Old age was creeping up on her. Magda, peace be with her soul, had shown him the sort of thing that could happen.

No, peace of mind was not to be found in this world. There is no tomorrow without sorrow, as the philosophers say. But even more powerful than the temptations from without were those born within man himself, in his brain, his heart. No hour passed without Yasha's being besieged by every sort of passion. No sooner did he forget himself for a moment than they gathered about him: empty fancies, daydreams, repulsive desires. Emilia's face would materialize from the darkness and refuse to be driven away. It would smile, whisper, wink at him. He would think of new tricks to perform, new jokes with which to entertain audiences, new illusions and stunts with which to bewilder them. Again he danced on the tightrope, turned somersaults on the high wire, sailed over the rooftops of cities, trailed by a jubilant crowd. He would chase away the fancies as diligently as he could, but still they would return like persistent flies. He hungered for meat, wine, vodka. He was consumed by a longing to see Warsaw again—the droshkies, omnibuses, cafés, confectionaries. Though he suffered from the colds and rheumatism and though there was a constant burning in his stomach, his lust had not diminished. With no woman about, he thought of sinning like Onan.

He had only two defenses against these assaults from within and without—the Torah and prayers. Night and day he studied, memorizing many chapters and reciting them as he lay on his straw pallet. "Blessed is the man that walketh not in the counsel of the ungodly." "Lord, how are they increased that trouble me! Many are they that rise up against me. Many there be which say of my soul, 'There is no help for him in God.' Selah." He repeated these passages so often that his lips swelled. In his mind he compared the Evil One to a dog which both barks and never stops biting. The creature must be constantly kept off with a stick, one's injured limbs pulled from its jaws, the wounds tended with salves and plasters. The fleas from its furry hide required also an eternal vigilance. And this until one's last breath.

He would surely have died had there not been an occasional respite. The Dog of Egypt did not always bite with the same ferocity. Now and again he withdrew, slumbered. But one had to stay on guard lest he return with renewed power and insolence.

4

One after another they all came with their troubles. They spoke to Yasha the magician as if he were God: "My wife is sick. My son must go to the army. A competitor is outbidding me for a farm. My daughter has gone mad . . ." A small dried-up man had a growth the size of an apple on his forehead. A girl had been hiccuping for a week and could not stop: at night, when the moon shone, she sounded like a hound baying. Evidently, there was a dybbuk in her, for she chanted hymns and prayers with the voice of a cantor. Now and again, she spoke in Polish and Russian, languages with which she was unfamiliar, and at such times she had a desire to seek out a priest and be converted. Yasha prayed for all of them. But each time he pointed out he was no rabbi but merely an ordinary Jew and a sinner, besides. The supplicants responded by repeating their requests. A deserted wife, whose husband had been missing six years and who had been searching throughout Poland for him, screamed so loudly that Yasha had to stuff his ears. She hurled herself at the building as if determined, from sheer bitterness, to demolish the structure. Her breath stank of onions and rotting teeth. Those standing behind her on line demanded that she make her complaints briefer, but she waved her fists at them and continued shouting and wailing. Finally, she was dragged away. "Scum, whoremaster, murderer!" she shouted at Yasha.

A melancholy young man confided that demons battled with him, knotting his fringed garment, putting elflocks into his beard, spilling out the water he had prepared for his morning ablutions, putting handfuls of salt and pepper, along with worms and goat-dung, into his food. Every time he sought to perform his bodily functions, a she-devil prevented him. The young man had letters from rabbis and other reliable witnesses to prove the truth of what he was saying. There were also learned sophisticates who sought out Yasha to discuss religion with him and asked him all sorts of impossible questions. Young idlers came to mock and discredit him with unfamiliar quotations from the Talmud, or with words in Chaldaic. He had resolved to receive people only two hours each day but, as it worked out, he stood at his window from dawn until nightfall. His legs grew so weary that he would collapse onto the straw pallet and would say the evening services sitting down.

One day Schmul the Musician, Yasha's former drinking companion, came to see him. Schmul complained that his hand ached so much it prevented him from playing his fiddle. No sooner did he lift his instrument than the pain began. The hand with which he fingered the strings had become stiff and bloodless, and he showed Yasha yellow, wrinkled fingertips. Schmul wanted to go to America. He brought greetings from the Piask thieves. Elzbieta had died. Bolek was in the Yanov prison, Chaim-Leib in the poorhouse. Blind Mechl had lost the sight in his good eye. Berish Visoker had moved to Warsaw.

"Remember Small Malka?" Schmul asked.

"Yes, how is she?"

"Her husband's passed on, too," Schmul said. "He was beaten to death in jail."

"And where is she?"

"She's married to a shoemaker from Zakelkow. Barely waited the three months."

"Is that so?"

"Perhaps you remember Zeftel? She was the girl who was married to Leibush Lekach," Schmul said slyly.

Yasha blushed. "Yes, I remember her."

"She's now a madam in Buenos Aires. Married some fellow named Herman. He left his wife for her. They own one of the biggest brothels."

Yasha paused for a moment. "How do you know?" he asked.

"Herman comes to Warsaw to take back ships full of women. I know a musician who's on good terms with his sister. She lives on Nizka Street and runs the whole business."

"Really!"

"And what about you? Is it true that you're a rabbi?"

"No, it is not."

"Everyone's talking about you. They say you bring the dead back to life."

"Only God can do that."

"First God, then you . . ."

"Don't talk nonsense."

"I want you to say a prayer for me."

"Let the Almighty help you."

"Yashale, I see you and I don't recognize you. I can't believe it's really you."

"We grow older."

"Why did you do it? Why?"

"I could no longer breathe."

"Well, and is it any easier in there? I think of you . . . I think of you day and night."

Schmul's arrival had been in the evening. Esther, herself, had announced him. It was a warm summer night. The moon was up, the sky filled with stars. One could hear frogs croaking and now and again the cawing of a crow. Crickets chirped. The old comrades looked at each other, each from his side of the window. Yasha's beard had become almost white and there were gold flecks in his eyes. Two disheveled sidelocks trailed from beneath his skullcap. Schmul's sideburns were also threaded with gray and his face was sunken. He spoke mournfully: "I'm disgusted with everything and that's a fact. I play here, I play there. Another wedding march, another good-moring dance. The wedding jesters repeat the same old weary jokes. Sometimes right in the middle of things I feel like running away . . ."

"Where?"

"I don't know myself. Perhaps to America. Every day somebody else dies. As soon as I open my eyes I ask: 'Yentel, who died today?' Her friends bring the news first thing in the morning. Soon as I hear who it is I get a pain in my heart."

"Well, and don't people die in America?"

"I don't know so many people there."

"Only the body dies. The soul lives on. The body is like a garment. When a garment becomes soiled or threadbare, it is cast aside."

"I don't want, as they say, to irritate you, but were you ever in heaven and did you see the souls?"

"So long as God lives, everything lives. Death cannot arise from life."

"But, nevertheless, one's scared."

"Without fear, man would be worse than an animal."

"He's worse anyway."

"He could be better. It's up to him."

"How? What should we do?"

"Harm no one. Slander no one. Not even think evil."

"And what will that help?"

"If everyone conducted himself this way, even this world would be paradise."

"It will never happen."

"Each of us must do what's in his power."

"Will the Messiah come then?"

"There is no other way."

5

Immediately after the Feast of Tabernacles the rains came. Cold winds blew and the apples, fallen from the trees, rotted, the leaves withered, the grass turned from green to yellow. At daybreak birds chirped once and then remained silent the rest of the day. Yasha the Penitent was troubled by a cold. His nose was clogged and would not clear. Pains shot across his forehead and into his temples, his ears. He had become hoarse. At night Esther heard him coughing. She could not stay in bed and went to him, in robe and slippers, to plead that he forsake his self-imposed prison; but

Yasha answered, "A beast must be kept in a cage."

"You're killing yourself."

"Better myself than others."

Esther went back to bed and Yasha returned to his pallet. He stayed dressed and bundled himself up in his blanket. He was no longer cold but still sleep would not come to him. He heard the sound of the rain on the shingle roof. There was a rustling in the earth as if moles were digging there or a corpse had turned in its grave. He, Yasha, had killed both Magda and her mother, had brought about the imprisonment of Bolek, had helped Zeftel become what she had. Emilia, he felt, was likewise no longer among the living. She had often said that Yasha was her last hope. No doubt she had done away with herself. And where was Halina now? He thought of them every day, every hour. Mentally, he called to the souls of the dead and begged them to give him some sign. "Where are you, Magda?" he muttered in the dark. "What has happened to your martyred soul?" Does she know I long for her and do penance? Or is it as it is said in Ecclesiastes: "And the dead know nothing." If that is so, then it has all been in vain. For a moment he imagined he saw a face in the darkness, a figure. But soon all dissolved into the dark again. God was silent. And so were the angels. So, too, the dead. Even the demons did not speak. The channels of faith had clogged up like his nose. He heard the sound of scratching—it was only a fieldmouse.

The lids of his eyes closed and he dozed. In his

dreams the dead came to him but they revealed nothing, speaking only nonsense, performing insane antics. He awoke with a start. He tried to reconstruct his dreams but as he did so they misted away. One thing was certain—there was nothing to remember. His dreams had been perverse, inconsistent—the babbling of a child, or the gibberish of a madman.

To drive away his evil thoughts Yasha intoned the Treatise of Benedictions: "From what time in the evening may the Shema be recited? From the time the Priests enter the temple to eat of their heave offering . . ." As he passed from the first paragraph to the second, he lived through a new fantasy. Emilia was still alive. She had purchased an estate in Lublin and had a tunnel dug from her bedroom directly to his cell. She came and gave herself to him. Just before daybreak she hastened back. Yasha trembled. For one moment he had relaxed and fancies had burrowed through like mice or hobgoblins. They dwelled in the mind ever ready to defile him. But what were they? What was their purpose in human biology? He quickly went on to the second paragraph: "From what time in the morning may the Shema be recited? As soon as one can distinguish between blue and white. Rabbi Eliezer says 'between blue and green.' " Yasha wished to say more but lacked the strength to continue. He ran his hand over his emaciated torso, his heavy beard, his coated tongue, his teeth—most of which had already loosened. Will it be like this until the end?

he wondered. Will I never rest? If so, let the end come!

He wished to turn on his other side but feared to disturb the blankets and rags with which he had covered himself. The frost was all about him, ready to penetrate to him at any moment. Once more he felt the desire to urinate but he did not yield to it. How did so much urine collect within him? He marshaled his strength and began to mumble the third paragraph: "The School of Shammai say, 'In the evening all should recline when they recite the Shema, but in the morning they should stand up, for it is written; and when *thou* liest *down* and when *thou* risest *up* . . .'" He fell asleep and dreamed that he must urinate. He walked into the outhouse but Emilia was standing there. Despite his embarrassment she said with a smile, "Do what you have to."

At daybreak the rain stopped and snow began to fall—the first snow of the winter. Clouds gathered in the east but, at sunrise, the sky became pink and yellow. The flame of sunrise caught the edge of a cloud and blazed in a fiery zigzag. Yasha rose, shook off his nocturnal weariness, and the nocturnal doubts. He had once read about snowflakes and now he verified what he had learned. Each flake that fell on the window sill was hexagonal, complete with stems and horns, with designs and appendages, formed by that hidden hand which is everywhere—in the earth and in the clouds, in gold and in carrion, in the most distant star and in the heart of man. What can one call this force, if not God? Yasha asked himself.

And what difference does it make if it's called nature? He reminded himself of the chapter in Psalms: "He that planted the ear shall not hear? He that formed the eye shall not see?" He had sought a sign, yet every minute, every second, within him and outside, God signaled His presence.

Esther had already risen; he could see smoke coming from the chimney of the main house. She was preparing food for him. The snow continued to fall but nevertheless the birds sang longer than usual this day. From their hiding places these holy creatures who possessed nothing but a few feathers and an occasional crumb chirped joyfully.

Well, I've dawdled long enough! Yasha said and, removing his jacket and shirt, he began to wash himself with water from the jug. He collected snow from the window sill and rubbed it over his body. He inhaled deeply, coughing up all his phlegm. The congestion in his nose cleared as if by a miracle. Once more he filled his lungs with the cool, morning air. His throat felt better and he began to say the morning prayer in a resounding voice. "I thank Thee." "How goodly are thy tenets!" "Oh my God, the soul which Thou gavest me is pure; Thou didst create it; Thou didst form it; Thou didst breathe it into me; Thou preservest it within me; and Thou wilt take it from me, but wilt restore it unto me hereafter." Then he put on his prayer-shawl and phylacteries. Praised be God that he, Yasha, was not confined in a real prison. Here, in his cell, he could pray aloud and could study the Torah. Just a few steps away from him was his devoted wife. Worthy Jews, the grandsons of martyrs and saints, sought his advice and blessings as if he were a rabbi. Although he had sinned greatly, God in his pity had not permitted him to perish in sin. Fate had decreed that he must do penance. Could greater benevolence exist? What more could a murderer expect? How would an earthly court have judged him?

After "Hear O Israel," he offered the Eighteen Benedictions. When he came to the words, "Yea, faithful art Thou to quicken the dead," he stopped to meditate. Yes, a God who could fashion snowflakes, form a man's body from semen, control the sun, the moon, the comets, the planets, and the constellations, was also capable of reviving the dead. Only fools would deny this. God was omnipotent. From generation to generation this omnipotence grew increasingly evident. Things which once had seemed impossible for God were now performed by man. All heresy was based on the assumption that man was wise and God a fool; that man was good and God evil; that man was a living thing but the Creator dead. As soon as one left these wicked thoughts the gates of truth swung open. Yasha swayed, beat his breast, bowed his head. Opening his eyes, he saw Esther at the window. Her eyes were smiling. She carried a saucepan from which rose a cloud of steam. Since he had already said the Eighteen Benedictions, he nodded and greeted her. Every bitter thought had left him. He was again filled with love. Esther apparently detected this in his face. Man can judge, after all. He sees everything if he chooses to see.

Esther brought a letter with his food. The envelope was wrinkled. It bore Yasha's name on it, and the name of the city. There was neither street nor street number.

He put away his phylacteries and washed his hands. Esther had brought him rice with hot milk. He ate at the table, putting aside the letter which he had decided not to open until after breakfast. This half-hour belonged to Esther. She would stand there, watching him and speaking to him as he ate. It would be the same old refrain, he feared: his health, the fact that he was killing himself, ruining her life, but—no—this morning she did not indulge in her usual complaints.

Instead, she smiled at him maternally and told him of the orders she had received, gossiped about the workshop and the seamstresses, told of her plan to have the house painted for Passover. He did not want to eat all of the rice but Esther insisted, swore she would not stir until he had swallowed the last spoonful. He felt strength returning to his body. The milk he was drinking had come from his own cow, the rice had been grown somewhere in China. Thousands of hands had labored to bring the food to his mouth. Every grain of rice held within it the hidden powers of heaven and earth.

After he had finished the rice and the coffee with chicory, he tore open the envelope. He glanced quickly at the signature and his eyes misted. He felt a mingling of joy and sorrow. Emilia had written to him. So Emilia was alive! But he did not begin to read at once, first offering up his praise to God. Then, wiping his eyes with a handkerchief, he began:

My dear Pan Yasha (or should I address you as Rabbi Jacob?), This morning I opened the *Courier Poranny* and saw your name—for the first time in more than three years. It was such a surprise that I could not read further. My first thought was that you were performing again—here or abroad—but then, eagerly, I read the whole article and my being grew sad and still. I recall that we often discussed religion and you expressed opinions which I regarded as deism, a belief in God without dogma or revelations. After you left us so suddenly in that unusual fashion, I thought many times that this was proof of how little help a faith without discipline was to a person in a spiritual crisis. You went away, leaving no trace behind you. You sank out of sight, as the saying goes, like a stone in water. Often I composed letters to you in my mind. I want to tell you first of all, should this letter reach you, that I accept all of the blame. Only after you left did I realize how badly I had behaved. I knew you had a wife. I drove you to this affair, so I am morally responsible. I have wanted to tell you this time after time, but I was under the impression that you had gone away to America, or God knows where.

The story in today's paper, describing how you have imprisoned yourself in stone, how you have become a holy man, and how Jewish men and women wait at your window for your blessing, has made an indelible impression upon me. I was unable to continue reading because of my tears. I have often cried over you but these were tears of joy. Twelve hours have gone by yet as I sit here and write this letter, I am crying again: first, because you have shown such great conscience; secondly, because you are atoning for *my* sins. I myself seriously considered entering a convent but I had Halina to think of. I could not hide from her what had happened. In her own fashion she loved you too and admired you exceedingly, and it was a great blow to her. Night after night, we lay in bed together and wept. Halina, in fact, became seriously ill and I was forced to send her to a sanitorium in Zokopane, in the Tatry Mountains. I could not have managed it (you must recall my financial situation) if an angel in human form had not come to our assistance, a friend of my dear departed husband, Professor Marjan Rydzewski. What he did for us cannot be related in one letter.

Fate chose that just then his wife should pass away (she's suffered for years from asthma) and when this good man suggested I become his wife, I could not refuse. You were no longer there; Halina was in the sanitorium; I had been left alone in God's world. But I told him the whole truth, omitting nothing. He is already an old man and a pensioner, but quite active; he reads and writes the whole day long and is extremely good to me and Halina. That's as much as I can say here.

Halina regained her health in Zokopane and when she returned, I could scarcely recognize her, she had grown and blossomed so. She is already in her eighteenth year and I earnestly hope that she will have more luck than her mother. Professor Rydzewski is as kind to her as a real father could be and indulges all her caprices. This new generation seems egotistical, without restrictions and with the conviction that everything the heart desires must be granted.

Well, enough about myself. It isn't easy for me to write you. I cannot picture you with a long beard and sidelocks as the journalist describes you. Perhaps you are not even permitted to read my letter? If this is so, forgive me. All these years I've thought of you, not a day passes that I don't think of you. For some mysterious reason I sleep badly and the human brain is such a capricious organ. In my fantasies I always pictured you in America in a huge theater or circus, surrounded by luxury and beautiful women. But reality is full of surprises. I do not dare to tell you what is right or wrong, but it does seem to me that you have inflicted too severe a punishment upon yourself. Despite your strength you are a delicate person and you must not endanger your health. The fact is you've committed no crime. You always showed a good and gentle nature. The short time that I knew you was the happiest period of my life.

This letter is already too long. They speak of you once more in Warsaw, but this time only with admiration. We have a telephone at home

now and several friends who knew of our friend-
ship have called me. Professor Rydzewski himself
suggested that I write you and he sends his best
wishes although he does not know you. Halina is
delighted to know that you are alive and will
write shortly—a long letter she tells me. May God
watch over you.

Your eternally devoted,
Emilia

Translated by Elaine Gottlieb
and Joseph Singer